HEART OF GLASS

FAIRY TALES REIMAGINED
BOOK 6

LAURA BURTON

JESSIE CAL

COPYRIGHT

Edited by Susie Poole

Proofed by Vanda O'Neill

Published by Burton & Burchell Ltd

First Edition

For film, TV and translation rights please contact Bethany Weaver @Weaver Literary Agency

❀ Created with Vellum

1

KILLIAN

Killian swam through the portal from the Underworld and rose up to a pool in a cave. He climbed out of the water, his boots thumping the stone ground as he shook water out of his shoulder-length hair and squared his shoulders, ready for a fight.

But surprisingly, he was alone.

He glanced up at the dancing reflections of the water on the cave ceiling, searching for the formidable sea monster, Neri.

He'd heard rumors that Neri was dead. Killian had thought it was a joke, but now he could see it was true.

Relaxing, he strode through the cave and set his mind on the task at hand.

First, he needed a boat.

Outside, the salty sea breeze whipped through his

hair, and a small fishing boat with two men bobbed in the water not far off the shore. The corners of Killian's mouth lifted, and he rolled up his sleeves to reveal the bulging muscles on his forearms. Then he marched toward them.

KILLIAN BATHED IN THE GOLDEN SUNSHINE AS HE leaned against the railing on one of the King of the Shores' royal ships. He had snuck in under the disguise of a servant. It was not easy finding someone his size to steal clothes from.

He stood a foot taller than any man on the boat, and his broad shoulders and arms were big enough to make even Hercules nervous.

He looked around the boat again, the music drawing him back to the party. A server walked by, and Killian picked up a glass of sparkling wine to dull the buzzing in his veins. That world heightened his senses to an unimaginable degree, and it was uncomfortable having to keep his thoughts and feelings in check so as to appear more human. He gulped down the drink, then surveyed the small group surrounding a bride and groom.

He thought it was the oddest selection of guests for a wedding. But then, it was an odd pairing. Never in all his years had he heard of a pirate marrying a mermaid. But there they were, making history.

A lobster sat in the prime position between the bride and groom, holding two sparkling rings in his pincers.

A seagull stood proudly to one side, wearing a black tie. And a dolphin watched from the other side of the boat with a top hat on its smooth head.

If Killian had not been so focused on his mission, he'd have cracked a smile. Maybe even made a sarcastic remark. But he needed to keep a low profile. A sacrifice was called for. The Underworld was missing a soul, and it was his job to get it.

The happy couple exchanged vows, and the guests cheered as the two of them kissed. The seas were calm for the entire day, and thousands of mermaids bobbed in the waters near the ship, flooding the air with their sickly-sweet tunes.

Men often whispered about the beautiful mermaid melodies, and their deadly abilities, but the siren's trance had no power over Killian.

The sky turned crimson as the sun began to set over the ice mountains. Only then did Killian step forward and show his true colors. He knew that his eyes had flashed cyan blue, because Lexa, the bride, looked at him like she was seeing a ghost. Then she muttered something Killian didn't care to hear to her new husband and kissed his cheek as they stopped dancing.

"I'll be right back," she whispered. But Killian heard her clearly. He had a keen sense of hearing and could hear even the faintest of sounds if he really focused.

Lexa rushed through the crowd of dancers, grabbed Killian's arm, and pulled him aside, taking him to the darkest corner of the ship. When she turned, her green eyes shone like two emeralds, and her face had turned ashen white. The pretty pink color of her cheeks completely faded.

"Please, just let me have tonight," she said, her voice shaky. "Just one night."

Killian smirked. As if anyone could barter with a guard of the Underworld.

"Don't worry, Princess, I'm not here for you," he said, before taking a long swig of his drink. The bubbles tickled all the way down. He had missed sparkling wine. It had so much more flavor than the grim drinks he had back home.

Lexa's eyes stretched wide. "But I sang the forbidden song, I made an oath…"

Killian raised a brow and surveyed the mermaid's look of disbelief. Lines had appeared on the corners of her eyes, and he wondered if she had gotten any sleep since she had sung the forbidden song.

"Let me explain a few rules of the Underworld..." He tucked a strand of hair behind her ear, but she shrugged away like she'd been zapped by an electric eel. Undeterred, Killian set his drink down. "You summoned your beloved pirate's soul back from the Underworld..."

"Yes, I know but—"

Killian raised both eyebrows and gave her a firm look. She stopped and shut her mouth.

"As you are aware, the Underworld delivered. But now we need something in return," he explained, keeping his eyes on Lexa.

She swallowed loudly. "And I'm ready to go, but not tonight. Please, can we wait until morning? Just give me one night with my husband—"

"You're not listening, Princess." He leaned forward and sniffed her, his nostrils picked up the sickly-sweet scent. And the sound of her racing heart thumped against his ears as though it was his own. "I can't take you to the Underworld. You have too much life in you."

Lexa took a step back, pinching her brows and looking at Killian like he'd said a bad word. "But you said you need..."

"A life for a life. That is correct," Killian confirmed, standing tall again. He smiled, but Lexa looked more terrified than ever, then her eyes flew in all directions, looking at the happy people dancing on the ship.

"If you're not here for me… who are you here for?" Her words barely came out in a whisper.

He took a big breath of the sea air, and all manner of scents mingled together, flooding him with information. He could sense the emotions of every person on the ship. And of them all, there was one that had a delicious scent. One that made him burn inside.

"I can only take a soul that has given up the will to live, one so tormented by life that putting them out of their misery would be a kindness."

"So, you're not taking me to the Underworld?" she asked in disbelief. "I can live out my life with Ryke?"

"Correct."

Lexa's frown deepened. "Who will you be taking then?"

Killian inclined his head with a gruff laugh. "Go and please your husband. Enjoy your life together. I have no business with you."

Reluctantly, Lexa ran back to the arms of her groom, who started to dance with her again. Then the crowd parted and a figure with the darkest aura met his eyes.

Killian strode across the ship, never taking his eyes off the woman, delighting in the sweet, addicting scent of guilt and hopelessness.

He stopped less than a foot from her. A pair of pretty blue eyes blinked up at him, framed with golden hair that fell in soft waves below her shoulders. She wore a pale blue gown with a tight corset, giving him an eyeful of her pert bosom.

"May I have this dance?" He held out his hand, and when she placed hers into it, he marveled at how tiny she was compared to him. Her feeble body was so delicate, it was like dancing with a doll.

The blonde maiden was a skillful dancer; not once did she stumble or step on his feet. And all the while, she held his gaze, her plump lips spread open to form a perfect O.

"To whom do I owe this honor of a dance?" she asked, her voice prettier than any of the thousands of mermaids.

Killian tightened his grip on her waist and led the dance, holding her slender body pressed up to him. The closer he got, the stronger the scent of her was, and it had him more intoxicated than drinking a gallon of bourbon.

"The name is Killian," he said, dipping her as she arched her back. His mouth hovered mere inches from hers, and he couldn't help but notice the swell of her chest heaving under his gaze.

"I'm Ella," she said between breaths.

Killian lifted her up and spun her around before setting her down to continue their dance. By now, the dancers had moved away to give them room and some people stood by and watched. But Killian paid them no attention. Ella was all he had eyes for. Her scent and sweet, tormented soul were his for the taking. And he was ready for it.

"Pleasure to meet you, Ella," he said in a low tone. "And I came for *you*."

"What do you mean?" she asked, batting her lashes.

Killian smirked and twirled her on the spot before he pulled her in again. "I know what you did to the King. I know you're wracked with guilt over it, too."

"I—I am not."

"Don't lie to me, Ella. I can sense it on you."

"You can sense guilt?"

"Yes, and you reek of it."

Ella stiffened in his grasp, but Killian did not let her go.

"What do you want from me?" Ella asked, her voice tight.

Killian saw a flash of defiance behind her eyes. He smirked again, then leaned forward and whispered into her ear while she trembled in his arms. "I want your soul. I've come to take you to the Underworld."

Ella pulled back to look at him with horror, then she drove her knee into his groin. He bent over in pain, and she ripped herself from his arms.

"Stay away from me," she huffed, then turned on her heels and fled through the crowd of dancers.

Once the blinding pain faded and Killian could follow, he saw her running down the sandy beach, and a small-heeled shoe lay on the deck by the wooden ramp.

Killian picked it up and chuckled as he looked out at the tiny, flowy dress disappearing into the night. He thought it extremely amusing that Ella thought she could hide from him.

2

ELLA

Once the horses slowed to a stop near the town square, Ella jumped down from the back of a wooden vegetable cart with a wave to the driver.

The bearded old man holding the reins replied with a nod, then flicked the reins, prompting the horses to continue toward the market. Ella's dirty and disheveled gown tugged her back as it got caught on a nail sticking out of the cart. Before she got a chance to free the dress, the fabric ripped, and she let out a heavy sigh. Not only was that the only gown she owned, but it had become an ironic representation of her life. Once elegant in a palace as a handmaiden, now ripped to shreds.

The village was bustling with people going about their affairs, and Ella skimmed the crowd, wondering if the bounty hunter had followed her. Though she had left him back on the ship, she wouldn't be surprised if he knew how to find her. Tales of Hades's hunters were spoken in whispers like horror stories. People talked about how the hunters tracked humans with ease, then dragged them down to the Underworld against their will without so much as a trial. She had always believed them to be fairy tales intended to scare thieves, but having met Killian, she now knew with absolute certainty that all those stories were true. As charming as his dancing was, the sharpness in his eyes was like that of a killer.

Ella's stomach churned, and she leaned against the fountain's edge in the middle of the square. According to *him*, he could sense her guilt. She had no idea how that was possible, but if that gave him the ability to track her, she needed to find a way to suppress her feelings. To get rid of her guilt. But how? Her heart weighed heavy, like an anvil crushing her chest, not only from what happened with the King of the Shores, but also with her family.

"Ella?"

Startled, she swung around with her heart racing, but then her eyes landed on a young man with shaggy brown hair. He approached her with a widening smile.

"Finn!" Ella threw her arms around her childhood friend and gave him a tight hug. "It's so good to see you!" Her tension eased as his familiar scent soothed her.

"I had no idea you were coming back," he said as they broke apart. "Your sisters didn't say anything."

Stepsisters, she wanted to correct him but decided not to bother. She forced a smile instead. "They don't know I'm here."

"Why not?" Finn rested his hands on his hips and gave her his signature stare. The one he reserved only for times when he caught Ella doing something he disapproved of. Ella avoided his discerning stare. She didn't want to tell him about the bounty hunter. She didn't want to get him involved.

"I just came to grab a few things," she said, looking down to avoid his eyes. He always knew when she was lying. "I won't be staying."

When she lifted her eyes, the concern on Finn's face was unmistakable as he continued to stare at her. "But where will you go? You know you can't go back to your stepmother's manor. Not after what happened last time."

Ella sighed and rubbed her arms, a sudden chill washing over her. "I'll just be in and out. I'm hoping they won't see me."

Finn looked at her from head to toe as if only just then seeing the sorry state she was in. "What happened to you?"

She ran a hand through her disheveled blonde curls, then flattened her ripped dress. "Long story."

"Does it have anything to do with…" Finn looked shiftily from right to left, then leaned in to mutter in her ear. "The death of the King of the Shores?"

Nausea rose inside Ella, even though she knew he was merely fishing for information. The news had spread like wildfire throughout the kingdom, but no one knew the details. Only that the King had been killed, and the Prince had risen to power.

She rested a hand on Finn's shoulder and gave him a polite smile. "Please, it's been a long day and my feet are throbbing."

He looked at her dusty feet with an arched brow. "Where are your shoes?"

She shrugged. "At this point, who knows?"

Finn's shoulders shook as he chuckled, and Ella was relieved when he didn't push the subject. "Nice to see some things are still the same," he said.

Oh, how she wished that were true. As nice as it was to see someone from her past—from a time when she was innocent and free of guilt—nothing would ever be the same.

"Come on." Finn reached for Ella's hand and pulled her with him. "Aunt Mara will prepare you a hot bath."

AUNT MARA RAISED FINN AFTER HE LOST HIS PARENTS. She was the personification of warmth and comfort. Just hearing her name brought a smile to Ella's lips. She was like a mother to Ella. The woman was short and petite, with a gentle nature. That was, until they got on her bad side. When they were kids and they would sneak off with a couple of cupcakes without asking. Cakes that were usually baked for a sick neighbor, or new mother in the village. Aunt Mara would make them bake a fresh new batch, even if it took them all night, and then deliver them with an apology.

Being back in Aunt Mara's cozy cottage flooded Ella with a comfort she desperately needed. She could not remember the last time her body relaxed. Not since that night in Neverland.

She shuddered at the dark memory, then pushed it out of her mind.

Replaying past events would not help her to erase her guilt. And if she didn't want the bounty hunter to find her, she needed to keep a handle on her emotions.

She nestled her sore body deep under the bath water and breathed long and slow, listening to Aunt Mara's bubbly voice from downstairs.

After bathing, Finn gave her some of his aunt's clothes to wear, including a simple cotton dress with short sleeves. She pulled on a thin pair of tan pants for added warmth and shrugged on a sheepskin vest. By the time she finished dressing, his aunt had beef stew and crusty bread ready on the table.

Ella inhaled the glorious scent of sizzling meat, and her mouth watered. "Smells delicious, Mara," she said, taking a seat at the table, feeling fifteen again.

"Thank you, dear. Here you go…" Aunt Mara handed Ella a bowl. "Eat as much as you like. Don't be shy."

Ella wasted no time in filling her bowl. Not only was she famished, but she had no idea when she would be eating again. She hadn't returned home to stay, that much she knew. As much as she loved being in Aunt Mara's home again, showered with unconditional love and friendship, all the reasons that made her want to leave in the first place were still there. Ghosts of a painful past haunted her, memories that she wanted to leave behind.

"So, tell me, dear…" Aunt Mara took a seat next to Finn. "What brings you home?"

"Oh, I won't be staying. I just came to get a few things," Ella said between sips of broth.

Aunt Mara cocked her head to the side, giving Ella the same discerning look that Finn had given her earlier.

"Were you unhappy in the Kingdom of Shores?" she asked.

The last time Ella was happy was when her parents were alive and her family was still together, but that wasn't what Aunt Mara was asking.

Ella sighed. "As much as I enjoyed taking care of Lily, the Prince's niece, I long to do more with my life."

"Like what?" Finn asked with his mouth full.

"I don't know. Sew dresses and sell them?" Ella said with a nervous laugh. Though, it wasn't as far-fetched as it once had been. In her village, she didn't get any attention for sewing her own clothes, but in the castle, with so many lavish fabrics available, the gowns she had made for Lily had most certainly turned heads. The gown she had worn to Lexa's wedding was one of Ella's masterpieces. It was too bad that it had gotten ruined. And all because of that Underworld bounty hunter, Killian.

Yet another reason why Ella couldn't stay. If Killian really was out to get her, she wouldn't want to lead him to her home village. To the few people she still cared about. To Finn and Aunt Mara.

Ella shifted her attention back to Aunt Mara. "I heard that whenever you see a shooting star, that means someone from the Underworld has entered into our world. Is that true?"

Aunt Mara chewed on a piece of bread as she

thought about it. "I believe that when there's a shooting star, it means that the Underworld has claimed a soul."

Ella ignored the weight pulling at her heart and leaned across the table, intrigued. "Tell me more."

Aunt Mara lowered her voice as if someone in the Underworld would somehow be able to hear her. "Ancient tales say that Hades will give up the throne for whoever claims a specific number of souls."

Ella stared at Aunt Mara with eyes unblinking. "What number is that?"

"No one knows," Aunt Mara said with a shrug, then leaned back. "But one thing I heard is that the soul only counts if it's guilty of some sort of wrongdoing. Otherwise, if an innocent soul is claimed, their count goes back to zero."

"Wait, so..." Finn dropped his spoon with a clatter. "The Underworld guards claim souls as some sort of competition for the throne?"

Aunt Mara nodded. "Seems so, but then again, those are just ancient tales. No one knows for sure if that's even a real place."

Ella knew. But she didn't want to unsettle them even more. Judging by how unnerved Finn looked, he was already going to have nightmares.

"Hypothetically speaking," Ella continued, turning back to Aunt Mara. "If someone has been targeted by one of Hades's guards, is there anything they can do to escape their fate?"

Aunt Mara gave Ella a curious look. "Hypothetically speaking… because they can sense guilt, the only way to get rid of them is to right your wrongs and get rid of that guilt before they catch you."

Ella nodded, remembering her dance with Killian and how he mentioned she reeked of guilt.

Aunt Mara narrowed her eyes at Ella. "Why the sudden interest in the Underworld?"

Ella leaned back with a shrug, trying her best to seem nonchalant. "I was just thinking about shooting stars. Anyway, I should be on my way. Thank you for the food and clothes, Aunt Mara."

"Where are you going?" Finn asked, turning to her with concern in his eyes.

"I need to sneak into the manor and collect some of the possessions I left behind." And figure out how to right her wrongs before Killian found her. "Thank you so much for everything," she said, rising to her feet.

Aunt Mara stood and pulled Ella into a hug. "If you're ever looking for answers, dear, follow the sundrop flowers."

Before Ella could ask how she knew about the flower, Mara pulled back and started clearing the table.

Finn approached, still concerned. "You don't have

to go back there, you know? We could provide you with anything you need for your travels."

Ella had considered grabbing a handful of clothes from Aunt Mara and never stepping foot in her stepmother's manor. It would have made her life much easier since even the thought of her horrid stepmother had her stomach knotting. But there was one item that Ella simply could not leave behind.

Ella chewed her lip in thought. "I need to sneak into the manor unnoticed," she said, giving Finn a mischievous look. "Will you help me? For old times' sake?"

Finn grinned. "When have I ever said no to you?"

Upon arriving at her stepmother's manor, Ella tiptoed up the stairs, trying not to make any noise. She could hear the servants busy in the kitchen. The thought of stopping by and saying hello crossed her mind—since she'd spend more time with the servants than with the family—but first she needed to grab her things before anyone spotted her trespassing. Especially her stepmother.

If the King's men ever came looking for Ella, her stepmother would gladly hand her over, no questions asked. She wouldn't even care to find out if Ella was guilty or not. She would surely take whatever reward was offered and buy herself new jewelry.

Ella snuck into her old room and hurried to a mahogany drawer. She pulled out a handful of the clothes which had once belonged to her and shoved them into a bag.

"Ella, hurry up!" Finn's voice was hushed but urgent as it came from the ground floor, just outside her window.

She picked up the rug that was in the center of the room and folded it in half, exposing a broken floorboard. She crouched and yanked up the board, revealing a box wrapped in sackcloth. Ella eagerly pulled it out and unwrapped it. As soon as her eyes caught sight of a scorpion engraved on the cover of the wooden box, she grinned.

Her father's box. It was all that he had left for her before he died. When she had gone to work for the King of the Shores, Ella hadn't been allowed to enter the manor. Her stepmother had forbidden her from getting her things, so she left with nothing but the clothes on her back. And the dress she supposedly stole from her stepsister. But how could she have stolen it, if she was the one who sewed it?

"Ella!" Finn urged.

"Coming!" she hissed back, hoping he would hear

and stop calling her name. She wrapped the cloth around the box again, then shoved it inside her bag.

"Ella?" Her stepsister's voice came from the door, and Ella froze. She pulled the strings of her cloth bag until it closed, then turned around slowly.

"Daphne, hi."

"How dare you show your face here, you thief," Daphne snarled, her rat-like features twisting into a scowl. "And in my room, no less." Though she was shorter than Ella, she crossed her arms across her petite frame and gave Ella a look that could kill. But her attempts to frighten Ella were futile, for Ella had bigger problems on her mind.

Ella could have pointed out that just because Daphne *wanted* the dress, it didn't make it hers. And that room had been Ella's since she was born. But none of that would've made a difference.

"I was just leaving," Ella said, swinging her bag over her shoulder. But as she headed toward the door, Daphne blocked her way.

"Not until you show me what's in the bag," Daphne demanded.

"It's just my clothes."

Daphne's eyes turned to slits as she gave Ella a suspicious look. "Yet, you're in *my* room. Now, open the bag."

"Hey, what is that?" Ella pointed behind Daphne,

feigning a look of horror. Daphne swung around, confused as to who could possibly be standing behind her.

As soon as Daphne's attention shifted, Ella darted toward the window, throwing her bag down to Finn, who caught it in midair.

"Ella!" Daphne screeched, clawing at the air as she tried to grab her with her tiny fists. But Ella was too fast. She jumped out the window and climbed down the thick vines growing on the wall. She moved quickly, scraping her elbows and knees on the thorns.

"Mommy!" Daphne's pitiful wails grew faint as Ella continued her descent. Once her feet touched the ground, she broke into a sprint with Finn next to her. They ran into the forest, laughing as they always did when they were young.

"Did you see her face?" Finn laughed. "I could see the veins in her forehead all the way from where I was standing."

When Ella laughed along with him, her lungs ached. She stopped running and held her side. Last time she had done something similar, with Finn next to her, had been ten years ago. "I can't believe she still falls for the *look behind you* trick."

"Some things never change," Finn said, slowing to a walk. "What did you take from her, anyway?"

"From her… nothing."

Finn gave her a pointed look. "You know they will send guards out to get us, right? The least you could do is tell me what I'm getting in trouble for."

Ella huffed. "Fine. It's a box that my father left for me. There, happy?"

For a second, Finn just stared at her with two bushy brows raised. He didn't need to say it, she could tell he was baffled by the thought of going into so much trouble for a sentimental item.

"What do you plan to do with it once the guards catch us?" he asked, placing his hands on his hips again.

Ella waved him off. "If we could hide from her guards when we were kids, I'm fairly certain we could run circles around them now that we're adults."

"You think so?"

"I know so."

Finn watched her for a moment, then scratched the back of his neck, lost in his thoughts. "Is that why you're here? Are you running from the King's guards?"

Ella arched a brow. "What are you talking about?"

Finn pulled out of his pocket a folded parchment paper. When he unfolded it, Ella's breath got lodged in her throat.

It was a sketch of a woman with golden curls cascading from out of a cloak, a shadow obscured her face. Above the sketch was the word "*Wanted*," and at the bottom was a generous reward for whoever captured the mystery woman.

"Apparently, she killed the King of the Shores," Finn said, lifting the paper higher. "Does she look familiar to you?"

Ella looked away from the sketch and snatched her bag from Finn's shoulder. "You should go home, Finn."

"As soon as you tell me the truth," Finn said, following after her. "Did you do it? Did you kill him?"

He jumped in front of her, and when their eyes locked, she sighed. As much as she wanted to put him at ease and assure him that she didn't do it, she could never lie to him. Finn wasn't just her best friend, but he was like a brother to her.

"Finn…" She touched his shoulder with a frown. "The less you know, the better. Now go home before they come for you too."

She walked past him, but he followed her. "I'm not leaving you alone, Ella."

"Finn!" She turned around and gave him a stern look. "Go home."

"Yeah, go home Finn." A deep voice came from behind Ella and she froze. She didn't have to turn around to know exactly who had found her. His rumbling voice was unmistakable.

"Who the heck is he?" Finn asked in a low tone as he looked over her shoulder.

Ella's eyes widened in panic. "Run!"

She took off in a sprint, dragging Finn with her. He stumbled at her unexpected yank but recovered quickly. They ran through the woods, weaving through the trees. Ella's heart raced with adrenaline and fear, and she pushed her legs harder.

"Ella." Killian appeared in front of her, and she halted, slipping on the muddy ground.

Finn reached for her arm and pulled her up. They darted to the right as Killian stood in place with an amused smile. "Running is futile and you know it." His voice was so clear behind her, it flooded her with fright.

"Who is that?" Finn yelled, his voice strained as he ran next to her. "Why is he following us?"

As much as she wanted to answer, her lungs were screaming and her muscles throbbing, and the only thing keeping her from feeling the pain at full force was her focus.

Until they came to a halt at a cliff. Ella bent over, panting.

"Well, that's not good," Finn said between his heavy breaths.

Ella peeked over the edge to find rapids at the bottom of a thirty-foot drop. "We can make it," she assured him. "We've done much higher jumps before."

Finn reached out his shaking hand. "Just like old times, then?"

Ella handed Finn her bag, and he swung it over his shoulder.

"Don't do it," Killian warned as he strolled into view, his broad shoulders and strong arms the size of a bear's. He could break every bone in Finn's body if he so wished. Ella wondered how it was possible that he was not out of breath—he had not even broken a sweat.

Ella took Finn's hand with a frown. "On three," she mouthed. "Three!"

She ran with Finn to the edge, but then stopped and slipped her hand from his, leaving him to jump alone. He screamed her name all the way down, then splashed into the rapids below as he had so many times in the past. She watched him for a moment as the current took him down the rapids. She knew he would make it out alive. They had always made it out alive.

She, on the other hand, was doomed.

Turning around to face Killian, she was surprised to find that he hadn't drawn any closer.

"That was a ruthless move. A jump like that could've killed him, you know?" Killian said, cocking a brow. He looked almost impressed.

"I am certain he's safer down there than up here with you," she snapped.

Killian's brows shot up in surprise. "You encouraged him to jump off a cliff to protect him from me? Clearly, you don't know much about me."

"I know enough," she said, clenching her fists. "I know why you're here, and why you want to take me."

"Is that right?" Killian crossed his arms, then flashed her an amused smile. "Please, do tell."

Ella gulped, beads of sweat forming on her temples. "I know about the competition in your world. The Underworld." Her voice shook despite her efforts to conceal her fear. "Whoever claims the most souls wins the throne. Isn't that right?"

Killian watched her for a long moment, a suppressed smile tugging at his lips. "I must say, humans are fragile creatures, but how they manage to find information never ceases to amaze me. Now, enough stalling."

In two strides, he was in front of her, picking her up and throwing her over his shoulder. Her head hovered over the edge of the cliff, and she let out an ear-piercing scream as she looked at the raging waters below.

"You are making a mistake," she said, slamming her fists against Killian's back as he carried her back into the woods. "I am not the person you're looking for. I'm innocent!"

Killian's back vibrated against her hands as he chuckled. "I don't make mistakes, darling. And you may try fooling me with many things, but your guilt isn't one of them."

Darling? Ella scowled. "Listen here, genius. Just because I struggle with feelings of guilt, doesn't mean I'm *guilty*." When he ignored her, a frustrated grunt ripped through her throat. "I didn't kill the King of the Shores!"

"The potency of your guilt says otherwise."

"Are you willing to risk your record on that?"

Killian stopped walking, and her question hung in the air for a long time.

"I know about your collection of souls," she added. "I also know that if you claim an innocent soul, your record is erased and you start back at zero. Do you really want to ruin your streak with me?"

The world spun once more before her feet found the ground. Killian stood in front of her, his expression serious.

"If you didn't kill the King, then who did?" he asked firmly.

She placed her hands on his chest to keep him from inching any closer. "I don't remember," she said.

"How convenient."

"It's true." She looked him in the eyes, noticing several shades of blue. "The memories of that night are hazy. I remember sneaking onto the King's ship, then waking up with a mermaid pushing my small boat back to the shore."

Killian studied her for a moment, and she wondered if he could also sense lies. Except, she wasn't lying. She was simply omitting having woken up in the boat with blood on her hands and arms, and all over her clothes. Everything else really was a blur.

"So, you *could* have killed the King?"

Ella pressed her lips to a tight line. "That is a possibility, yes. However…" She lifted a finger. "I also may not have done it. So, until we know for sure, you would be gambling your streak."

"Then how do we find out for sure?" he asked, his peppermint breath brushing her face.

She stepped back, casting him out of her personal space. "I'll need to retrieve my memory of that night."

Killian stroked his stubble for a moment, then huffed. "All right. You have until the next blood moon to prove your innocence. Otherwise, I will take my chances with you."

Ella let out a breath she didn't even know she was holding. "Thank you." She bowed her head nervously at him, then tried walking past him.

Killian stepped in front of her. "I'm coming with you."

Ella looked at Killian as if he'd slapped her. He might as well have. "Excuse me?"

Killian crossed his arms, his bulging muscles the size of her head. "You have already wasted a lot more of my time than I had planned. So, I want to be there the moment you find out you're a killer."

She glared at him. "You are unbelievable."

"And you have no idea where to even start looking," he said curtly. "Well, I do. So, either we go together, or I'll take you to the Underworld now. You decide."

She grunted, then turned on her heels, all the while wondering how on Earth she was going to get rid of him.

3

KILLIAN

Searing sunshine beamed down between the dancing leaves above as Killian and Ella walked in silence. They kept off the main road and instead followed the natural paths that ran along the riverbank.

Though Killian could no longer hear the waves of the ocean, the salty sea breeze floated in the air. The forest was alive with so many sounds. He listened to the croaking toads hiding in the overgrowth. The birds whistled and chirped as they flew from tree to tree. And then there was the gentle hum from old ash trees while their branches swayed lazily in the breeze.

Being in the human world is invigorating, Killian thought as he tuned into the vibrations of so many living things around him.

From the soft hum coming from the blades of grass

to the rapid thumping of a hare's heartbeat. Finally, he was drawn back to the delicious scent of inner turmoil that was like the most exotic wine. He shot Ella a sideways glance. Her watery eyes were narrowed on the crooked path ahead, and her hands were balled into tight fists. Killian wondered if she was trying to act confident.

But she had her bottom lip rolled inward and pinched by her top teeth. He thought it mildly amusing that this woman thought she could hide something from him. He could see right to her soul, and it was a pretty, swirling mist of pink and red. With a dark purple at the heart.

He knew Ella was not lying. She couldn't remember exactly what happened that night. But he was certain Ella was guilty of *something*. Hades had chosen her, after all. But if Ella's guilt and despair were not based on actual guilt, but rather the honorable concern of being guilty, that would be a problem. Part of him expected this to be a trick from Hades, since he was in no hurry to give up the throne.

Killian looked at Ella again, trying to see her as a murderer.

Though why a pretty maiden like her might want to kill a king was beyond Killian's comprehension. And if Ella had *not* murdered the King of the Shores, as she insisted, then Killian would lose everything if he dragged her to the Underworld.

He couldn't let that happen. Not when the throne was his for the taking. Just one more soul. After hundreds of years, that was all he needed. And after all this time, to risk going back to square one was too much to fathom.

He shook his head, the thoughts evaporating. He made the right call to confirm the reason for Ella's guilty aura. The method in which that would happen, however, he wasn't as sure. The only person he knew that could possess such information in that world was Rumpelstiltskin. Killian was not excited about the idea of seeing Rumple again. Especially since Rumple was known for offering nothing without expecting something in return.

"So, Rumpelstiltskin. How would he know how to help me?" Ella asked, stealing glances at Killian.

He could feel her eyes on him, but he kept his expression neutral and avoided her gaze. "He's a formidable human," Killian replied, his voice gruff and grating the back of his throat at the thought of seeing Rumple again.

Ella seemed to pick up on his thoughts. "Why do you say that? Do you two have some sort of history? How could he help me with my memory?"

Killian raised a skeptical brow and met Ella's

inquisitive stare. "Do you always ask these many questions?"

Ella's aura darkened. "Fine. Keep your secrets, then." She scowled, but the intensity of her look was softened by the sunkissed curls framing her angry face.

Then Killian picked up another sound: a grumble coming from her stomach. "You need to eat," he said, slightly annoyed at such human frailty.

Ella marched on. "I'm fine."

Killian grabbed her arm in one swift motion.

Ella spun around with a jolt, her eyes lit with fury. "What are you doing? Get your hands off me."

Killian released her but crossed his arms. "I'm going to need you to stay put while I go get some food."

Ella scoffed, tossing her bouncy curls over her shoulder. "We're at least half a day's walk from a tavern, and in case you haven't noticed, we've not passed a single living creature all morning."

Clearly, she didn't know how to hunt. It wasn't about what they could see, it was about what they could hear. Killian felt out for the heartbeat of a wood pigeon cooing in the trees above. But then he caught the sound of another hare nearby. He pulled back his cloak to reveal the handle of his dagger. "I said I'll get us food."

Ella rolled her eyes, but then she caught sight of the rope Killian pulled out of his satchel. "Hold out your hands."

Ella stepped back. "What for?"

"I'm afraid I don't trust you to stay put."

Ella's eyes shot up to meet him again, and her lips formed one tight line. "That will not be necessary."

"And I am not asking. Now, hold out your hands."

Ella's mouth twisted in all sorts of ways as nonsensical sounds came out of it. A flurry of emotions raced through her, and Killian could sense every flutter of emotion. Fury, confusion, fear… and resolution.

Killian could easily pin her down with one hand and tie her up with the other. At least this way he was allowing her some dignity. Slowly, she clasped her hands and held them out.

Killian stepped closer and looked at the cascade of golden curls flowing over her shoulders to her narrow waist. She wore a cotton gown with an ivory corset, narrowing her waist and lifting her breasts. But he kept his focus on her wrists. He tied them together with an expert knot, then looped the rest of the rope around a tree trunk. The motion pressed her against the tree.

"You barbarian!" she spat at him as she tried loosening the knot.

Killian sighed and tapped his lips. "Keep quiet, you're going to scare away our catch. You want me to come back with a kill before sunset, do you not?"

Ella's mouth shut at that. But she didn't break eye

contact. Instead, her neat brows pinched and her cheeks flushed pink.

Satisfied the maiden had been subdued, Killian turned on his heel and ventured deeper into the forest.

He walked like a tiger on the hunt, not putting any weight on his heels as he walked over the grass. The sea breeze flowed softly, rustling the leaves to make sounds like the ocean. A hare leaped out from a bush and right into his line of sight. Killian slowly went for his knife, but before he could get it, the hare's ears pricked up and it leaped away.

Killian let out the breath he had been holding and tuned into the sound that had disturbed the hare.

It was Ella.

Clearly, the woman had the attention span of a gnat. She had already forgotten all about his warnings and was grumbling about the rope being too tight.

Killian was forced to walk farther, until he was confident that Ella would not frighten his prey. He ran along a fallen tree trunk to cross the riverbank, scaled a hill, and found a small deer grazing in a meadow. Thousands of butterflies floated in the air like petals fluttering in the wind.

Killian crouched and took out his knife, squinting to keep a clear target on the deer. He had hunted so many times that with a single flick of the wrist, the knife flew through the air and landed dead on its target. The blow was fatal.

Gray clouds hung low, and the forest grew dim as Killian returned to the place he had left Ella. He frowned as he drew closer because her tantalizingly tormented aura was no longer clinging in the air. Neither could he hear her grumblings.

Killian ignored the quickening of his heartbeat as he raced ahead. When he returned to the tree where Ella had been tied, he saw nothing but a length of rope on the ground.

He picked up the rope and cursed under his breath.

4

ELLA

Ella tore through the forest, her heart racing in her chest, part exhilaration, part nervousness. The optimistic side of her brain cheered at her wit in setting herself free from the rope. After all, he wasn't the first to ever tie her up. Her stepmother had him beat. But the negative part of Ella's brain kept telling her that running was nothing but a waste of energy. Killian would find her anywhere she went. With him hunting her, she couldn't run or hide.

Perhaps Rumpelstiltskin could help her with more than just her memory. Maybe he would know how she could get rid of Killian.

Ella willed her legs to run faster. The odds may have been against her, but she was not going to give up so easily. Surely, she could find Rumple's place on her own. She just needed to make it to a tavern. Drunken men were the easiest to pry information from.

As she reached the main road, the sound of a cart came from around the corner. She waited until it drew closer, then waved to the driver. A bearded man that resembled the butcher back in her village pulled the two horses to a stop, then motioned for Ella to jump in.

She hastily climbed through the back, only to find a group of men sitting scattered between crates filled with vegetables. The smell of tobacco and grease made her reconsider the ride for a tenth of a second, then she remembered the roughness of Killian's grip as he tied her up, and decided the risk was worth taking.

She held her breath, then went to sit between two crates. The space was tight, but at least she didn't have to sit beside any of the men. Sure, three of them sat across from her, eyeing her in the most uncomfortable way, but at least they weren't close enough to touch.

Ella closed her eyes and leaned her head on one of the crates, hoping that if she dozed off for a bit, time would go by faster. The sun had already begun its descent, and the sky was growing darker, which meant that by the arrival of the moon, they would have reached the next village.

Ella wasn't sure how long she'd been out, but her neck was stiff from being in an awkward position for so long. Her spine ached from the hard wood pressing against her back, and she didn't have to open her eyes to know that the sky had turned black. The hooting of owls could be heard above the hooves of the horses against the dirt road.

"Where do you think she came from?" a whiny voice whispered across from her.

Though her eyes remained closed, her ears perked up with attention.

"Maybe she's lost," a gruff voice replied. He was curt, as if uninterested in continuing the conversation, but the whiny man next to him didn't seem to grasp the intention.

"Lost women don't own expensive boots," the whiny man said. And by the pitch of his voice, Ella wouldn't be surprised if she opened her eyes to find him ogling her boots. Even in the dark.

Dang it, Finn. Those were probably stolen boots. She should've checked before accepting anything from the best thief in town. Though he could have won them, fair and square, in a game of poker.

"Don't touch her boots, you fool," the gruff man said, then the sound of a slap came from near her feet.

Ella fought against the urge to curl up and hug her legs.

"I just want to see if they're made of fine leather."

"I said no, Theo. Now, get some sleep. You want to be well rested when we meet with One-Eyed Joe."

"Why?" Theo asked.

"Because…" the gruff man hissed. "When I tell him that you gambled half of his money, you just might have to run for your life."

Theo gulped, and there was silence for a long time.

"I think Theo is on to something," a new, raspy voice added. The weight inside the cart suddenly shifted, as if the man had leaned toward his gruff companion.

"What is this?" the gruff man asked. The sound of parchment paper ruffling between them made Ella's stomach churn.

"Look at her hair," the raspy voice whispered.

When the glare of a lantern shined in front of her, Ella opened her eyes. The three men across from her were staring as if they had just opened a chest full of gold.

Ella cleared her throat, then rose to her feet, wincing as she stretched her legs. "Excuse me," she called out to the driver. "This is my stop."

"Are you sure?" the driver replied. "Plover village is just ahead."

"I prefer to get off here."

"What's the rush?" The man with the gruff voice

stood, the parchment paper still in his hand. Ella didn't have to see the front to know that it was one of the Prince's wanted posters.

Ella chewed on the inside of her lip for a moment, but when the man with a raspy voice lifted the lantern and the light illuminated her face, she swung around and jumped onto the railing.

Multiple hands grabbed her arms and pulled her back before she jumped off the cart. She was thrown on the floor, then two men pinned her down.

"Get your dirty hands off me!" Ella yelled.

The cart came to a stop, and the driver turned around. "Fellas," he called out in a calm tone. "Is that really necessary?"

"Afraid so," the man with a raspy voice said, picking the wanted sign that had fallen on the floor and handing it to the driver. "She's worth quite a pretty penny."

While the driver read the sign, Ella looked at two men sitting in the corner, her eyes begging for their help with a silent plea. But they averted their eyes and lowered their heads.

Cowards.

"Are you sure this is her?" the driver asked.

"Of course that's not me!" Ella barked, trying to wiggle from the gruff man's grasp. "I can't even get you off of me, how can I kill a king?"

The driver cocked his head as he looked down at her. "Interesting…" He lifted the paper for her to see. "This wanted sign doesn't say anything about the crime committed."

Drat.

A wicked smile spread across the gruff man's face as he kept her pinned to the floor. "Looks like our days of working for One-Eyed Joe are over, fellas. We're about to be rich."

A whiny-pitched laugh came from the scrawny man who had to be Theo. He dropped to his knees by Ella's head. "Rich! We're going to be rich!"

Ella jerked her knee upwards, ramming the gruff man between his legs. He grunted and bent over, the strength in his arms gone. She pushed him off her, but before she could even think of getting to her feet, the driver had her pinned down again.

"Get me that sack of potatoes," he said to Theo. "Pour out the potatoes and give me the sack."

"No!" Ella screamed with her last bit of oxygen. Then the sack was forced over her head. Panic rose from her chest as her lungs tightened under his weight. She couldn't breathe.

A strong thud made the floor beneath her shake. "I believe the lady said no," Killian's thunderous voice came from only a few feet away, and for the first time, his voice filled Ella with hope instead of dread.

The weight of the cart shifted as if all four men had hurled together. "I don't believe this concerns you," the gruff man said. "But, I'll tell ya what, if you turn around and walk away, we'll let you live—"

A sudden screech ripped through the man's throat, and his piercing scream grew faint as if he was hurled across the forest.

When the weight above her lifted, Ella ripped the sack from off her head and took a greedy gasp of air. The driver had risen to his feet to join the raspy man who stood against Killian with a knife. The gruff man was nowhere in sight, and neither were the cowards in the corner. Theo jumped off the carriage with a terrified yelp and sprinted into the woods.

Killian stood tall, watching as both men attempted to slice him with their knives. He swerved out of the way, pulling out a long sword from its sheath. The men stepped back, then looked at each other for a moment.

The man with a raspy voice turned around to run away, but Killian grabbed him by his cotton shirt and yanked him back. The man grunted as Killian pinned him against a stack of crates.

"Whoa, hey, all right." The man threw his arms in the air. "You can keep her, man. She's all yours."

"Well, that much is obvious," Killian hissed, bringing the sword to the man's neck. His blade reflected the silver moon, but it wasn't metal. It was glass. Ella had never seen anything like it.

"Please, don't kill me!" the man cried. "Please."

Killian pressed his blade into the man's jugular but didn't pierce the skin. "Apologize to the lady."

"I'm sorry!" the man cried. "I'm so sorry!"

The sound of slicing flesh made Ella gasp. Killian grimaced, then turned around to find the driver holding a knife with Killian's blood dripping from its blade. But not just any knife. It was a knife also made of glass. The man seemed to have taken one of Killian's weapons while he wasn't looking.

Killian loosened his grip on the raspy man, then turned toward the driver. The raspy man stumbled past Ella and jumped off the cart, then ran away in fright.

Upon realizing he'd been left alone, the driver gulped, and the hand holding the weapon began to tremble.

With a flick of a wrist, Killian's sword knocked the knife from the man's hand. The knife slid to Ella's feet. He swung around to jump off the wagon, but Killian grabbed him in midair, yanked him back, and threw him to the floor. The man grimaced with the impact, then grunted when Killian pinned him down with his large boot.

"Killian, don't." Ella rose to her feet and stepped forward. "Please, don't kill him."

Killian glanced at Ella, but then his eyes flickered to her wrists and his expression turned dark. He grabbed her arm and lifted it between them. "Look what they've done to you. And you're defending them?"

She looked at her wrists and saw her raw, scraped skin. "It's a rope burn," she said.

"And for that, he's going to die." Killian grabbed the hilt of his sword with both hands and lifted it over the man's chest.

"He didn't do this to me," she said, lowering her voice. "You did."

Killian stood over the man for several heartbeats without moving. For a moment she didn't think he would listen to her. But then he swung his sword back into its sheath and stepped back. The man staggered to his feet, and after stumbling out of the wagon, he limped away as fast as his injured body would allow.

After the man disappeared into the woods, Ella sighed.

"Does it hurt?" he asked, turning to face her.

"I'm fine."

He grabbed her hand and turned it so that her bleeding wrist was illuminated by the moonlight. "This…"

Her eyes dropped to her wrist. With all the tugging and pulling she did to free herself from his knot, she hadn't even realized how badly it had scraped her skin.

Killian's jaw locked, and his blue eyes flickered with a hint of guilt. He dropped her hand and stepped back as if creating an invisible barrier between them. "This will not happen again." He said it like a promise, and though his jaw was still clenched, there was a softness in his eyes she had never seen before.

Was that his version of an apology? She couldn't tell.

"Can I ask you a question?" Her voice was soft in the night. "If you want me dead, why didn't you just let them take me?"

Killian leaned into her until her back touched the stack of crates. He locked his eyes with hers. "If anyone else kills you, I don't get to claim your soul."

The reality of his words hit her like a bucket of ice water, and a wave of irritation washed over her. She shoved him away with a scowl.

"Make yourself comfortable and eat some vegetables while I take the reins." He picked up his knife from the floor, then climbed into the driver's seat. "And don't try anything. Otherwise, I will sit you next to me."

"I'm fine back here. The more distance between us, the better," she grumbled.

Killian guided the horses down the dirt road. "Suit yourself."

5

KILLIAN

Killian shrugged his shoulders back as the knife wound itched, healing itself at rapid speed.

Though he was immortal, he still had blood running through his veins and he still experienced pain. His body worked overtime, sealing up the cut and flushing out the toxins, but the discomfort was nothing compared to the throbbing ache in his chest.

Seeing those dirty men pinning Ella down, their greasy hands all over her body, made his heart hammer against his ribcage and lit a fire of fury inside of him.

It took every ounce of self-control to not tear each man limb from limb.

The only reason he didn't was because he turned out to be the worst of them all. What he had done to her wrists… The smell of her blood sent his mind into a spin. So, when she pleaded with him to spare those men's lives, he did. But not because of them. Because of her. She was worried about feeling more guilt should those dregs of society lose their lives because of her. But that would have been noble guilt, the kind of guilt that heroes have after winning a bloodbath of a war. Then live out the rest of their days obsessing over the cost of victory.

That kind of guilt had no place in the Underworld. Neither did her fierce will to live. And it would have certainly made Ella a poor fit as a prize.

He gritted his teeth, whipping the reins against the flanks of the two horses. A flash of indignance washed over him, and he sensed the horses muttering under their breaths as they pressed on.

But Killian had no time to let them rest. The moon was rising, and he knew it was best to get Ella out of the forest before they faced a much larger foe than mere humans.

They were edging closer to ogre territory.

He took a turn down a windy path, and soon enough, the horses' hooves struggled over the loose gravel. Finally, the overgrown trees forbade them from passing any farther, and the horses came to an abrupt stop.

Killian jumped down and strode to the back where Ella was curled up and shivering. He looked up at the night sky, now a deep shade of purple with silver streaks of moonlight. He had not noticed the cold, but Ella's arms had goosebumps as she hugged herself.

"Do you not have a cloak?" Killian asked, his voice more curt than he intended it to be.

Ella scowled at him. "I gave my bag to Finn."

"Well, that was foolish. We go on foot from here," Killian said, thinking that the sooner they got inside, the better.

Ella's shallow breaths came thick and fast, and Killian could sense her heart racing as she stumbled out from between the crates. He offered his hand to help her down, but she gave him a look of pure repulsion.

"I can get down by myself," she huffed.

She jumped down and landed like a cat beside him. The air shifted, and an entirely new scent wafted over Killian as he watched her straighten her skirt, which had lifted to her knees.

He noticed the sheepskin pants over her legs and lifted a brow. When Ella was done, she caught his expression.

"What?"

"Nothing," Killian said. "It's just that I've never seen a maiden wearing men's clothing before."

Ella scowled. "I don't know how long you've been in the Underworld, but it is normal for women to wear these. Besides, it's more practical when one is being dragged by a ruthless captor."

Killian didn't argue. But couldn't help smiling at her attempt to offend him. Then he pointed to her round bosom pushed up by the corset.

"A cloak would've been more practical, if you ask me."

Ella followed his line of sight and crossed her arms over her chest with an outcry of fury. "Let's just go. I'm freezing."

The corner of Killian's mouth ticked upward as she stormed off ahead of him. He picked up the empty potato sack and tore it open with one quick motion. The sound of it ripping made Ella yelp with surprise and jump back. But then he handed it to her and she took it.

"Wrap that round your shoulders," he said. "The last thing I need to worry about is you catching a chill."

Ella hesitated for a moment out of pride, but then took it and wrapped herself up. "Oh, Underworld forbid I get a chill and you can't take my soul."

Killian knew she was joking, but the thought of Ella dying was far from funny.

They walked on in the night and followed the

narrowing path. Owls hooted in the distance, and Killian picked up the sound of a wolf cry. It was at least two miles to the south. They were safe for the time being, but soon enough, Ella was muttering again.

"This sackcloth is so itchy. I'm going to break out in hives." She wrestled with the sack and muttered various complaints for several minutes until Killian could not take it any longer.

With a heavy sigh, he ripped the cloth from her. She yelped in surprise, but then stared at him as he took off his cloak and draped it around her shoulders. "Now, stop complaining, will you? I'm getting a headache."

Ella pulled the cloak around herself and let out a shuddering breath. "I didn't know bounty hunters from the Underworld got headaches."

Killian paid her no attention. But Ella kept talking. "That said, I didn't think bounty hunters from the Underworld bled, either. Do you want me to take a look at—"

"That won't be necessary," he said. And it was true. His wound had already closed, and the scar would be gone by morning.

Ella was about to talk again, probably to ask another ridiculous question, but they reached an iron gate, ornate and tall. Through the bars, they could see a vast garden with gravestones and statues that loomed like gargoyles. Then they saw the crooked house, black as though it had been on fire at some point. And only one window was lit orange.

Ella's aura grew fearful, and she hugged Killian's cloak more tightly around her.

"That's where Rumple lives?" she whispered. "It looks so evil. Why don't you take *his* soul to the Underworld?"

The gate squealed as Killian pushed it open. "He's made a deal with Hades. None of us can touch him. Believe me, I would be the first in line."

Ella sucked in a nervous breath but didn't say any more. Her silence was a welcome relief as Killian led the way up the garden path toward the front door. He pounded his fist on the oak and the house seemed to tremble in response. When the door creaked open, there was no one in sight.

The inside of the house was just as menacing as the outside. A damp, musty smell flooded Killian's nostrils. He peered at the dull, dusty paintings looming over them in the narrow hall.

Killian strode through the house toward the soft flickering glow of candlelight farther down the hall and found an old man sitting in an armchair by a single candle. His moth-eaten armchair stood beside an empty fireplace, and Killian couldn't help but frown at the sorry state. It was difficult to believe this to be the formidable Rumpelstiltskin. All he saw was a tired, lonely man unable to even light a fire.

Rumple looked up, his dark eyes landing on Killian for a moment, then stretching wide with recognition. But his expression quickly turned neutral again.

Killian couldn't sense any emotion from the man. It was as though he were a soulless shell of a human, void of any humanity at all.

What was most shocking was the Rumple he was looking at was not the man he met many years ago. This new Rumple, with hair as silver as the moon, must've killed the last one and taken his place. It wouldn't have been the first time that had happened in the centuries Killian had been alive.

"How nice to have visitors," Rumple said, rising to his feet. "Can I offer you a drink?"

"Whiskey," Killian said.

Rumple smiled as he reached for a crystal glass in the center of the table, then poured Killian his drink. "And for the lady?"

When his attention turned to Ella, he gasped. Ella stepped back like his gaze hit her like a flash of lightning.

"Good grief, Ella, is that you?"

Ella's thin hands clamped over her mouth as she stared at him, eyes blinking rapidly. "You're Belle's father," she said in nothing more than a horrified whisper. Her aura flashed all sorts of colors as she processed several emotions at once. It made Killian's skin tingle.

Rumple's eyes darkened. "You may call me Rumple now."

Ella opened and closed her mouth several times, and Killian could tell she had so many questions that she was struggling to choose which one to ask first.

But Killian had a feeling it would be about their past and growing up alongside his daughter, which had nothing to do with the problem at hand. And his patience was running thin.

"The girl needs to recall an event that happened several weeks ago," Killian said, picking up his drink and knocking it back in one gulp. "It's imperative we get her to remember."

Rumple cocked his head at Killian. "I fail to see how her memories are any of my concern."

Killian sensed Ella's disappointment as she stood next to him, and it stirred within him a strange urge to make Rumple eat his words. "Well, she's my concern, so…" He reached over the table and grabbed Rumple's shirt, balling it into a tight fist. "Tell me what you know."

But then a zap like ten million volts of current shot through Killian, and he jolted back.

Rumple straightened out his shirt with a soft laugh. "You can't hurt me, remember? That was part of my deal."

Killian grit his teeth. As much as he would have loved to wipe that smug smile off his face, the man couldn't be touched by anyone from the Underworld.

He poured himself another drink and downed it in one. "Then how about a trade?"

Rumple raised an intrigued brow. "What could you possibly have to offer me that I don't already possess?"

Killian looked around the forsaken building they were in. It was hardly a palace, with splintered, squeaky floorboards and colorless walls. The man clearly did not value ordinary treasures. Rumple was a collector of very particular items. Or knowledge. There was only one thing Killian had that would be of interest.

Killian withdrew his knife and placed it on a small table in front of him. The candlelight reflected in the glass blade revealed the blue tint. Rumple's demeanor changed, and he picked up the knife like it was a newborn baby.

"Well, now this…" he said in awe.

"That's right. A blade forged from the fires of the Underworld," Killian said. "Now, tell me what you know."

Rumple turned his attention back to Ella, and she stepped behind Killian to hide from the intensity of Rumple's stare.

"Your memories are not lost, so the water in Neri's cave is of no use," Rumple said. "Your memory loss is due to a drug in your system."

"A drug?" Ella asked, her voice rising in pitch. "Could you be referring to pixie dust?"

Killian wanted to groan. If Ella's problems were around pixie dust, then this was about to get a lot more complicated.

Rumple nodded. "Pixie dust, indeed. Your memory is impaired because you have a pixie dust ailment. And it's exceedingly difficult to cure. Practically impossible. Unless…"

Killian gave Rumple a hard look. "Unless what?" When Rumple didn't respond, Killian rolled his eyes. "All right, now he's just toying with us." He went to pick up the dagger, but Rumble slammed his palm on the table and Killian withdrew.

"There is one place in this forsaken land that may have the answers you seek."

Killian huffed in frustration, his annoyance building by the man's cryptic words. "Well, out with it, then."

Rumple swaggered across the dim room to the mess of parchment littered across a desk. He picked one and offered it to Ella.

Killian looked at the map as she rolled it open. "Fairy Forest? You've got to be kidding me."

Rumple raised a brow. "I never kid. If you want Ella to be cured and regain her full memory of that night… you need to speak to the fairies."

6

ELLA

Ella leaned against a tree, panting. "I don't think I can take another step." Her legs ached, and she couldn't even feel her feet anymore. And that was with a pair of expensive boots. "Why do fairies have to live so high up, anyway? And why aren't there horses that can hike to this altitude?"

"The air up there makes it easier for fairies to fly. And I do have a horse. I just wouldn't bring him to the fairies because…" Killian stopped talking once he caught Ella giving him an *I-couldn't-care-less* look. "Oh, I see. You were simply complaining as opposed to asking an actual question."

"Yes. Now, can we please break camp here? My feet are killing me."

"There are a million things that can kill you, but your feet aren't one of them."

"Killian, please?" Ella leaned her head against the tree trunk and closed her eyes. Her body was throbbing with exhaustion. Thankfully, Rumple had offered them food because if she were tired *and* hungry, she would be the one dragging Killian's soul to the Underworld.

When Killian didn't respond, she opened her eyes and found him staring at her.

"What?" she asked.

He shook his head as if shaking off a spell. "Nothing. I'll go gather some wood to make a fire."

"Thank you," she spoke under her breath as she slid down to the ground, hugging her legs and wrapping Killian's cloak around her thin frame.

Killian stopped a few feet away and glanced at her. Ella could tell he was hesitating to leave. She gave him a lopsided look.

"I'm not going to run away. I promise." As much as she hated to admit it, she was safer with him for as long as the Prince wanted her dead. Also, she doubted her legs would oblige even if she did change her mind.

Killian's tense shoulders seemed to relax, and he nodded. Then he walked away without as much as a *be-right-back.*

THE HOWLING OF A WOLF ECHOED IN THE DISTANCE, and Ella shot her eyes open. Killian was already sitting by the fire on top of a thick log. She hadn't even noticed he'd returned, let alone started a fire.

Another howl came deep within the woods, and Ella sat up, her eyes adjusting to the darkness. She had heard of stories about a beast devastating villages, but that was in the Chanted Forest. Not at the mountain peaks to the north.

"These are just regular wolves," Killian said, picking up a long stick from the ground and poking it into the fire. "Not shifters."

"What do you mean, *shifters*?"

He gave her a side glance. "Have you really never seen a shifter?"

A chilly wind blew, and Ella went to join him closer to the fire, still engulfed by his cloak. "How is it that you're not afraid of wolves? They're ferocious creatures."

"They're just wolves," he said with a shrug. "Not much of a threat to someone like me."

Ella arched a brow. "Someone like you?"

"Let's just say that I can dilacerate them," he said, still poking the fire. He winced with the movement of his shoulder, and Ella could tell he was still in pain from his wound.

"All right, that's it." She turned to face him. "Remove your shirt."

"It's fine. It'll heal on its own."

"That's what you've been saying, and yet, it's still not healed."

"That miscreant cut me with my own knife," he hissed. "It takes longer to heal when we're cut with glass."

"I'll be back." She was about to stand when Killian grabbed her arm. But he wasn't as rough as previous times, which surprised her.

"Where are you going?" he asked.

"To make a poultice for your wound," she said, leaning toward him. When her lips inched closer, he stiffened. "Go ahead and look through me, tough guy. Am I lying?"

His eyes dropped to her lips for a fraction of a second, then he cleared his throat. "Fine." He let go of her arm, then turned back to the fire.

Ella suppressed a smile, surprised that she was able to make him uncomfortable.

She left to forage the poultice, then came back with all the ingredients on a large leaf. She took a seat next to him again, and after combining all the ingredients with a bit of water, she mixed it with the tip of her fingers until the black dirt turned to a thick goo.

"All right, let me see your wound," she said, turning to face him.

"I still don't think this is necessary," he grumbled.

She gave him a hard look. "You're clearly in pain. If nothing else, at least the poultice is going to numb it so that you don't feel any pain while it's healing."

"Fine, then answer me this..." He leaned into her personal space, and a surprising wave of heat rose within her. "Why do you care?" His eyes were so close and so blue.

"Because not only did you get hurt defending me," Ella said. "But I believe the reason you didn't tear their limbs apart was so that I wasn't subjected to such a horrific sight. And given your nature, that was very gentlemanly of you."

Killian held her gaze for a long moment, and she wished she knew what he was thinking. But he simply nodded.

"Good. Now, stop being so stubborn and show me your wound."

In one quick move, he pulled off his shirt, exposing the mountains and valleys of muscles across his upper body. Ella's mouth hung open as she stared at the scars crisscrossing his skin. If human weapons didn't do much damage, then he must've gotten those in the Underworld.

"My wound is on my right shoulder," he said,

ripping her attention away from his scars.

"Right." Ella cleared her throat, then rose to her feet. She carefully approached his seated form. The wound was open, and the skin around it was a mixture of red and purple. "It's infected. It needs to be cleaned."

Killian reached for his satchel and pulled out a sheepskin. "Here. Use this." He opened it and handed it to her.

The strong smell of alcohol burned her nostrils as well as her eyes. She blinked. "Wow. And here I thought it was water," she mumbled.

"Water is too weak for my line of work."

She placed the poultice next to Killian on the log, then held the sheepskin steady. "You might want to bite down on your shirt," she warned. He crumpled his shirt in his hand instead, and Ella wondered if he'd been through worse pain. Judging by the scars on his back, she was fairly certain he had. "All right. Here we go."

She poured the alcohol onto his open wound, squirming at the thought of how much it must've been burning. But his muscles barely twitched. She could very well have been removing a splinter from his skin.

"Does it hurt?" she asked.

"Not yet," he said.

"What do you mean, 'not yet'?" When she leaned

forward to see what he was doing, she spotted him holding his open hand over the fire. "What are you—?"

The red and yellow flames turned blue as they continued burning. Ella stared at the blue flames in awe. It wasn't like anything she'd ever seen. Then Killian picked up his glass sword and hovered the tip of the blade over the blue flames.

Ella's admiration soon turned to shock. "Killian, what are you doing?"

He handed his glass sword to her, the tip glowing a bright red. "Cauterize it."

Ella gasped and stepped back. "Are you out of your mind?"

He glanced over his shoulder to give her a look. "Didn't you say that goo numbs the pain?"

"Well, yes, but…" Her eyes dropped to the poultice next to him on the log. "What happened to letting it heal on its own?"

"That was before I knew it was open," he said. "If we leave it like this, the infection will spread. It has to be done."

"Can this kill you?" she asked.

Though she couldn't see his face, she could swear she heard him chuckle. "To your disappointment, no, this can't kill me. But I could lose an arm if this infection spreads, and I rather keep my limbs if at all possible. So, please... do it."

She took the sword reluctantly. It weighed heavily in her small hands. "How much would you say this will hurt?" she asked in a shaky voice. When Killian bit down on his shirt and gripped the log beneath him, she sucked in a terrified breath.

He yelled something to her, but it was muffled by the shirt in his mouth.

"What's that? I don't understand."

He spat out the shirt. "Don't think. Just do it."

Without another thought, Ella pressed the tip of his sword to his open wound. He jerked forward with a grunt as the blade sizzled against his skin. The smell of burning flesh hit Ella's face. She held her breath while he shoved his shirt back into his mouth.

She was careful in covering every inch of his wound, even though her hand wouldn't stop trembling. Once she was done, she stepped back and dropped the sword on the ground.

Killian's shoulders sagged as he spat the shirt from his mouth. His skin was glistening with sweat as it reflected against the blue flames.

"Thank you," he said through ragged breaths. "Well done."

"Actually, I'm not finished," she said, reaching for the poultice. She scooped some with the tip of her fingers, then gently applied it to the wound. His shoulder twitched, but he didn't pull away. And for a long moment, they were both silent. Other than the sound of crackling fire burning in front of them, the night was quiet.

Ella rubbed the poultice on his skin. For some reason, she had expected his skin to feel rough and rugged, but it was soft and smooth. It was nothing but lean muscle.

"Is this what healers do in your world?" she asked, trying her best to keep her strokes gentle. "Burn your wounds closed?"

"We have no healers in my world."

"Of course not, everyone is dead," she joked, but Killian swung his legs around until he was facing her. His eyes were bluer than she'd ever seen.

"Offering your healing services is not going to make me change my mind about claiming your soul."

"Healing services?" Ella frowned down at him. "I'm helping you because you're hurt. This may be a foreign concept to you, but it's called kindness."

"It's called leverage, and I do not wish to be indebted to you. So, name your price."

"My price?" Ella echoed. But then she crossed her arms. "Fine. I request my freedom as my price."

"That I cannot do."

"Why not?"

Killian sighed, then turned toward the fire again. "Because you've been marked."

"Marked?" Ella tossed the poultice aside, then took a seat next to him on the log. "By whom?"

"Hades."

"And why would he mark me?" she asked.

Killian watched the flames. "When your friend Lexa sang the forbidden song, she requested that her love's soul be spared. That means his soul left a void that needed to be filled. So, another soul was marked to take its place. Yours."

Ella shook her head. "I still don't understand… Why mine?"

"The soul with the most guilt and despair, and weakest will to live, is the one that gets marked."

Ella stared at Killian with eyes unblinking. "And my soul is the darkest of everyone in the kingdom?"

"Of everyone connected to the event that propelled the forbidden song to have been sung," Killian explained. "Out of everyone in Neverland that night, your guilt was the strongest, and your will to live the weakest."

Ella turned toward the fire and watched as the flames licked the air. "My will to live was the weakest? That doesn't make any sense. If that were true, I wouldn't be trying so hard to survive."

Killian picked up the stick from the ground again and poked into the fire. "Surviving and feeling deserving of life are two different things," he murmured. "I do not know the reason for your despair, but the depth of it has weakened your will to live. Whatever it is that you did, it makes you feel guilty to be alive. Whether you want to admit it or not, the marking does not lie."

Ella watched the fire in silence, not knowing what else to say. She wanted to tell him he was wrong, that the marking was wrong, but that meant she would have to admit that she never once had contemplated ending her life, and that wasn't true. She had contemplated that many times before, and for the exact reason Killian had just mentioned. She didn't feel deserving of life. Not when everyone else in her family had died. Living in a world where they no longer existed was never the plan for her. And how she'd managed to survive that long without them had been a miracle.

When the flames blurred in front of her, Ella realized her eyes had filled with tears. She wiped at them discreetly with Killian's cloak.

"I don't make the rules," Killian said, his voice surprisingly softer. "I just follow them."

She sniffed back the tears, then recomposed herself. "Will you be able to make new rules when you win your foolish competition and take over the throne?" she asked.

"Do your questions ever end?"

"Do they annoy you?"

"Yes."

She glanced at him with a devilish grin. "Good. Then at least I'll have the satisfaction of making you as miserable as you make me."

When he glanced at her, she saw a flicker of amusement in his eyes. "You should get some rest," he said. "We have a lot more hiking tomorrow."

"One more question," she pressed, and Killian let out a frustrated huff. "If you answer, you will have paid my price. You will be debt free."

He turned to her with a skeptical brow. "Fine."

She turned her body to face his. "How many more souls do you need to win the throne?"

Killian watched her for a long moment. "One."

Ella's face fell at his answer. "One, as in… *one*?"

Killian nodded, then looked away from her. "I made a bed of leaves over there. You can have it," he said, pointing behind him.

"What about you?" she asked.

"I'm not tired."

She looked at the bed of leaves, then back at him again. "Then why did you make the bed?"

He didn't respond, but then again, he didn't have to. He had made it for her. The realization filled her with warmth.

"For someone who wants me dead, you're taking quite good care of me," she said teasingly.

"If that's what you think, take a look at your wrists again," he replied, his tone firm. His eyes flickered to her wrists, and his jaw clenched. The sight alone made him angry. But not at her. At himself for having done it.

"What, this?" She lifted one of her wrists. The burn wasn't as red anymore. "You promised me that it wasn't going to happen again, and it hasn't. Thank you for that."

Killian's blue eyes shot toward her in surprise, and as he held her gaze, she wondered what was going through his mind. Then his eyes fell to her lips and something inside of her stirred.

He looked away and cleared his throat, breaking the still moment between them. Whatever that was.

Ella took in a breath, then rose to her feet. "Well, thanks again for the bed." She walked past him, then settled onto the bed, wrapping his large cloak around her body like a blanket. "Good night," she whispered.

He replied with a single nod, and for the millionth time that night, she wished she could see into his mind. Or at least sense his emotions like he was able to do to her.

She rolled onto her side, away from him, and closed her eyes. As closed off as Killian appeared to be, Ella knew there was more to him than he was letting on.

7

KILLIAN

The next morning Ella handed Killian his cloak back. "Thanks," she said, not quite meeting his eyes.

The leather was still warm. He shrugged it on, and the scent of Ella became all-consuming to his already heightened senses. Like flowers in full bloom with just a hint of fragrant spice.

He tensed his jaw and muttered, "Don't mention it."

Ella frowned back at him. "Is there something wrong?" she asked.

Killian picked up his satchel and sheathed his sword. "No," he said, but it came out too harsh. He flexed his hand, trying to ignore the fact that the strong scent had his veins buzzing.

Killian grabbed his sheepskin bottle and took a

large gulp. When the buzzing subsided, he focused on the sound of rushing water a mile ahead. The thought of bathing in cold water helped him to regain his focus. Ella seemed unable to hear the waterfall yet. He thought it remarkable how humans were able to exist in this world with such weak senses.

When they reached an opening in a line of trees, Killian marched through and helped Ella jump down the slippery bank to the water's edge. The air was crisp and cool now that they were high up. Ella's chest heaved as she took greedy breaths.

"Slow your breathing down," Killian muttered. "The air is thinner at this altitude, and if you keep going like that you'll pass out."

Ella did as she was told, and as her breaths slowed, she looked around the vast lake with fog rolling above the water's surface. The morning sunshine was too weak to burn them, but it cast a dazzling golden glow over the scenery. The dewy grass and leaves on the trees shimmered gold and green. And thousands of birds tweeted to each other.

But it was the waterfall that drew Killian's attention. Ella turned to him, having looked about the area, and hummed in disapproval. "Great. It's a dead end."

Killian took off his cloak and dropped it to the floor. "No, it's not," he said, pulling off his shirt.

Ella stepped back. "What are you doing?"

He bundled his sword in his clothes, then yanked off his sheepskin pants before kicking off his boots. Ella's eyes boggled. Her breaths grew short and ragged again as she watched him undress to his cotton underpants.

He wondered what was wrong with her. Her cheeks had turned beet red, and her eyes kept darting in every direction so as to avoid looking straight at him. That was when he realized she must've never had a man undress in front of her before. Still, the mixture of emotions swirling within her was pleasant. He even picked up a dash of arousal coming from her.

The sensation made his skin prickle, and his heightened senses shot through his veins like electricity. He shut his eyes and gave his body a few seconds to recompose.

"Your turn," he said, pushing through the lump in his throat.

Ella's cheeks flushed. "What do you mean, 'my turn'? I'm not taking off my dress."

"Do you want to get your memory back?" he asked, trying to block off her nervous flutters from his senses.

Ella crossed her arms. "And how does taking off my dress help my memory?" she asked.

Killian pointed to the waterfall. "We're going through that. And the less clothing you've got on, the less likely you are to drown. Besides—" He turned back to her. "Fairies are not the most trusting species. They'll be much more inclined not to cut our heads off at first sight if we arrive bare of any threats."

Ella's dainty hands flew to her mouth, then rested on her neck as though she was checking her head was still on. "Are you telling me that if I keep my dress on, the fairies will cut my head off?"

Killian wished he was lying. Fairies were obnoxious, self-righteous, and prideful. Of course, they also happened to be the only creatures in this world that knew everything there was to know about this land and its properties.

"Trust me, I am less thrilled than you to have to deal with them," Killian said. "But if we want that memory, they're the only ones who can help. Now, please, let's not waste any more time."

Ella started to grumble again as she fumbled with the ties on her corset. Killian turned his back to give her some privacy and listened out for any sign of danger. The closest beast was a mama bear and three cubs grazing half a mile down the mountain. They were completely alone with the twittering birds.

Finally, Ella came into view in a thin underdress that barely covered her thighs. She tied her curly hair back with a rag and met Killian's stare with her cheeks burning. Her aura was a blend of humiliation and fury, sending Killian's senses wild. He felt a strong urge to give her his cloak, but that would only drown her. He shook his head and turned away, resisting as his body stiffened.

Then, without a word, he jumped into the water, glad that it was cold. Ella jumped in after him, and they swam toward the waterfall.

"Take a deep breath and don't stop swimming until you get to the other side," he said. "If you panic half-way, just hold onto me. If you try to go back, you will drown."

"What inspiring words. I feel so encouraged now," Ella said, her voice dripping with sarcasm. She took a gulp of air and buried herself in the water.

Killian followed her kicking legs amongst bubbles as they swam past the waterfall. They dove deeper to avoid getting hit by the plunging water, and as they reached it, an undercurrent took them. Ella cried out, a mass of bubbles exploding near her face as the two of them went tumbling forward.

Soon enough, the golden sunlight flooded the water again, and Killian grabbed Ella's arm to pull her up with him. Their faces broke free of the water, and Ella coughed between gasps.

"That was horrid!" she started to say, but then her eyes turned big and glassy as she looked around them.

Wild exotic plants surrounded the glittering lake with oversized flowers of reds and purples. Butterflies fluttered about lazily, and a dragonfly the size of Killian's palm zoomed by. Tall, lustrous trees loomed over them like giants, and the mixture of floral scents was almost enough to cover up Ella's aura. Almost.

They climbed out and shook like wolves, sending sprays of water drops everywhere. Ella squeezed her hair and pulled it forward to cover herself up. Killian turned to check on her, but as he caught sight of the thin cotton fabric stuck to her bosoms, leaving nothing to the imagination, he froze.

When she caught him staring, he ripped his eyes away. Before he could say anything, the pressure of a steel blade at his back made him pause, and he picked up the pungent aura of a fairy standing behind him.

"Who are you?" the fairy demanded. "And what in the roses are you doing in our forest?"

Killian raised his palms. "Relax, fairyman. Don't get your wings in a knot. We come in peace."

The pressure on his back disappeared and the air shifted. Ella looked on with big eyes as a tall, slender man dropped from the sky in front of Killian and narrowed a pair of citrine eyes at him. His sleek, black hair was braided away from his face and spilled down his ice-blue robes. "What did you just call me?"

Killian supposed that the fairy was trying to be menacing, but Killian couldn't take him seriously. Not with the huge delicate silver wings sticking out from his back.

"I'm Killian, and this is Ella—" He stepped in front of her, covering her from the curious eyes that no doubt had noticed the curvy figure underneath the wet clothes.

The fae leaned closer and rested a small knife on Killian's neck, then sniffed him. "You're not fooling anyone. What I want to know is, what is a bounty hunter from the Underworld doing here?"

A flurry of movement drew Killian's attention, and he knew they were surrounded. There must have been a hundred fairies hiding in the trees, probably with arrows pointed at him.

Killian gritted his teeth. He had hoped they wouldn't know he was from the Underworld, but of course, the fairies would notice he was not fully human.

"As you can see, we are bare. We mean no harm to any of you," he said, keeping his voice steady. The fairy's nostrils flared as his eyes narrowed on him, but he didn't retort, so Killian took that as a good sign. "If you will just take us to your leader."

Whispers flew all around them like ruffling leaves. "The Queen? Is he planning to take her soul?"

Killian sensed the rising tension and knew he wasn't going to get anywhere without true transparency. Fairies honored pure truth. It was perhaps the reason why the only other creatures they would deal with were their cousins, the elves and pixies.

Killian took a breath. "I am to bring this woman to the Underworld." He motioned to Ella, who was standing behind him. "But first, I must find out if she is guilty of a crime."

The fae standing in front of him twisted his face into a puzzled look, and he whipped around to look at Ella, who was now shivering, hugging herself, and still soaking wet. "What crime, exactly?" he asked Ella.

She grabbed Killian's arm, but he knew the fae no longer wanted to hear from him. They needed to hear her voice to sense her truthfulness. Killian gave her a reassuring nod. She swallowed so hard, Killian was sure the fairies could hear it from within the trees.

"Murder," she said hesitantly.

The fae's wings twitched. He moved back to Killian and brought a hand to his throat. "You bring a murderer to our midst?" he hissed. "Tell me why I shouldn't kill you both right now."

Killian wished he had brought his sword. His patience was wearing thin, and he wasn't getting anywhere with the bone-headed fae gripping his neck in his skinny fingers.

"She believes she is innocent."

The air changed. All the tension dissipated as

though Killian had uttered a sacred password. Whispers of the word "innocent" spread around the trees.

Finally, the fae dropped his hand and turned back to Ella. "You believe you're innocent?"

Ella nodded. "This man has been hunting me for a crime I did not commit. The problem is… I have lost my memory of the night in question. So, we were hoping that someone here could help me."

Killian knew Ella was putting on a show. Though she spoke in a feeble voice, her aura was blazing with confidence. He thought the fae would see right through the damsel-in-distress act, but to his surprise, the fae's wings folded back and his shoulders relaxed.

"Well, in that case. Come with me." He whistled, and two more fairies jumped out from the forest and took Killian by each arm. Then the first fae offered his for Ella to hold.

Killian resisted the urge to roll his eyes. Fairies might have honored pure truth, but they lacked the wisdom to recognize it. He figured these pretty boys with wings couldn't resist a distressed, helpless maiden.

They walked deeper into the forest, and all manner of fragrant flowers in full bloom overwhelmed Killian's senses. And the forest's vibration was so powerful and strong, it was like walking through a hurricane. He tried to ground himself. The only thing to stop him from losing his temper with the overstimulation was the gentle, spicy scent of Ella. Not her aura. Her scent.

As he tuned in to it, his body relaxed like it was stepping into a warm bath. By the time they reached the fairy capital, Killian's mood had lifted considerably.

The group stopped before a vast square with an elaborate stone fountain. Behind the fountain was a treehouse—no, tree-*palace* —with peaks and turrets, and climbing flowers of purple and yellow. A searing sunshine poured over the place while somewhere a choir sang in harmonies that could rival mermaids.

The earthy path had been leveled, and sweet peas filled the borders. Ella gasped and her aura glowed brightly as she looked around in awe. "This place… is beautiful."

"This is Fairy Capital," the fae with dark hair remarked, a note of pride in his voice. He let go of her hand. "Wait here. I will talk to the Queen."

He swaggered off and disappeared behind the doors of the palace. Once he was gone, the two fairies holding onto Killian let him go and the air grew light and giddy. Killian supposed that fairies did not often have visitors.

"Sorry about Alvin. He's a water fairy. Not so great with manners," the fairy with long red hair said, offering Ella his hand. But when his eyes dropped briefly to her chest, Killian stepped in front of her once more.

The fae turned his azure eyes to Killian and beamed. "I'm Aalish." He gestured to his burnt orange robes. "Fire fairy."

Ella peeked from behind Killian with a smile, and her aura was brighter than the noonday sun. "Do you think you can help me recover my lost memory?" she asked.

He nodded to the fairy to his left, who Killian noticed wore the same colored robe. He wondered if it was a uniform of some kind to distinguish their class.

"Not us fire fairies, no," Aalish said, "You need an earth fairy, I reckon. But it all depends on the Queen…"

The other fairy nudged him in the ribs. "Stop jabbering, you fire nymph. The Queen will have your head for spilling out secrets like that."

Aalish rubbed his chest with a scowl but didn't say any more. Ella did not seem to be concerned by the reaction. "If you two are fire fairies, I don't suppose you can do anything about this?" Her wet garments clung to her body no matter how much she tugged on them.

Aalish looked thoughtful but then laughed. "You want me to set fire to you? You'd be roasted on the spot."

He whistled, and a female flew down with her hair flowing like crimson waves over her shoulders. She wore a white robe. Aalish's cheeks grew red as she grinned at him. "Mistyblue, will you do the honors?"

Mistyblue had eyes so light, they were almost silver. She took a look at Killian and Ella, then placed her palms together, raising them to the sky.

Killian watched with fascination as the fairy spun around at a speed of epic proportions. A gust of warm wind rushed over them, nearly knocking Ella off her feet. Killian grabbed her waist to steady her.

When the fairy stopped, Ella and Killian were completely dry, but also a little disheveled. Ella's curls had turned frizzy and wild.

She patted herself down. "Thanks," she muttered.

Aalish looked smug. "That's Mistyblue." Then he jerked his head to the fairy while looking at Ella. "Wind fairy."

Killian thought that fact was obvious but inclined his head all the same.

Finally, the doors to the palace opened, and Alvin reappeared. "Come." His words were spoken with such authority that they boomed in the square, and birds flew up into the sky.

Killian and Ella exchanged looks and walked up the earthy path to meet Alvin.

"You have three minutes to make your request," Alvin said.

"Thank you," Killian said. And they walked on. When they entered the palace, Ella sucked in a breath with a little squeak. The ceiling was a huge glass dome that let in a flood of sunlight and lit up a vast mosaic tile floor. The colors danced before their eyes, as though the picture of four fairies had come to life. Wings fluttered and robes flowed as Killian moved his head, studying the picture.

Two young fairies in olive green robes approached them and offered them clothes.

Killian took the gray robe and tossed it over his head, while Ella gratefully accepted a yellow one. Now dressed, they were led up an oakwood spiral staircase that creaked beneath their feet.

When they reached the top, they were taken to a throne room with all manner of fine furniture and tapestries hanging on the walls. On the throne sat a female. She was smaller than the other fairies, with long, bushy golden hair. She wore a glittering gown that shimmered like it was made of a million diamonds. Her youthful face and tiny hands gave Killian the impression that she was young.

She must have inherited the throne recently, judging by the way she sat, with slight stiffness, as though she was trying to look important and confident.

But her aura reeked of insecurity. Killian thought he could use that to their advantage.

"Your Majesty, thank you for your time," Killian said, taking a knee. "You are most gracious to accept us in your forest during our time of great need."

Killian hated having to speak like a sycophant. But the Queen's shoulders settled, and her aura warmed at the sight of him.

"I must confess, this is the first time I am meeting a bounty hunter from the Underworld," she confessed.

"Please, call me Killian."

The fairy's mouth lifted at one corner. "You may call me Queen Zaria."

Ella dropped to her knees beside Killian. "Queen Zaria, I am Ella of the Kingdom of the Shores, and I humbly ask for your help."

Queen Zaria turned to look at Ella and studied her for a moment. "You wish to retrieve a lost memory?"

Ella nodded, and the Queen hummed.

"First, I need to know how you lost it."

Ella bit her lip and looked at her toes, peeping out from the bottom of her robe. "I remember being on a ship. I was assisting the King and then… nothing." She glanced at Killian, her eyes misty. "The next thing I know, I'm waking up in a small boat with blood on my hands and clothes."

The Queen sucked in a breath with a hiss. "I can

certainly see why everyone thinks you are guilty. Nonetheless, you mention a ship? Where were you headed?"

"Neverland, Your Majesty," Ella said.

The Queen rose from her throne and took thoughtful steps. "And you have absolutely no memory at all that might explain the blood on your hands?"

Ella nodded. "I get nightmares sometimes. About… that night. But everything is so broken up and just flashes, really."

The Queen hummed again, squinting at Ella. "Have you noticed any change in behavior since then? Depression, anxiety, mood swings?"

"Definitely, a bit of paranoia too," Killian chimed in.

Ella and the Queen looked at him like he had just broken wind.

"What? I'm just making an observation," Killian added.

Queen Zaria scowled. "Neverland, you say..." she said, turning back to Ella. "Well, I'll have one of the healers look you over. But my first impression is you've been poisoned with pixie dust."

"Interesting," Killian muttered. Rumple was right after all. "Do you know if the pixie dust is still affecting her?"

She nodded. "Pixie dust stays in the system for a long time. Side effects only worsen as time goes on.

Especially if the victim was made to do something…" She glanced at Killian. "Traumatic."

"Like kill someone?" Killian asked, raising a brow.

"What can be done?" Ella asked, sounding hopeless. Tears leaked from her eyes and slid down her pink cheeks. She wiped them away in a flash, but her tormented aura grew all-consuming for Killian, and there was no way for her to hide the anguish she held inside.

The Queen tutted. "There's a flower with medicinal properties that can help."

"Does it reverse the damage?" Killian asked.

"Although the flower will cure her of the pixie dust poison, it will also put her in a very deep sleep, which will enable her to see into her own mind," the Queen explained.

"What?" Killian and Ella asked in unison.

But before they could ask more questions, the Queen flicked her dainty fingers and two fairies came forward. "Pixie dust. It causes hallucination, amnesia, loss of self-control, to name a few… and as time passes on, the mind creates its own barriers to any memories relating to the period that you were first poisoned."

"Can she drink the medicine and just be cured of the poison without having to go inside her own mind?" Killian asked.

"It is not possible to have one without the other," the Queen explained.

Ella shook her head, pressing her fingertips to her temples. "Are you saying I need to get inside my own head and…"

"Break down the barrier, and root out the last fragments of pixie dust," the Queen finished.

Ella and Killian exchanged worried looks. Killian did not like the idea of Ella walking around inside her head. The idea was so abstract. He wasn't even sure it was possible.

"I must warn you," the Queen added, breaking through Killian's thoughts. "The mind is a very powerful, alluring place. Anything in there is possible. Anything at all. Your greatest fears come alive. As do your biggest wishes. Many have tried to venture into their mind… only to never return."

"I've seen worse realms," Killian muttered. Although he wasn't going to refute that the mind was a powerful enemy, and not something to take lightly.

The Queen stepped forward and touched Ella's arm. "My aids will show you to the healer's cabin if you wish to proceed. But you must consider the risks."

Ella nipped her bottom lip and took a deep breath. Then she looked long and hard at Killian, but he couldn't make the decision for her. She sighed. "If that is the only way to prove my innocence and clear my body of the pixie dust poison, what other choice do I have?" She hugged herself. "I'll do it."

"Indeed, you will." The Queen nodded to the fairies who stood beside Killian and Ella, waiting to take them. "The flower will need to be stewed in the silver rays of moonlight for a time to extract its medicine. The healer will check you are in good health, and I invite you both to join me for a fairy feast tonight."

Killian bowed his head. "That's very generous. Thank you, Your Majesty."

THE GENTLE MOONLIGHT RESTED ON THE TABLES LADEN with all manner of fine food. Hundreds of fairies were seated within their ranks. Wind fairy with the wind fairies. Water, earth, and fire.

The owls hooted joyfully as the fairies sang, and even the crickets sounded chirpy as they joined in the celebration. Killian did not know the reason for the elaborate affair. A choir of fairies sang while everyone else ate. The boughs of red and yellow flowers hung from the branches, and everyone wore exquisite clothes.

Killian glanced at Ella just as she lifted a small bowl to sip the liquid. Her soft, golden curls had been smoothed out into elegant waves down her back. She wore a pink cotton dress with a corset. A thin veil fastened by a clasp on the back of her head rested just below her waist. If Killian hadn't known any better, she looked ready to be married.

Killian shrugged against the tight cotton shirt, not quite large enough for his stature. And his dress pants were itchy. He missed his thick boots and dragon-scale armor. The clothes he wore in the Underworld. He would have even been happy to wear his cloak again.

Clothing was so thin and weak in the human world. Especially in the Fairy Forest. But Killian did not complain. Instead, he enjoyed the food and watched as Ella asked question after question to the fairies seated nearby. The Queen had them at the head table with her and kept glancing at them, as though wondering when Killian and Ella might do something. Though what exactly she expected them to do, Killian couldn't be sure. Perhaps she was waiting for them to change their minds. But she didn't know how stubborn Ella could be, which in this case, worked to their advantage.

He looked at the steaming pot over the open fire, the sleeping medicine bubbling inside. Killian would be lying if he said he had no concerns about Ella diving into her own mind. But not because he thought Ella was weak—it was because her guilty aura no doubt had darkened the deepest corners of her mind. And unless she gave him permission, there was no way he could follow after her.

Even if he did, that was one of the few realms Killian had never entered. One thing he feared was not having control, and having to deal with the unpredictability of the mind would surely drive him to insanity.

"This bread is sweeter than sugar," Ella said, leaning into one of the fairies sitting next to her. Killian watched as Ella nibbled on the corner of a yellow crusty roll.

Aalish chuckled. "Don't eat too much of that. It's faedough. All of the nutrients your body needs for a day are in just one bite. Fairies use it for going on long journeys."

"And how often do fairies travel outside of Fairy Forest?" Killian asked, lifting a brow.

There was a hush in response, and every pair of eyes landed on him, unblinking. The air grew cold as their offense encircled the fairies like a dark cloud.

Somebody cleared their throat.

Killian smirked. He knew fairies never left their home. Though the reason behind it had never been mentioned. Perhaps they were afraid of the dangers that lurked outside their safe haven. They kept to themselves in the world, probably completely unaware that the Chanted Kingdom had been under three different Queens in less than two years. And he wondered if they were even affected during the days of eternal winter. He glanced at the fire fairies, the edges of their wings glowing like embers, and thought probably not.

"Well, we have it for the day we need it," the Queen said. And that was final.

She forced a smile, and everyone continued eating their food. Except for Ella, who had gone from sipping to gulping her bowl.

Once it was empty, she plopped down from her stool and grabbed Aalish's arm. "Dance with me," she said merrily.

The fae seemed more than happy to oblige, and they danced their way toward the fairies who were playing musical instruments.

Killian leaned back and watched Ella as she laughed at herself, trying to twirl. Her aura was an adorable blend of pink and yellow. The purple stain of guilt was faint, like a forgotten bruise. And for a fraction of a moment, he caught the corner of his lip twitching at the sight of her so joyful and carefree.

It was a side of her he'd never seen, and he found himself wondering what could have driven someone so lively to lose their will to live. Over the centuries, he'd claimed many dark souls, but not once had he questioned what had brought them to that condition. It was easier that way. It helped him avoid distractions and kept him focused on his goal: Winning the throne.

But there was something about Ella's soul he couldn't shake. And it wasn't for lack of trying. She was like an enigma to him, a blend of many colors, bright and dark alike. And he found himself wondering what could possibly have happened in her life that caused her bright soul to darken so much.

Ella threw her head back with a cackle, and even though the music was loud, her laughter landed in Killian's ears like vodka to his senses. His body relaxed and a soothing calm came over him. The thought of shutting his eyes for a moment crossed his mind, until the music grew louder and the tempo grew faster. He would've been able to block it out had the joy in Ella's heart not been sending vibrations into his chest. He shifted in his seat, uncomfortable with the waves of happiness that kept crashing onto him. He thought about blocking the connection with her, but he knew that if he did, he would end up connecting with the fairies and the relentless buzzing of their wings would send his senses into overdrive.

So, as much as he hated the warm and fuzzy feeling that beat like a drum in his chest, Ella's scent was the only thing keeping him steady.

"How much longer until the medicine is ready?" Killian asked the Queen.

She placed her wine glass down, then dabbed her lips with a napkin. "Time goes by faster when you're having fun, you know?" She motioned toward a rosy-cheeked Ella on the dance floor. "You should learn a thing or two from her."

Killian leaned back and gulped down his glass of wine. He didn't look forward to spending the entire night enduring the thumping of joy. Not that he didn't want her to have fun. He just didn't care to feel it himself.

But then the music changed and the tempo slowed, and something shifted within Ella. Killian stiffened in his seat and scanned the crowd of dancers until he spotted her under the dim light. Her eyes were closed as she swayed to the rhythm of the song. He sensed heat rising within her, and her sensuality sent an electric shock down his spine.

When Aalish's hands moved down to her hips, Killian waited for Ella to slap his hands away. When she didn't, he knew she'd had too much to drink.

He stood and walked across the dance floor, which consisted of oversized palm leaves woven together to make a bouncy surface, and it creaked under their feet. "I'll take it from here," Killian said, cutting between them.

Ella's eyes widened in surprise at the sight of him.

"Well, look who decided to join the fun," she said playfully.

"And you're having a bit too much fun, don't you think?"

"Nonsense." She threw her arms around his neck and swayed to the music. "There's no such thing as too much fun."

She tried making him sway with her, but he didn't move. He wasn't there to dance. He cut in to make sure she didn't do anything she would regret in the morning.

"Come on, Killian, if you're going to cut in, then dance with me. Otherwise, I'm going to find someone who will."

Killian grunted, then wrapped an arm around her waist and pulled her close. "How much alcohol have you had?"

She giggled. "What alcohol?" When her eyes sparkled with innocence, Killian knew she wasn't lying.

In one swift motion, Killian grabbed Aalish by his robe and ripped him away from his new dancing partner. "What has she been drinking?" he demanded.

Aalish gave Ella a lopsided grin. "It's kaavah. It's to lower her inhibitions and open up her mind. She was too guarded. She would never have entered the dream world in that state of mind."

"Let him go," Ella said, tugging on Killian's arm. "I feel fine. Better than fine."

Killian let go of the fae and turned to Ella. She was not better than fine. She was tipsy and heated to her core, which made his blood boil like a volcano.

"I'm hot," she said, lifting her hair to cool down the back of her neck. "Why am I so hot?"

"I think we should call it a night." He tried putting space between them, but Ella grabbed him again and leaned forward. Her natural scent washed over him like a tsunami until all of his senses tingled.

"Not until we finish this dance!" This time, she wasn't so playful, and the words came out like an order.

Killian took her hand, and she twirled herself, lifting his arm up over her head.

"Hey! You're good at this," she said, genuinely surprised. "I'm impressed."

She took Killian's other hand and placed it on the curve of her waist. Heat lodged in his chest, and he pressed his eyes shut, trying to keep his emotions from igniting.

He could not lose control. She was not being herself. But Killian couldn't think straight. Ella's addicting scent was luring him in like a Venus fly trap, and his body was electric.

For the first time in more than three hundred years, a new sense took over Killian. Though it was a sensation that was so distant in his memory, he hardly remembered it.

When a gentle gust of wind wafted through her luscious hair and a fresh plume of floral scent flooded his nostrils, he opened his eyes again.

Her fingers ran down his arms at a tantalizing pace, and it made his skin tingle everywhere she touched.

She must've noticed the effect she was having on him because she bit her bottom lip. Her lips were glossy and pink, and the urge to taste them burned in his veins. He flexed his hands, fighting against the urge to taste every part of her mouth.

She pressed her body up to his chest, and her warmth set off an explosion inside of him. He simultaneously broke into a sweat and got goosebumps. As she continued moving her body, all of his muscles tensed and blood rushed to all sorts of places.

Just before the feeling became all-consuming, Killian placed both hands on Ella's shoulder and stepped back. "And we're done here."

Ella dropped her arms, blinking at him with a deep frown. "You're leaving already?"

"We both are." Before she could argue, he bent over, grabbed her legs, and threw her over his shoulder.

"Killian! You're such a caveman…" Her grumbles faded to mumbles until they were no longer coherent words. Killian thought for sure she had fallen asleep as he marched into the night.

He didn't stop until they were safe inside the cabin

that had been offered to them. Upon entering the bedroom, he laid her on the soft bed, her blonde curls spread sensually over the goose-feather pillow. As her body relaxed, a satisfied smile spread across her lips.

"Your eyes are so blue," she whispered, looking up at him. Then her bottom lip was in between her teeth again, and her entire aura grew rich with need, like a primal hunger ripping through her senses as she ran a finger down Killian's chest.

He grabbed her hand and placed it gently back on the bed. "You should rest. It's going to be a long day tomorrow."

She nodded and closed her eyes. Killian figured she fell asleep because the vibrations in his chest finally subsided, and he let out an exhale.

As he was about to stand, Ella grabbed his cotton shirt and pulled herself up. Before he could stop her, she kissed him.

It was soft and tender, but as suddenly as it happened, it was over. She pulled back with her eyes still closed and let herself fall back onto her pillow.

Killian sat frozen for several heartbeats, unsure of what to do. Finally, he grabbed a blanket and covered her with it, then made a makeshift bed on the floor. He laid down and closed his eyes, relieved to have his emotions still like a lake in the night.

He rolled onto his back and silently reprimanded

himself. He could not let that happen again. Ella was his last soul. If her memory was restored and they discovered she was guilty, he would be taking her to the Underworld, and she would belong to Hades.

He couldn't have any feelings for her. She was his mission. A mere pawn in a game set long before she was even born. When Hades set the challenge, that whoever was the first to collect one hundred thousand souls for him would be worthy of the throne, Killian had his doubts.

But now he was so close. It would be a tragedy to throw it all away for a human. Even a human as captivating as Ella.

8

ELLA

A mixture of emotions swirled inside of Ella as she settled on a bed next to a group of fairies. It was morning and she was full of jitters.

Although she had a feeling that had something to do with the kaavah drink they gave her the night before. They said it would help open her mind, but it did the opposite. She couldn't remember anything from the night before. Aalish had said he enjoyed dancing with her until Killian cut in, but when she asked Killian about it, he said they never danced at all. He said they drank a little and then went to sleep. Sounded like a boring night, which was exactly what she needed to prepare for whatever was about to happen.

There was a hushed silence as the fairies busied themselves around her. One of them placed a warm blanket over her body as she lay on the bed, while another was stirring something in a big pot.

Ella took in a deep breath as Ensley, one of the earth fairies, leaned over to give her an intense stare. Killian was at her side, watching the fairy's every move with narrowed eyes, as though he was on high alert and ready to attack should things go wrong.

"Here, drink this," Ensley said, bringing a bowl with her. When Ella tilted her head up, she noticed the bowl was half filled with water, and a large yellow flower floated inside. Ella recognized the flower. It was a sundrop flower.

Aunt Mara had told Ella before she left that if she ever needed answers, to look for the sundrop flowers.

"Remember, the longer you stay under, the harder it will be for you to return. And if you stay past midnight, you will be trapped in your mind for good," Ensley explained, her gray eyes boring into Ella's. "Also… if something kills you in there, your brain dies here."

Ella swallowed hard, pushing through the lump in her throat. It wasn't so much the risk of going brain dead, but the fact that something deadly even existed inside her mind was terrifying.

"Are you ready?" Ensley asked. When Ella nodded, the fairy brought the bowl to her lips.

"Wait." Killian placed a hand between Ella and the

fairy. Ensley pulled back as Killian looked down to meet Ella's eyes. "Are you sure about this?"

Ella stared up at him, confused. "Wasn't this the plan?"

"Did you not hear the risks? You could die in there."

"And if I don't get that memory, you'll drag me to the Underworld and I'll die anyway." She gave him a puzzled look. "What's gotten into you?"

Was he concerned about her safety? Sure, her soul was his winning prize, but that wasn't what she was sensing from his gaze.

He ran a nervous hand through his hair. "I guess what I'm asking is if you're ready?"

"Yes," she said, trying to mask the fear in her voice. Yes, she wanted to find out what really happened that night, but that didn't mean she wasn't terrified.

"What if you don't return?" he asked, his Adam's apple bobbing as if he also had a lump in his throat.

She leaned her head down again, then let out a nervous breath. "Then I need you to kill me."

Killian's brows shot up. "What?"

She turned to meet his eyes. "If something goes wrong, and returning is no longer an option, I can't stay trapped in my mind forever. I don't know what darkness lies in there. So, I need you to promise me that you won't leave me trapped in there."

Killian shook his head as if he wasn't hearing her correctly.

She reached for his hand. "Promise me, Killian."

He narrowed his eyes, clearly not wanting to say the words. But she needed to hear them. She needed to hear him say it. "Killian, please?"

"I promise," he finally said. "I will not leave you trapped in there."

A heavy weight lifted from her chest, and she let out a relieved breath. "Thank you." She gave his hand a light squeeze, then turned to Ensley. "I'm ready now."

Ensley looked at Killian, who still had his arm separating them. He pulled back with a huff as Ella focused on the bowl Ensley brought to her lips once more. The water tasted metallic against her tongue, but she forced two gulps down her throat.

Ensley placed the bowl aside, then went to stand above Ella's head. Two small fingers touched her temples, and suddenly, Ella became overcome with sleepiness, her heartbeat slowing. "Close your eyes," the fairy's voice entered her mind like a thought. "And remember, if at any given moment you would like to wake up, you must find a way to jolt your subconscious. Usually, that works best with the sensation of falling."

Ella took in a deep breath as if she were about to dive underwater. Then, before her eyes closed, she glanced one last time at Killian, his face etched with concern. Warmth washed through her at the thought that maybe, just maybe, he grew to care about her for more than just her soul.

He gave her hand an encouraging squeeze. "I'll be right here if you need me."

She gave him a single nod, then closed her eyes.

THE SMELL OF FRESH FLOWERS FILLED THE AIR AS ELLA'S eyes fluttered open. She was lying on a bed with etchings of mermaids and tridents carved into the ceiling above her. She had seen those carvings before. And as she sat up, she recognized the room.

It was Lily's bedroom.

The Prince's niece, whom she'd spent years caring for while she worked for the King of the Shores.

Why was she in Lily's bedroom? Out of all places for her mind to take her, why back to the Shores' castle?

She jumped from the bed and opened the door. The hallway was dark, but even with the limited lighting, Ella could see that it wasn't the same hallway she so often walked through in the years she'd been a maid there. The stone walls lacked windows, making it feel like a dungeon.

"Hello?" she called out into the darkness, her voice echoing down the seemingly endless corridor.

A little girl's giggles echoed back, and Ella's breath hitched in her throat. "Lily?"

The torch on the wall lit up, making Ella jump. Silence washed over the hall, then another wave of giggles echoed in the distance.

"Ella, come play with me!" Lily's playful voice came from down the hall, and Ella forced herself to remember she was in a dream world. None of that was real.

She grabbed the torch from the wall with a shaky hand and walked slowly down the tunnel, illuminating the way.

A door appeared to her left with light coming from the space beneath. Ella pushed it open. The entrance hall came into view, but there was no one in sight. No guards. No maids. Not even Arnold, the butler who oftentimes stood outside the King's throne room. Seeing the palace so devoid of people and the usual hustle and bustle was eerie and sent the hairs on the back of Ella's neck on end.

As she stepped into the entrance hall, the door behind her slammed shut with a bang. She swung around, startled, only to find that the door had vanished.

Lily's little footsteps against the marble floor grew closer, and Ella turned toward the sound. "Ella!"

Lily's small frame crashed into Ella's side, hugging her legs, and burying her face into Ella's dress. Her blonde curls were as light as the sun, and when she looked up to smile at Ella, her innocence was as refreshing as a summer's breeze.

But then Lily frowned.

Ella crouched until they were eye to eye. "What's wrong, sweetie?"

"You left," she said with trembling lips and teary eyes. "And didn't even say goodbye."

When a single tear slid down her cheek, Ella wiped it away, then tucked a golden strand of Lily's hair behind her ear. "I'm so sorry. I didn't have a choice."

"If I help you find what you're looking for, will you come back?" Lily asked.

Ella studied Lily for a moment. "You know what I'm looking for?"

Lily nodded with a smile. "Come with me!"

She pulled Ella by the hand as she often did when her tea party was ready and she didn't want to leave her dolls waiting. Normally, Ella would tell her not to run, but in that moment, rushing was necessary. The quicker Ella found what she came for, the sooner she could leave.

Lilly let go of Ella's hand and ran ahead, her

golden curls bouncing on her little shoulders. Ella followed Lily through the narrow halls toward the back of the castle until she stopped in front of a mahogany door to the left. Lily pushed the door open and ran inside. Though Ella hadn't yet caught up, she knew it was the King's study.

Ella peeked her head in before stepping inside. The room was empty, and Lily was gone.

"Lily?" Ella called out. "Where did you—" The rumble of an earthquake trembled beneath Ella's feet, and she jumped back, grabbing onto a sofa by the wall. The room, though small at first, began to expand. Growing bigger and bigger as the ground rumbled. Ella's mind spun at a dizzying speed. She closed her eyes, gripping the sofa as the floor shifted under her. When the movement came to a halt, Ella opened her eyes again. A gasp escaped her throat as she witnessed the transformation before her.

The King's study had become one of the largest libraries Ella had ever seen. Books lined the walls from the floor to the ceiling. Only one wall across the room was bare, with nothing but a balcony leading to a small courtyard outside.

The gentle sound of a ballerina music box started, catching Ella's attention. She followed the melody, scanning the row of books. As she drew closer to one particular shelf, the music grew louder. One book was out of place, and she ran a finger down its thick spine. When she pulled it out, the music was crystal clear. She opened it, expecting to find words written on a page, but instead, it was blank. The music died suddenly, and Ella stared at the blank pages, puzzled.

What was the meaning of that?

She flipped through the pages, searching for anything she might've missed, but the entire book was blank.

She thought back to the melody that had been playing a moment ago. It was familiar. But the memory was faint.

She closed her eyes and began humming the melody. After a few heartbeats, the blank pages began to glow.

Ella shot her eyes open and watched as the ink smeared on the page. But instead of words, an image appeared like a sketch. A portrait of her parents. Her mother's curls resembled hers as they fell loosely down her shoulder, and her father's almond-shaped eyes resembled her own. Her heart swelled at the sight of them, looking happy and vibrant.

When the melody started again, a baby appeared in her mother's arms. The page began to glow once more, and Ella brushed the tip of her finger over the sketch. Her parents began to move as if they were alive inside that very book. Ella hadn't seen her parents since before her teen years, but she still remembered every trace of their features. Her heart swelled at the sight of them. Of missing them.

A soft smile tugged at the corner of her lips as she finally understood what she was holding.

It was a memory. Her memory of them.

Her breath hitched as her heart picked up speed. She stepped back and scanned the rows of books once more. If each of them were different memories, then all she needed was to find her memory of that night.

She closed the book and its glow faded. Though she could no longer see the pages, she was pretty certain the image of her parents had vanished. She swallowed through the lump in her throat, then placed the book back on the shelf. She scanned through the rows of books again, having no idea how they were sorted. How could she possibly find the one she needed?

Okay, Ella. Focus. She reached out her hands as if she could touch all the books at once. *This is your mind. Narrow it down. Find the book you need.*

The shelves in front of her began to shake as if experiencing an earthquake. Two books flew off the shelf and onto the floor by her feet. Ella picked them up and flipped through its pages as quickly as she could.

The longer you stay under, the harder it will be to return, the fairy's warning echoed inside Ella's mind.

Ink bled through the pages, showing images of the day she first arrived at the Shores' kingdom. She tossed it aside and grabbed the next book. But there were only images of Ella leaving the kingdom and returning home.

What about everything in between? That was what she needed.

She looked up to see if there was a book she'd missed, and although she had two books in her possession, there seemed to be a book missing, leaving an empty space.

The huff of an animal came from the corner, and Ella froze in the middle of the room. She turned around slowly to find a wolf the size of a grizzly bear lying by the fire, sleeping. Its breathing vibrated the ground.

As Ella moved slowly toward the door, a man wearing regal clothes strode in. He stood tall, confident, and refined as Ella took in his appearance. She gasped and stepped back.

"Prince Tristan." Ella curtsied, but then shook her head, reminding herself that he wasn't real.

"How dare you come back here after what you've done?" he said venomously as he took a threatening step toward her.

She moved away from him on wobbly legs. "I didn't… I couldn't have…"

"If you're so sure, then why are you here?" he hissed. "You know you killed the King. We all do. Guards! Seize that murderer!"

Ella sprinted in the opposite direction and burst through the nearest door. She rushed down the stone steps to a courtyard. A wave of footsteps forced her to a halt, and she spun around to see a group of guards surrounding her. Their uniforms as gray as the sky above them.

"Wait, don't, please," she pleaded as they closed in on her. "Please! I didn't do it!"

All hope seemed lost as one of the guards reached out to grab her. But an angry growl came from behind her. The wolf was now very much awake as it landed in front of her, ready for a fight. A screech escaped Ella's throat—until she realized the animal wasn't attacking her. It was protecting her.

The guards jumped back, but before they could draw their swords, the wolf attacked. Their screams filled the air as the wolf grabbed them with its jaw and threw them to every side.

Ella was frozen in place. She had never seen a wolf so large. She had heard about the beast but never had she encountered anything like it.

Then the wolf turned toward her, panting. It had golden brown fur, and its yellow eyes peered into Ella's shocked expression. "Run, Ella!"

Ella cocked her head, recognizing the voice that entered her mind. "Belle?"

"Run!"

Ella broke into a sprint toward the stone steps that led to a forest. The sounds of the guards screaming and their bones crunching faded into the background as she entered the woods. Her heart raced while her lungs burned, but the thought of slowing down was the farthest from her mind. Her brain was too busy trying to process the reason as to why a wolf would have sounded like her childhood friend, Belle.

Ella pushed her legs harder, ignoring her throbbing muscles. Once the castle was far behind her, she slowed her pace and leaned against a tree, panting. Her heart thumped so hard it ached. The air was getting colder as the dark clouds rolled in.

She needed a new plan to find her lost memory. Wandering around aimlessly wasn't going to be practical. She was looking for a book. But where would she find a book in the middle of the forest?

She looked up to find a clearing ahead. She approached the field of orange flowers, looking for anything unusual. Anything that could guide her as to what direction to take.

She took a step forward and a hard crunch came from underneath her feet. A piece of orange fruit lay broken on the ground. Suddenly, Ella noticed it wasn't a field of flowers. It was a vast pumpkin patch.

Though a vine of pumpkins was not itself unusual, something about that one seemed strange. As Ella dragged her feet through the dirt to clean off the orange goo that was stuck to the bottom of her shoe, a faint screeching came from the center of the vine. A sound that reminded Ella of the rats that lived in her stepmother's basement.

She stopped dragging her shoe and stood still. The screeching drew closer, and Ella stepped back. Another pumpkin crunched under her feet, splashing the juices up her leg. She jumped back with a grunt. *Gross.*

As she dragged her feet on the dirt ground again, a movement inside the crushed pumpkin caught her eye. When she caught sight of what it was, a gasp lodged in her throat as her eyes widened in horror. Every hair on her body stood on end.

A scorpion the size of a cat crawled out, wobbling as if he'd hatched prematurely. With his tail curled upward, he was as tall as her waist. He turned toward Ella, then froze in place. She couldn't tell if he was more afraid of her than she was of him.

Then a hiss came from his tail, and a piercing scream ripped through Ella's throat. She bolted back into the woods. The screeching of legs hitting the ground at a fierce speed came from behind her. Adrenaline coursed through her body, and she pushed her legs harder.

Her foot caught an overgrown root, sending her flying to the ground. A sharp stab shot up her arm as it scraped over the rocks. She bit back the pain and staggered to her feet again. But as she looked up, she spotted the scorpion ahead of her. She jerked back, wondering how on Earth he had run past her.

A hissing came from behind her, and Ella froze. Nausea rose within her stomach at the realization that there were two of them.

Pushing through her paralysis, she swung around. The second scorpion stood a few feet away. She walked to the side, angling her body to keep both of them in her line of sight. Not that it would make a difference. She had no fighting chance against one of them, let alone two. Their claws clicked like a lobster, and Ella stopped breathing.

That was it. She was going to die.

A flaming torch fell from the tree above, hitting the ground between them with a thud. One of the scorpions scuttled back, frightened of the fire. But before he could turn around to run away, a shadowy figure jumped down from the tree and pierced the scorpion with its sword.

Ella looked away as the crunch echoed in the darkness. Her stomach churned and that fairy bread almost came back up. The other scorpion hissed, his tail high above his head. The shadowy figure pulled an arrow from their quiver and shot the creature in the side. The scorpion screeched in pain, then ran away, disappearing into the woods.

Ella let out a shuddering breath as she turned toward her rescuer. The burning branch on the ground illuminated the space between them.

The figure turned around, revealing the soft features of a woman. Her long blonde hair was tied in a single braid over one shoulder.

"Are you all right?" she asked.

Ella stared at the woman with eyes unblinking. Unlike everyone she had seen thus far, this was the first person that didn't look familiar. "Who are you?"

"The name is Aurora," she said, picking up the flaming torch from the ground and handing it to Ella. "Here. You might want to hold on to this."

Ella's body trembled at the thought that she would need to use it against more of those creatures. "Are there more of them?"

Aurora pointed a thumb over her shoulder. "A whole field of them."

"The pumpkins?" Ella muttered.

"Yes. Those are eggs that hatch at the slightest sound."

"Sound?"

Aurora pressed a finger to her lips with a soft shush. "We have to be extremely quiet."

Ella looked at the torch in her hand, then moved closer to Aurora. "If they're repelled by fire, why don't we just set them all ablaze?"

"They're not repelled by fire," Aurora said, tapping her knuckle on the torch. "It's cedarwood oil they hate. It kills them on the spot. My arrows are also made of them." She then pulled out a knife and sliced the nearest cedar tree. A clear liquid leaked from the bark as if the tree was bleeding. Aurora touched the clear goo, then rubbed it on her arms. "This will keep their claws away from you, but you still have to be careful with their tails."

Ella took a handful of the cedarwood oil from the bark and rubbed it on both of her arms and legs as well as the back of her neck.

"I don't understand," Ella said, wiping her hands on her dress and reeking her clothes with the oil for good measure. "If this is my dream world, where do those creatures come from?"

"They were created by your mind to attack when you get too close to a protected memory," Aurora answered, coating her arrows with extra oil.

"But why would they attack me?" Ella asked.

"They guard your darkest memories," Aurora

explained. "Especially the ones you want to lock away and forget."

Ella turned toward the direction of the field. "So, to get to the memory I need, I'll have to go through them?"

Aurora gave Ella a quizzical look. "Why would you want to retrieve a dark memory?"

Ella sighed. "It's a long story, and I don't have much time. The fairies said that if I stay past midnight, I may never wake up."

Aurora's expression fell, and she lowered her eyes to the sword she was coating with oil. "The fairies are correct. I suggest you listen to them. Otherwise, if you don't... you will wish you had."

Ella watched Aurora for a long moment, the flames from the torch casting shadows on her skin. "You're not from my mind, are you?"

Aurora shook her head but didn't look up.

"How long have you been trapped in here?" Ella asked, her voice barely above a whisper.

Aurora looked up and sucked in a deep breath as if trying not to let the truth overcome her with sadness. "Too long. Now, you should go. No memory is worth the risk of being trapped in here. Trust me."

Ella didn't expect Aurora to understand, and there was no time to explain. "I need to get this memory. Otherwise, I'm as good as dead, anyway."

Aurora let out a long breath. "You're making a mistake."

"Yes, I have a knack for those. Now, will you please tell me how I can get through that field without getting eaten alive?" Ella pleaded.

Aurora sheathed her sword, then turned to face Ella. "You have until midnight before you reach the point of no return."

"How do I know when it's midnight?" Ella asked.

"You will hear a bell. But until then, you can look at the eclipse." Aurora pointed to the waxing crescent moon in the sky. "When it reaches a total eclipse, you know it's midnight. Keep an eye on it at all times. And just to be safe, you should leave before then."

Ella nodded. "Fine. So, what's the plan?"

Aurora whistled, and a black stallion came galloping into view. She climbed on without even waiting for him to come to a full stop. "This is Midnight," Aurora said, caressing the horse's mane. "And yes, I see the irony. Now, come on."

She offered Ella a hand and helped her climb on behind her. They rode quietly through the woods until they reached the edge of the field. "Okay, get down."

Ella climbed off, careful not to make any noise as her feet landed on the ground.

Aurora reached into her satchel and pulled out a midsize horn. "When you hear the sound of this horn, run through that field as fast as you can." She kept her voice barely above a whisper.

"Wait!" Ella's whisper came out panicked as she grabbed Aurora's leg. "You want me to run on foot? Are you out of your mind?"

"Trust me, I'm going to need Midnight more than you."

"But where will I run to?" Ella asked.

Aurora peered into the distance. "I have no idea how your mind works, but… my guess is that tower over there."

Ella followed Aurora's line of sight and spotted a tall tower of gold looming at the top of a hill.

"All right. Get ready," Aurora said, grabbing onto Midnight's reins. "It was nice meeting you, Ella."

Aurora took off into the field, galloping Midnight deep into the nest of the creepy crawlers. The large pumpkins began to shake as they hatched, one by one. Aurora turned a sharp right and galloped away. Most of the newborn scorpions crawled out of their pumpkins and followed the sound of the horse's hooves against the ground, leaving their hatched eggs behind.

Ella hid behind a tree, her heart beating at her throat. That was madness. She was insane for having even gone there.

She looked up at the eclipse. She still had time. But it did nothing to slow her racing heart.

The sound of Aurora's horn in the distance jolted the rest of the scorpions to follow. They ran blindly in her direction, and that was when Ella understood the plan. Aurora was clearing the way for Ella to pass.

Once the field was clear, Ella broke into a sprint. She pushed her legs harder as she crossed through the field, her feet smashing into the broken pumpkins. Aurora's horn sounded again, but this time it was faint in the distance.

When Ella came to a rope bridge, she dropped to her knees, panting. Her lungs were on fire, and her chest ached. She placed the torch on the ground with shaking hands. Her legs were throbbing, and every time she tried to stand, her knees would give out.

She looked ahead at the tower, the gold shimmering with the reflection of the moon. Her memory was in there. She was sure of it.

Ella, can you hear me? Killian's voice entered her mind as a whisper.

Ella looked around her. The lake under the bridge was still and the night overall was quiet. "Killian?" she called out in a loud whisper.

Ella, it's been too long. You need to return.

A wave of warmth washed over her at the sound of Killian's voice.

Forget the memory and come back, Killian hissed in her

mind. She felt pressure on her hand, and she wondered if he was squeezing it.

She looked up at the top of the tower, remembering what Ensley had said. *If at any given moment you would like to wake up, you must find a way to jolt your subconscious. Usually, that works best with the sensation of falling.*

If she could make it to the top of the tower, she could jump and force her brain to wake up.

Ella rose to her feet on shaky legs, grabbing onto the rope to steady herself. She crossed the bridge, careful not to miss a step.

A low rumble came from the lake beneath her, and Ella's eyes shot toward the sound. A round, dark boulder bobbed in the water, creating ripples in the lake. Upon spotting the rock, Ella let out a relieved breath, then continued crossing the bridge.

A cold water drop hit her skin and slid down her arm. Ella froze. She looked to the other side of the bridge, but it didn't seem to be raining. She looked behind her, but it wasn't raining there either.

Another rumble vibrated the bridge, and Ella held on. She looked at the lake again, only to find that the boulder was gone. A tall, dark pillar took its place, and as her eyes followed the parallel ridges stretching above her head, she gasped.

Two ginger eyes peered down at her. And when

their eyes locked, the creature bared his teeth with a hiss. When his hot breath hit her face, Ella screamed.

A water dragon!

She took off running across the bridge, then a jolt to the rope sent her flying forward. The bridge split in two, and she grabbed onto the rope as her half of the bridge fell into the cold water.

The loud scream from the water dragon creature vibrated the water, and fear rippled through Ella's body. He jumped up out of the water, then slammed back down, sending a large wave toward Ella. She gripped the rope with all of her strength as the wave crashed against her.

The murky lake water filled her mouth, the taste of mud and decaying leaves choking her as she coughed. She tried climbing the bridge, but yet another wave crashed into her, and her foot slipped on the wet wood.

When another rumble from the creature came from behind her, she glanced over her shoulder and found him swimming toward her.

With nowhere to go and her energy fading, she pressed her eyes shut, and only one thought overtook all others.

Killian, help!

9

KILLIAN

Ella's plea landed like a thunderclap inside Killian's mind, and without hesitation, he picked up the bowl next to Ella's bed.

"Don't drink that!" Ensley cried out, scrambling forward.

Killian scowled over the rim of the bowl. "Don't you dare try to stop me."

Ensley dropped her hands as her eyes widened. "It's very dangerous. You may not make it out alive."

Killian didn't argue. He knew the risks. Diving into the dream world could result in them both ending up dead. But Ella needed him, so he gulped the last of the tonic without another thought.

The effects on his body were instantaneous. A weakness spread throughout his limbs. His knees buckled under his weight, and his body fell as he faded into oblivion.

When he woke up, he focused on sensing Ella. Her aura was fading. His time was limited, so he took no time taking in the unusual surroundings.

He marched through the dark woods, reaching out for Ella. He could sense her soul. It wrestled between life and death, and an overwhelming sensation of choking took hold of Killian's being.

He powered through and found a circle of bubbles in the water dividing him from a tall tower. As he watched the bubbles, Ella's scent grew faint. He knew she was in trouble, and he only hoped that he wasn't too late.

But before he jumped in the water, a ferocious roar rumbled the ground beneath his feet. Then there came an unearthly screech. Killian watched as a creature like a water dragon, with an extended neck, eyes like slits, and fins the size of tree trunks, rose from the water.

The monster snaked back and forth. To get to the tower, he had to deal with the monster first.

Killian looked up at a stone statue of a knight, and without a word, he climbed up and forced the stone sword from its grip. Then he held his right hand up, focused on building heat and energy from his palms until they glowed blue. He swiped his hand along the sword until it exploded into blue flames.

He held the sword with both hands, shook his shaggy hair out of his eyes, and glared at the beast.

He waved the blue sword above his head, and it was the perfect distraction. The monster was no longer interested in Ella as she sank into the dark waters.

The silver moonlight flooded the water and lit up the monster's inky eyes. Killian side-stepped just as the monster lurched forward and its terrible head was mere inches from his body. But then Killian thrust his sword, sinking the flaming tip into the monster's flesh.

The smoky scent of burning flesh clung to Killian's nostrils but then a monstrous tail whipped around, nearly knocking Killian off his feet. He jumped back just in time, and an ugly howl flooded the air before the beast fell back into the water with a mighty splash.

Killian's heart thumped against his ribcage as he focused on sensing Ella. Her heartbeat had slowed, and she was no longer breathing. The thunderous sound of a war cry ripped through Killian's throat as he held his flaming sword high and watched the monster coming at him.

The monster bared its razor-sharp teeth and snapped at Killian. He swung his blazing sword, and just as the monster launched forward again, Killian took the hilt of his sword in both hands and jumped. He landed, diving the sword deep into the cranium of the beast. With a groan and the sizzle of burning flesh, the monster sunk into the depths of the water.

Without wasting any time, Killian shrugged off his jacket and dove in after Ella. When he crashed into the water, everything lit up an ice blue and he could see that his hands were glowing too.

Ella's limp body was sinking like a boulder to the bottom of the moat, and her wavy hair covered her face. From the limp way her body moved, Killian just hoped that Ella had not gone deeper into her consciousness. She would delve deeper into her mind, to a place that even he could not help her escape.

Killian took her arms and yanked her upward. Her narrow frame was so light as he soared to the surface. As soon as the crisp air hit them, Ella coughed and sputtered several times. He threw her over his shoulder and climbed the broken wooden bridge until they reached the top. They fell to the ground, panting, and Killian hurried to brush her golden hair away from her pale face.

"You came," she whispered, her pretty blue eyes blinking back at him.

"Of course I came." He took her hands and surveyed her arms. Her dress clung to her slender body. "Are you hurt?"

Ella held on to his arms and pushed herself up to sitting. "I'm fine."

Killian helped her to her feet. "Have you found anything yet?"

"Yes. We're looking for a book," Ella said, squeezing water from her skirt. "And I'm certain it's inside that tower."

Killian looked up to find a tower looming over them. "Then let's go get it and leave this place before we're trapped."

They ran together into the tower, then he followed Ella's lead as she scaled a wooden staircase. As they walked deeper into the tower, the place shifted and transformed into the inside of a castle. They rounded a corner to find a dining room. A fireplace across the room came to life, illuminating a long mahogany table with candles placed at the center. The smell of food filled the room, and a meal suddenly appeared on the table.

Was Ella's mind creating these illusions? Killian had never seen anything like it in all the centuries he'd been alive. It was both fascinating and terrifying to think that one could be lost in a world so unpredictable.

Ella picked up a plate, and as she smelled the aroma, her eyes rolled back with pleasure. "Pumpkin spice," she murmured. "My favorite."

"I know," a woman's voice came from behind them, and Killian stepped protectively in front of Ella.

A woman in a long white gown stood by the

window. She had a golden braid over one shoulder and a lace shawl over the other. But as the light of the fireplace illuminated her face, Ella gasped.

Killian sensed her emotions growing stronger, more intense than he'd ever known. An overwhelming joy mingled with grief, like sweet and salty.

"Hi, sweetheart," a man in formal attire appeared next to the woman, and Ella's emotions overwhelmed Killian's senses to the point he could barely breathe.

He turned to find Ella's eyes glassy. She was crying. He could almost taste the salty tears that ran down her cheeks as she stared at the couple with eyes unblinking.

"Momma. Papa." She dashed to the man and woman, and they hugged her, their faces shining with joy. But there was something different about them. Killian couldn't hear a heartbeat or sense their aura. It was as though Ella was hugging soulless statues.

"Ella!" he called out. "They aren't real. None of this is. We need to keep moving."

Ella turned and looked at him, wiping her eyes. Then she nodded. "Right…"

"Must you go so soon?" Ella's mother asked, her voice as soft and gentle as her daughter's.

Ella bit her lip and looked from her parents to Killian. He knew that she was asking for more time with them. But Killian could hear Ensley's distant cries. *"Please wake up. Please."*

Time was running out, and if they didn't leave soon, they'd both be trapped.

"The memory," Killian said, giving her a hard look. "How do I find it?"

"It's a book," Ella said, but her eyes never left her parents. "That's all I know."

More information would've been nice, but judging by the intensity of Ella's emotions, Killian had a feeling that it was going to take a lot longer to pull her from her family than it would for him to go in search of the book himself.

He turned on his heel and hot-tailed it out of the room. He raced around the castle, searching through the endless rooms. Rooms full of ornate furniture and tapestries. But no bookcases.

Every room he raced into had no books. He gritted his teeth and circled back to the ground floor. As he reached a narrow hall, he caught sight of a study with a fireplace burning inside. He entered the room and scanned the bookshelves on the far wall, but it was empty.

"Did you find the book?" Ella's voice came from behind him, and he turned around. She stood by the door, watching him with her beautiful blue eyes.

"Not yet," Killian said, frowning at her damp skirt, the same pale blue that tied in the back. "I thought you stayed with your parents?"

"Like you said, they aren't real," she said with a shrug as she walked toward him. "But you are." She ran a hand across his chest as she circled him. Her touch ignited his senses in such a way that he had to ball his fists to suppress it.

"What are you doing, Ella?"

She stopped when she was finally facing him again. "Want to know something interesting about this realm?" she asked in a soft whisper, then placed a hand over his heart. "I can sense you too. And I know you want me."

He swallowed hard, and when his heart began to race, Ella flashed him a devilish smile before leaning in and touching her lips to his ear. "And I don't mean my soul. You want to claim something else entirely, don't you?"

When she pulled back and looked into his eyes, he noticed something off about her aura. And her scent was different.

"You don't have to hold back," she said, her voice sensual and alluring. "I surrender."

Killian's frown deepened as she slid her hands up his forearms and leaned forward. Her pert bosom brushed against his chest as she rose on her tiptoes to whisper into his ear again. "I surrender *myself to you.*"

Killian turned to search her eyes, still unable to read her aura. She bit her lip in a way so tantalizing, it made his mouth go dry. But he shook his head. "Nice try. You are nothing but an illusion."

Ella grinned and stepped back. "I'm not an illusion, Killian. I'm your *fantasy*." She slowly loosened the ties of her dress. Killian's heart sped up as he watched the material drop down her shoulders, the swell of her cleavage on full show. She shook her blonde curls, brushing them away to give him an eyeful of her womanly figure. "I'm here because your mind brought me here. I'm your deepest desire."

Killian shook his head. "You're not real."

She smirked. "I'm as real as your chances with Ella on the other side," she continued. "You know as well as I do that the real Ella would never go for a man like you. Someone who revels in darkness. A killer without remorse."

Killian winced at the truth of her words. Then her bare chest pressed up against him, and the heat of her body set his insides ablaze. "But *I* would go for a man like you. That's why you brought me here. Do you not want me?"

Oh, he wanted her all right. He wanted to rip the dress clean off her body and taste every inch of her. But held his ground.

"Have your way with me, Killian." Her breath brushed his cheek. "You know you want to."

He leaned forward, and Ella's smile widened.

"That's it. Don't hold back," she breathed, clasping her hands behind his neck.

Having Ella in his arms, undone and freely available, hardened all of Killian's muscles. He was blazing hot and icy cold all at the same time. He wanted this to be real. But as he leaned forward to kiss her neck, he inhaled deeply and shut his eyes.

She smelled like lavender.

"I want you, Ella," he whispered against her skin, and she moaned in anticipation. "The problem is… you're not her."

Killian dropped his hands and stepped back. Ella's smile fell and her aura grew dark. She shrugged her dress back over her shoulders with a huff, then her entire being vanished like a vapor, leaving only a thin layer of mist flowing in the air.

Something hard fell on the wooden floor with a thud. Killian looked down to find a leatherbound book resting at his feet.

The book.

A wave of adrenaline rushed through him as he picked it up. Flipping through its pages, he noticed they were blank. Perhaps Ella needed to be the one to look through it since the memories belonged to her. Even so, he knew he'd found it. He could feel it. Those were her memories.

Killian rushed out of the study and hurried up the

staircase toward the dining room. He focused on finding Ella, but as his senses connected with hers, a wave of turmoil and despair hit him like a brick wall.

He tumbled over and grabbed onto the railing to keep from falling down the steps. The intensity of her emotions was so overwhelming to his senses, it even knocked the air from his lungs. She was crying. No, sobbing. And he forced himself to push through until he found her.

She was on her knees, sobbing on her father's lap as he sat on a chair, rubbing her back comfortingly.

"I'm sorry, Daddy," she spoke through her sobs. "I am so sorry."

The guilt that came from her soul was heart-wrenching. Even for Killian.

He dropped to his knees next to her and cupped her wet face. "Ella, I need you not to lose your focus," he begged, looking deep into her eyes. "I know it hurts, but I need you to be strong and stay with me. Can you do that?"

Her red, puffy eyes blinked at him. Then she nodded.

"Your memory." He handed her the book. "Is this it?"

As she opened it, the pages flipped until they landed on a spot where a red glow beamed onto her face. Killian watched her eyes race back and forth as she took in what was on the page. But then the ground began to tremor with such force that debris and dust began to fall from the ceiling.

Ella dropped the book, her hands trembling as the tremors grew more violent.

"It's time!" Ensley cried so loudly it was like a roar in Killian's ears.

He grabbed Ella's hand and pulled her to her feet. "Come on, we have to wake up."

They hurried to the open window, and Ella climbed out, stepping onto a roof. Killian followed her out and the air grew freezing cold. They climbed even higher on the slated roof, scrambling over the tiles as their breaths came out in puffs of cloud.

"What now?" Ella asked, panicked, as the tower began to crumble around them. Killian took her hand and peered over the edge at the dark water below. "We need to jolt ourselves awake."

Ella followed his line of sight. "Are you saying we need to jump?" The pitch of her voice told him that she was not entirely thrilled by the idea.

But then her mouth dropped open and her eyes widened. Killian followed her line of sight to see her parents struggling to keep their balance as they walked along the roof toward them.

"My sweet Ella! Stay with us!" they called out, and

Killian could feel the weight of Ella's heart in his own chest.

"Momma, Papa!" Ella tried to reach for them, but Killian grabbed her hand and kept her in place.

"Ella, don't. It's an illusion. They aren't real."

"They're real to me," she said, yanking on his hand, but Killian remained firm.

"Ella. We need to jump, now."

"You go. I can't leave them," Ella said, struggling to get out of his grasp. But Killian refused to let her go. Part of the roof caved away to their right, and Killian pulled Ella close.

"You can't save them, Ella."

Ella's chest heaved against him as she began to sob. Her parents scrambled along the roof, crying out for their daughter. But clouds of red and purple circled above their heads and a thunderous roar filled the air.

"Ella, they're not real." But she wasn't listening. "Ella, *I'm* real. Look at me…" Killian grabbed her hands and pressed them to his chest. "Look at me. I'm real."

But her eyes were still glued to her parents.

Killian then grabbed her face and kissed her. She gasped against his mouth, and he sensed the heaviness inside her heart suddenly lift, like an anchor detaching from a ship.

When he pulled away, her focus was back and her

gaze was entirely on him. Her trembling body was completely pressed up to him, and he held her tight.

"They're not real," she said in a faint voice. Killian nodded. Then she looked out at the chaos around them, illuminated by the total eclipse. "None of this is real. We need to wake up."

"Yes." Killian took her hand, all the while keeping an arm wrapped around her waist. "We need to jump. It'll jolt us awake."

More of the roof broke away, leaving them on just a small ledge. Ensley's cries had now grown so faint, Killian was not sure if it was already too late.

"We'll do it together," he said, clutching her waist. Ella pressed her eyes shut, trying to drown out her parents' cries. She squeezed Killian's hand, and he could feel her heart hemorrhaging.

With a nod, they counted to three. The final drone from the clock striking midnight boomed somewhere in the distance as Ella and Killian leaped from the roof and fell into the tumultuous waters below.

10

ELLA

Ella took a greedy gasp of fresh air as she jolted upward in the bed. Ensley's pale face came into view. Killian was on the floor at her feet, but in one quick jump, he was standing at Ella's side. His eyes roamed over her body as if checking for injuries.

"Are you all right?" he asked, his breath quick.

"Yes." Her voice shook, but it wasn't until Killian grabbed her hand that she realized her whole body was trembling.

"Are you sure?"

She looked up to see his concerned expression, but all she could think about were her parents. Her father's arms, tight and warm around her. Her mother's voice begging her not to go. She'd failed them yet again, and the guilt knotted in the pit of her stomach like a thousand snakes. Killian's image blurred as her eyes filled with tears. "I…" Her lips trembled. "I failed them."

She began to cry, and Killian pulled her into his arms. She buried her face into his chest and sobbed, the cotton fabric of his shirt soaking up her tears.

He pressed his lips to her ear as he held her tight. "It's okay," he whispered. "It's over now."

Her heart lifted at the thought of her turmoil being over. Finally.

"Did it work?" Ensley asked.

Ella's eyes shot open, and she looked up to meet Killian's. "It worked," she breathed. "Killian, it worked!"

Killian's eyes widened with hope. "And?"

A smile spread across her face. "I'm innocent!" she beamed. "I didn't kill the King! Killian, I'm innocent!"

But Killian didn't seem to share her enthusiasm. Instead, he watched her with careful eyes. "Ella, tell me everything you remember," he said, his voice serious.

Flashes of memory swirled inside her mind, and she pressed her eyes shut, trying to single out the ones she wanted. "I was on the ship, the sky had turned dark, and…" The memory was clear as day, and she shot her eyes open again. "Someone stabbed the King. A man. I fell to my knees and tried to stop the bleeding. That's why his blood was on my hands and clothes. But it wasn't me. I didn't kill him. I was trying to save him."

Her heart soared inside her chest. Not only at knowing that she wasn't a murderer, but also at the hope that her soul could be spared.

But Killian still hadn't said anything.

She narrowed her eyes at him. "What's wrong?"

When his brows furrowed, her enthusiasm vanished and her face fell. He didn't even have to say it. She knew. "I'm still marked, aren't I?"

Killian's jaw tightened. "Seeing your parents again must've stirred up your hopelessness," he said. "Your will to live… it's weaker than it's ever been, Ella."

When he said nothing else, Ella couldn't tell if he was upset at having wasted so much time with her only to have come to a dead end, or if he was genuinely concerned for her life. And it wasn't just by the way he held her gaze in that moment. It was the fact that he came to her aid when she called for him. He didn't have to. He could've left her there to die, then gone off to find a less complicated soul to claim. He would've gotten what he wanted: The throne.

But instead, he risked being trapped inside the dream world to save her.

Too bad it was all in vain because she was still marked. And her will to live was crumbling by the second. The desire to survive was gone along with the illusion of her parents.

Her soaring heart dropped like an anvil inside her chest, and the air grew suddenly thicker.

Killian sat next to her and cupped her face, brushing a thumb against her soft cheek. "You said a man stabbed the King. Did you see who it was?" he asked. "If we can find the real killer, I can take his soul in place of yours. I will plead on your behalf and I'm certain Hades will not object."

Ella shook her head. "I… I didn't see his face…"

"Think harder, Ella," Killian demanded, his voice firm. "You were there. You saw the man stab the King. Focus on his face."

She tried, but… "It was dark."

"Try harder."

Ella jumped to her feet, her body buzzing with anxiety. "I don't remember!" She kept shaking her head as if the motion itself could somehow jog the missing memory, but it was useless. She swung around to look at Ensley, who stood quietly across the room, watching them. "Why can't I remember?"

Ensley shook her head. "I'm not sure. Everyone is different. Perhaps you didn't give it enough time—"

"We ran out of time!" Killian took an angry step toward the fairy, but Ella stepped in front of him.

"Killian, please." She placed a hand on his chest. His heart raced against her palm. "It's not her fault. She's right, everyone's mind is different. Maybe the memory will clear up on its own if I just give it a little more time."

"We don't have time, Ella. If you are still marked by the time the blood moon appears, your soul will be taken."

Ella could feel the blood drain from her face, and the room suddenly grew hot.

Killian stepped back and clenched his jaw, shifting his attention back to Ensley. "There must be more we can do."

Ella glanced at Ensley, hoping she had an answer.

Ensley stepped forward and placed a gentle hand on Ella's shoulder. "Perhaps all you need is a trigger."

"What kind of trigger?" Killian asked before Ella could.

Ensley looked from Killian to Ella. "You'll need to return to the place where the event occurred. Retrace your steps."

"What if I can't return to the exact place?" Ella asked. She couldn't imagine taking a ship and sailing back to Neverland without getting caught by the King's guards.

"Then the only other way is to find someone who shared the memory with you," Ensley continued. "Someone who was there. Who saw what you saw."

Ella knew who that person was, and her heart sank at the thought of seeing him again. Of him seeing her. Recognizing her. Capturing her, and sending her to the gallows, the rope tight around her neck.

"Is that the only way?" Killian asked.

Ensley nodded. "I'm afraid so."

Ella shook her head, but before she could voice the negativity swirling through her mind, Killian grabbed her shoulders and turned her to face him.

"You have nothing to be afraid of," he said firmly. "I will be with you the whole time."

"He wants me dead, Killian."

"He will not harm you."

She gave him a pointed look. "He's the Prince. He has an army."

Killian shrugged. "That's still no match for what you have."

She arched a brow. "And what is that?"

Killian pulled back, his chest puffed out. "Me. Now, let's go find the real killer before we run out of time."

Ella looked up at the night sky to find the moon, but storm clouds rolled in above the thick forest canopy, making it almost impossible for her to tell the arrival of the blood moon.

"What happens if the blood moon appears and I

still don't remember the killer?" she asked, walking next to Killian.

"We shouldn't concern ourselves with what hasn't happened," he said, keeping his eyes on the path ahead. "Let's just focus on using the Prince to trigger the rest of your memory and—"

"And what?" She stopped walking and stared at his back. "What if it doesn't work?"

Killian stopped a few feet ahead, then turned to look at her. Even in the dark, she could see the frown lines on his face. "It has to work."

She narrowed her eyes. "But what if it doesn't?"

Killian sucked in a deep breath before marching back toward her. "Why are you giving up?"

"I'm not giving up. I just want to know what my options are."

"Our only option is to find the real killer so you don't have to pay for a crime you didn't commit." His eyes were serious as he towered over her. "Now, let's stop wasting time. The blood moon is in three days."

"What does the blood moon have to do with any of this?"

"Enough with the questions," he said, rubbing his temples impatiently.

Ella cocked her head. "What aren't you telling me?"

He dropped his hands, and she caught sight of his

tight jaw. "When we're sent for a soul, we are given an allotted time to bring them in. If we don't, by the next blood moon, that soul becomes available for the taking."

Ella stared at Killian in disbelief. "What do you mean… 'for the taking'?" When he didn't respond, she placed a hand over her beating heart. "Someone else will come to claim my soul?"

That meant that even if Killian decided to let her go, someone else would come for her. And if by some miracle she was able to outrun the next bounty hunter, another would come after that, and there was no way she would be able to outrun all of them for the rest of her life. She was blacklisted. She was doomed.

Killian must've noticed her panic because he cupped her face with his strong hands and forced her to look into his eyes. "I need you to listen to me very carefully," he said, his voice soft but firm. "No one will touch one lock of hair from your head. Do you hear me?"

She grabbed his strong arms with trembling hands.

"Do you hear me, Ella?"

She nodded, though her hands were still shaking.

"I need you to say it," he whispered, brushing his thumb softly against her cheek. His touch was warm, and a wave of calm washed over her. Her heart slowed, and she sucked in a breath.

"Yes," she breathed. "I… I hear you."

"Good." His thumb traced the outline of her jaw. "Now, do you believe that?"

She opened her mouth to answer, but the words got caught in her throat when his thumb brushed over her bottom lip.

"Do you trust me?" he asked.

She did. She wasn't sure why or how, considering who he was, but she did. Something about the protective manner in which he was holding her and the blue flicker in his eyes made her feel safe.

"I trust you," she spoke against his thumb as he traced her upper lip.

The corner of his lips curved, and she felt a sudden urge to kiss him. Memories of his lips on hers on the tower roof flooded her mind, and her body grew hot.

But Killian pulled back, leaving her cheeks cold where his hands held her. "There should be a lake up ahead. We can break camp there."

Without waiting for a response, he started walking again. Ella blew out a nervous breath before following his lead.

Before long, they were sitting near the lake with a fire burning in front of them. Killian's sword rested against a boulder near the fire, and Ella could see her reflection in the glass. Her golden locks swirled over one shoulder.

"What's on your mind?" Killian asked, shoving a stick into the fire.

Ella twirled one of her locks around her finger. "I have my mother's hair," she said with a sad smile. "I had forgotten about that."

"Your mother was a beautiful woman," he said. "That is if what I saw in the dream world did her any justice."

Ella's cheeks warmed. "Thank you."

"I'm sorry you had to leave them."

She shook her head. "That wasn't them. None of that was real."

"I could tell it was still hard for you."

Ella's eyes fell to the crackling flames as the memories of long ago returned to her mind. "Not as hard as watching them die."

Killian turned to her as a tear slid down her cheek. "What is it about losing them that makes you feel so guilty?" he asked.

"I had a sister," she said, her voice barely above a whisper. "I lost her when I was seven. She was my mother's favorite. I was always closer to my father. After my sister was taken away, my mother refused to eat. She would sleep all day and cry all night. It was… unbearable."

Killian didn't respond. Perhaps he could tell she wasn't done.

"Eventually, she got very sick and… didn't make it. My father was inconsolable. I was twelve at the time and thought maybe I could find my sister before my father gave up on life too. So, I decided to look for my sister on my own."

"Did you find her?" Killian asked.

"No." Ella swallowed the lump in her throat. "I was caught trespassing a kingdom to the North and was taken to the gallows. My father tried to plead for me, but…"

Killian winced as if he could somehow sense the wave of guilt that rose within her.

"The only way to save me from the gallows was for my father to take my place." Another tear slid down her cheek. "I destroyed my family."

Killian frowned. "You were only a child."

She wiped the wetness from her face and sniffled. "I'm not a child anymore. Maybe I deserve everything that is happening to me."

"If you truly believed that, you wouldn't be trying so hard to survive."

Ella shrugged. "Perhaps I'm just selfish."

Killian leaned his elbows on his knees and shook his head. "A selfish person wouldn't give herself up to save a friend. Finn, was it?" He gave her a side glance. "You tricked him into jumping into that ravine while you stayed behind. You wanted to make sure he would be safe from me. That's not what a selfish person does."

Ella narrowed her eyes at him. "All you need is one soul to get everything you've ever wanted. And even though I didn't kill the King, I am still marked. My soul is filled to the brim with guilt and despair. You and I both know that if you dragged me to the Underworld right now and claimed my soul, the throne would be yours. Why haven't you already?"

Killian shifted his attention back to the fire, the reflection of the flames casting shadows on his face. "You don't deserve this, Ella."

Ella reached for his hand and gave it a light squeeze. "Thank you." When he said nothing else, she leaned closer to him. "Tell me something about you."

Killian was silent for a long moment, then he stood and scooped up a handful of mud by the water's edge before returning to Ella's side. She had to fight against the urge to snuggle closer to him. To his warmth. The chill in the air was more than the fire could warm.

She shook her head, expelling the thought of being in his warm arms, and focused her attention on the pile of mud in his hands.

"What are you doing?" she asked, watching as he molded the mud like clay.

"This." He reached out his hand toward the fire, and the flames transformed into a mixture of blue and white. He then skewered the thick mud into the stick and held it above the blue flames. "Here. Hold this."

As soon as Ella took the stick from his hand, he took another scoop of mud and rolled it in his hands. Ella couldn't tell what he was shaping it into. By the time she turned her attention back to the fire, the mud on the stick had turned to glass.

"Wow," she said, mesmerized. "Where did you learn this?"

"My mother taught me." Without saying anything else, he took the stick from her hand, and after dropping the glass on the ground, he skewered yet another molded lump of mud with the stick and returned it to the fire. Once the second piece turned to glass, he dropped it next to the first piece. He then scooped more mud with his finger and placed it between both pieces before throwing both into the fire.

The flames grew high. Ella pulled back as the heat of the fire licked a bit too close for comfort. But Killian didn't even flinch. They waited a few heartbeats, then Killian poked the stick into the fire again and flicked the glass sculpture from within the flames. It flew to the other side and dropped to the ground with a thud.

When Killian stood, Ella followed him to where the glass object had fallen. The glass was a mixture of red and yellow, and it had burned the ground underneath. Killian grabbed his sheepskin bottle and poured some of the liquid over it. It sizzled like a steak on an iron skillet, but it wasn't until the smoke cleared that Ella could tell what Killian had made.

"Here." The glass object had turned a striking clear blue, like ice. Like his sword. Except it wasn't a sword. It was a knife. He picked it up. "For you."

Ella stared at it, mesmerized. "That's... beautiful."

She took it in her hand. It was warm and heavy.

"That's the only material that could injure someone from the Underworld," Killian explained. "In the event that someone else comes, you should be able to defend yourself."

Ella gave him an amused look. "How do you know I won't use this to strike you in your sleep?"

He looked at the knife, then back at Ella. "I asked you to trust me. The least I can do is trust you too."

She tossed the knife from one hand to another. It was smooth but heavy. "Your mother must be proud," she said, turning to him with a grateful smile. "Thank you."

Killian gave her a single nod. "Keep it hidden, though. It's worth more than diamonds in this world."

"Good to know." Ella lifted her dress, but then froze when she caught Killian staring at her bare thighs. Butterflies exploded inside her stomach as his eyes continued to roam below her waist.

She found a place for her knife, but the sudden

thought that something Killian had made with his hands was now underneath her dress made her pulse in her core.

She threw her dress over her legs and cleared her throat. "We should get some sleep," she said, almost out of breath. "Good night."

She laid on a bed of leaves on the ground, then turned her back toward him. Behind her, she could hear him move, but she forced herself to stop thinking of the distance between them. Or wishing he was closer.

She pressed her eyes shut and forced herself to fall asleep.

11

KILLIAN

Faraway screams ripped Killian out of a deep sleep. He blinked up at the darkness, waiting for his eyes to adjust to the weak light peeping through the trees.

The air was heavy and flooded with terror. He could hear Ella's heartbeat racing like marching soldiers headed for war. He got up and lay beside Ella's sleeping form. She thrashed from side to side, letting out a moan, then a terrified scream.

He grasped her small shoulders. Her pretty blue eyes flew open, and she blinked up at him like she was staring at a ghost. "It was… It was…"

Killian dipped his head, finding her terrified gaze. "It was a nightmare," he said to her. "But you're all right. You're good."

Trembling from head to toe, she crawled onto

Killian's lap and took fistfuls of his shirt, burying her face in his neck.

Killian froze but held still as she sobbed against him. Her tears wet his skin, and he was enveloped in her bittersweet aura.

"It's all right. It was just a night terror." Killian swept her hair away from her clammy forehead and caressed her cheek. The touch soothed Ella, and it flooded Killian with a new scent. Like cinnamon. "Try to get some more sleep…" he said, ignoring the pang of hunger gnawing at his insides. But this type of hunger could not be satisfied by mortal food. It was a craving that would have to be endured.

Ella smoothed out her hair and looked furtively at the smoking fire. Only a few embers were still alive, and she shivered again.

"I'm so cold," she said. She looked at Killian again before glancing away. "And you're so warm."

Killian's body ran at a higher temperature than a mortal's. "Come on," he said, drawing Ella's small frame closer to him. He draped an arm around her body as she wriggled back until she touched him.

Ella's body pressing up to his set Killian's body ablaze, and he reasoned it was a good thing she couldn't sense auras. If she knew how deeply he wanted her, she'd run as far as she could to get away.

She wriggled again, pressing on all the delicate

parts of his nether regions, and he bit back a groan. The hunger magnified, and he fought to stop forbidden thoughts from crossing his mind.

Soon, Ella was settled back to sleep, but Killian couldn't close his eyes for more than a couple of seconds. Instead, he fought an internal battle between his urges and common sense. He focused on her steady breaths and busied himself with stroking her hair, which created a sense of calm.

When morning came, every muscle in his body was rigid and stiff. But Ella woke up and moved in his arms. He melted against her and forced a fake yawn as she sat up and shuffled away from him. The morning light illuminated her rosy cheeks, and Killian supposed that in the daylight, her actions were less scandalous.

"Thank you," she breathed, combing her fingers through her hair.

A rush of embarrassment colored her cheeks, and he smiled. "I couldn't let you freeze to death."

Then the gentle breeze picked up her sweet scent and floated it up to his nostrils. His body reacted and he jerked back to get more space between them. "Go ahead and bathe on this lake. I'll go to the waterfall farther out."

Ella frowned. "But the sun's hardly been up. The waterfall will be freezing."

Killian turned on his heel and walked away, but not before muttering, "Exactly."

KILLIAN KEPT SEVERAL STEPS IN FRONT AS HE AND ELLA entered the nearby village. The cold water did nothing to quash the raging emotions swirling inside of him, and every time he got a whiff of her delicious scent, it simply lit the embers of desire on fire again.

He marched through the street and towered over the nearby people, who scattered upon seeing him. They passed three pigs tied to an outpost, their snouts snuffling through the trough, eating rotten leftovers.

Killian set his mind on the task at hand. The fairy theorized that in order to trigger the part of Ella's memory they were seeking, she'd need to see the Prince again.

Which meant they needed a way into the palace.

Ella's stomach growled, and it broke Killian out of his thoughts. Before he could come up with a plan, they needed sustenance. He cast his eyes about the village square. A dusty gravel path divided two rows of buildings. The houses were made of wattle and daub, and there were shutters in place of glass windows. The people were poor in that village, and the place stank of body odor and urine. Unwashed children ran across the street, scrounging for food. And an old man in haggard clothes lay outside a bar, holding out a tin cup with a shaking hand.

Killian pulled out a coin and tossed it into the man's cup where it landed expertly with a light clang. The old beggar lifted his wispy white brows and his clear eyes sparkled. "Bless you, son," he said.

Killian glanced at Ella and caught her look of surprise. But then the corners of her lips picked up and he turned away.

"Don't look at me like that," he said.

"Like what?"

"Like it's a surprise to you that I haven't got a heart made of stone," he said, leading them to the door to a tavern.

He held the door for her, and Ella offered him a thankful smile. Once they stepped inside, Killian immediately regretted it. There was an overwhelming mixture of senses going on at the same time. The jarring sound of iron dragging along the stone floor. The steady *thud-thud* from upbeat patrons with their drinks.

And upstairs, Killian could hear the creaking of bed frames and the occasional thumping of a headboard hitting the wall.

The tavern wasn't crowded, but it was busy. And the people in it were equally as dirty as the bar. But this place also had a small-framed gentleman tinkering on a dusty piano in the corner of the room.

A group of men chatted loudly in the corner, cradling their drinks, deep in conversation. A few of them turned to look at Ella as she entered, and she turned away, running a nervous hand through her hair.

Killian didn't see any of the wanted flyers with Ella's picture on it, but that didn't mean people weren't carrying it with them. He took off his cloak and placed it over Ella's shoulders. She quickly threw the hood over her head to cover her curls.

As she took a seat at the bar, Killian sat where he could block her from the men's view. A big-busted woman turned around and her eyes snaked over Killian before she looked at Ella, her lips curling up. "Need a room?"

"No, just food," Killian said.

"Despicable if you ask me," one of the men grumbled from the corner.

"Aye. Holding another ball with all that fine wine and feast, yet here we are, settling for broth."

Killian and Ella glanced at each other.

"There's a ball?" she mouthed to him. "We need to find out more."

Killian nodded, then turned to stand. But Ella grabbed his arm before he even had a chance to move. "What are you going to do?"

"Get more information."

She must've sensed something in his tone because she gave him a look that reminded him of when his mother would warn him not to misbehave.

"Relax." He leaned back with his elbow on the bar and dipped his head. "I know how to get information, Ella."

Killian marched to the corner, and the group of men fell silent as they looked up at him. "What's this I hear about a ball?" Killian asked, his voice a tad deeper than usual.

The men stared at Killian in silence, their eyes wide and hollow as they took in his appearance. But then one of them took a swig of his drink and slammed the cup on the wooden table. Killian supposed it was to gather his courage.

"What's it to you?" he sneered. Then he turned to his friends as they all cackled.

Killian itched with mild irritation. For someone who commanded respect in the Underworld, to be challenged by a mere human was the greatest insult. He fisted the man's shirt and picked him up. The table flipped, and the drinks spilled to the floor as their tankards landed with a clang. The laughter was quickly replaced by horrified looks as his friends stared wide-eyed. Killian paid no attention and lifted the man even higher. "Tell me about the ball."

"Killian!" Ella hurried to his side and grabbed his elbow. Killian barely felt her attempts to move him, but her hushed reprimand was loud and clear. "There are better ways to get information."

Killian kept his hard stare on the man, whose eyes were about to jump out of their sockets. "Maybe. But this is the fastest."

The man threw his arms up and his limbs flailed like a scrambling bug caught in a spider's web. "I don't know anything, mate! I swear!"

Killian cocked a brow. He had to hand it to the man—most humans would just tell him what he needed to know. But the alcohol must've given him a bit too much courage.

Ella dipped her head toward the flailing man and let out a light chuckle. "My apologies. He's a tad impulsive…" She yanked at Killian's arm again and gave him a hard look. "And doesn't realize what a bad idea it is to call undue attention."

Killian pressed his lips to a tight line. She had a point. If anyone recognized Ella, they would also inform the Prince that she'd been snooping for information about the ball. Then they would miss out on their only way into the palace.

"Fine." Killian put the man down. "Then what do you suggest we do?"

Ella swung around with a beaming smile and

clasped her hands. "How about a round of beer for everyone!"

It was silent for a moment, then a wave of cheer erupted in the tavern, and Killian looked around, surprised at how quickly the mood had shifted.

The group of men put the table back in place, then lifted their cups toward Killian in gratitude. As they all returned to their seats, the man Killian had grabbed stood frozen and confused.

"You heard the lady, sit." Killian pushed the man back into his seat, then sat across from him. "Apparently, we're going to have a chat over drinks."

Another wave of cheers rose in the tavern, then the clangs of cups against the tables filled the room. That was their way of saying their cups were empty and ready to be refilled.

"I'll help you serve," Ella said to the woman behind the bar, but not before leaning into Killian's ear. "Remember, no violence."

As she walked away, one of the men at his table leaned toward Killian with a drunken smirk. "She's pretty. And those hips. Too bad that cloak covers everything."

Killian fought back the urge to snap the man like a twig. But that would go against Ella's request for no violence. So, he simply gave the man a side glance.

"Look below her waist again and I will snap your neck."

The man stared at Killian for a moment, then laughed and waved him off. "Oh, come on, we're sharing a drink." He slapped Killian's shoulder. "No need for furrowed brows, mate. We're all good here."

At that, Ella returned with everyone's drinks, as well as some food, and another cheerful roar erupted as the men lifted their cups.

She took a seat next to Killian, and her floral scent masked the odor of sweat and beer. For the first time that day, his body relaxed, and he leaned back as Ella engaged the group of men in conversation. She asked them about their jobs and their families, and after the second round of drinks, she asked about the famine and the Prince.

They had plenty to say about the Prince's inability to provide for his kingdom, but still nothing about the ball. Killian didn't care for the chitchat, but he was intrigued by Ella's method of gathering information. She had a way about her that drew them in and got them talking. The problem was that she got them so comfortable, their words were like an open faucet of useless information.

But Killian decided to trust her. If nothing else, at least he got to enjoy the sound of her voice.

After several hours of chatting about everything

under the sun, Killian thought for sure his head was going to explode.

He rubbed his eyes, trying to tune out the chatter. He wasn't sure how much longer he would be able to bear it. Not only were they running out of time, but Killian simply did not care to hear about what kind of life they wished they had.

Killian had not come to hear about their hopes and dreams.

"Killian, let me ask you a question." One of the men at the table craned his neck to look at Killian's back. "How long is your hair?"

Killian let out a frustrated sigh, then looked at Ella. "I need a break."

He shoved away from the table and went to find the privy. The tavern only had one for both men and women, but thankfully, it was unoccupied when he pushed the door open. He leaned his back against the door and closed his eyes.

"I didn't think I would see you again," a familiar voice spoke, and Killian opened his eyes to find Ella leaning against the water basin. Except it wasn't Ella because, despite the lavender smell, she had no aura.

Killian's face hardened. "How are you here?"

Ella lifted her hands in feigned innocence. "Don't blame me. I'm a figment of *your* imagination."

Killian huffed, then went to the basin to splash

water on his face. When he opened his eyes again, he was hoping she would be gone.

She wasn't.

"Is this some sort of hallucination side effect from having gone into that forsaken world?" he asked.

"Not exactly." Ella turned to meet his reflection in the mirror. "You see, you're immortal, which means your mind is far superior than that of a puny human. It's so enthralling getting into your mind."

Killian scowled at her through the mirror. "What does that even mean?"

"It means…" She flashed him a devilish smile, then leaned into his ear. "We can have loads of fun."

Killian moved away from her. "You're not real."

"I'm as real as you want me to be." Ella's voice dripped with sensuality as she prowled toward Killian, her hand slithering up his chest. "You just have to surrender."

Killian grabbed her hands and forced them off of him. "How do I get rid of you?"

"Now, that hurt my feelings." She feigned a frown. "Not good for the ego, you know?"

"Why are you really here?" he demanded.

"I'm your reality check, Killian." Her seductive voice was gone. "Look at what is happening out there. Are you really on board with her method?"

"She knows what she's doing."

Ella narrowed her eyes. "Does she? Or are you giving in to her wishes in hopes that she changes her mind about you? That she forgets how you dragged her against her will? How you tied her up like a prisoner?"

Killian didn't respond. But he didn't have to. If that was a figment of his imagination, then everything she was saying was coming from his own mind. His own doubts.

"You're not the nice type, Killian. You're a killer." Ella's voice was harsh, and her words stung. But she wasn't wrong. "You know she'll never go for a man like you. I, on the other hand…" The seductive tone was back, as was her touch against his chest. "Am quite a fan of the evil in you."

Killian grabbed her wrists and shoved her off of him. "You're a real piece of work, you know that?"

Her smile broadened as she clearly enjoyed getting under his skin. "At least I don't pretend to be something I'm not."

The door opened and Killian turned around to find the real Ella entering the privy. She looked around the otherwise empty space. "Who were you talking to?" she asked.

Killian shook his head. "No one. I just came to splash some cold water on my face. Those stories were getting a little… winded."

Ella chuckled. "I know, once you get drunk men

talking is hard to make them stop. Now, they're just slurring."

When Killian said nothing else, Ella stepped inside and reached for one of his hands. Her floral aroma enveloped him in the small space.

"Thank you," she said softly. "For letting me do it my way. That was nice of you."

The word *nice* rang in Killian's ears like a loud siren, and his brows furrowed. "You have to stop that."

Ella gave him a puzzled look. "Stop what?"

"Thinking that I'm going to be nice every time you ask," he said. "I'm not the nice type, Ella."

She frowned. "That is not what I meant."

"I'm from the Underworld. I claim souls without remorse. That is who I am—what I am—and that is not going to change."

Ella's frown deepened. "I know that."

"Good."

She stepped back and lowered her eyes. For a moment, they were both quiet. "There'll be a masquerade ball in two days," she said, not meeting his eyes. "I just need some privacy in here, then we can go."

Killian nodded, then walked out. As the door shut behind him, a wave of disappointment hit his back and he winced.

He cursed under his breath, forcing himself not to

care about her feelings. Not to care that her expectations for him shattered.

He marched back to the group. Most of the men were already passed out over the table while the few that were still conscious sang some sort of pirate ditty.

"Yeah, Killian. Come sing with us!" one of the men said, waving his hand. But Killian was not in the mood. He took a seat across from them and scowled at the wall, fighting back the urge to punch a hole through it.

"Where is that pretty maiden?" one of the men slurred as he leaned over the table. "Doesn't she look like her?" He held up one of the wanted flyers from the Prince with Ella's face on it.

Several of the men who were singing stopped. Their eyes stretched wide, no doubt at the reward, which surprisingly had doubled.

"Wait. It does look like her," another man said.

Killian balled his fists and cracked his knuckles, then turned to the fool who was already missing several of his teeth.

In the quiet tavern, Killian propped his feet up on the table and crossed them at the ankles as he took a swig of beer.

When Ella came out, he wasn't surprised to see her

eyes stretch wide and her mouth drop open. "Killian, what in the world…?"

She scanned through the tavern at all the men on the floor.

"We tried it your way," Killian said. "But the more they drank, the more nonsense came out of their mouths. And I have zero tolerance for nonsense."

Ella glared at him. "So you killed them?"

"They're not dead." He shoved one of the men with his boot, and the man groaned. "Besides, half of them were already down from the countless rounds of drinks, anyway." He placed the beer bottle on the table and rose to his feet. "Shall we?"

Ella's glare remained intact. "We already had what we needed. You didn't have to do this."

Killian sighed. "No. You got what you needed. What I needed was peace and quiet."

Ella crossed her arms, and he had to fight back the urge to undo the distance he was sensing between them. "Right, because you're not the nice type. I get it…" Her eyes roamed over the incapacitated men again before returning to him. "The message is loud and clear, Killian."

The flash of silver in her aura with the metallic scent of her sadness made his stomach churn.

She stormed out of the tavern, and Killian could feel the weight of her heavy heart in his own chest.

He could've told her he was protecting her, but it was better if she didn't know. The sooner she realized he wasn't capable of change, the easier it would be to let him go.

He was who he was. And when he found the real killer and removed the mark from Ella, he wouldn't be sticking around. He would be returning to the Underworld to claim his throne.

That was all that needed to matter.

12

ELLA

Despite the heaviness in Ella's heart, her spirit lifted the moment she caught sight of Belle's cottage in the woods. A flood of warm memories washed over her as the image of two little girls running in the yard while their fathers chatted on the front porch surfaced in her mind.

"What is this place?" Killian asked, carrying a pile of fabrics they had bought on the way.

"It belongs to my friend Belle," Ella said, welcoming the tug of excitement that came from being somewhere familiar. "I mean, it used to be hers when she lived with her father. Our fathers used to be good friends. I grew up just up that hill."

Killian turned toward the hill. "Then why don't we just go to your house?"

Ella's heart squeezed. "My stepmother sold the

property after my father passed. Anyway, Belle and I grew up together. I'm sure she wouldn't mind us staying here if she knew we had nowhere else to go. Besides, she has another life now."

"Another life, indeed. She's the Queen of the White Rose Kingdom, is she not?" Killian asked.

Ella arched a curious brow. "How do you know that?"

Killian chuckled. "Just because I don't live in your world doesn't mean I don't know what goes on here. Now, are you going to tell me what we're doing here?"

Ella reached for a hidden key by a potted plant near the door. She couldn't believe the key was still there after all those years. But instead of opening the door, she rushed around the house. A squeal escaped her throat at the sight of a shed. The key fit the iron lock perfectly, and the wooden door creaked open.

Killian peeked inside, probably wondering what he would find. But she didn't expect him to see it. He wouldn't even know what it looked like.

"You can place the fabrics on top of that," she said, pointing to a wooden table in the center of the room. She walked across the small space and began peeking under the various white sheets that covered Belle's father's tools.

"What are you looking for?" Killian asked, placing the fabrics on the table.

A metal box rested on a top shelf, and Ella reached up to grab it. It was higher than she expected, so only the tips of her fingers brushed against it. She tugged on a cloth beneath it to pull it closer, but the shelf buckled and the box tumbled down.

Ella yelped and shielded her head, but a strong hand grabbed the metal box in the air. When she turned around, Killian was towering over her, his body pressed up against hers as he held the box above their heads.

"Are you all right?" He was so close, his breath brushed her face, sending shivers down her spine.

She opened her mouth to reply, but the smell of pine trees and waterfall coming from him enveloped her senses. And it didn't help that his eyes were so blue.

"Ella?"

"I—I'm fine." She walked around him and exhaled his scent out of her system. That shed was too small for the both of them. "How good of a hunter are you?" she asked.

Killian turned toward her. "Is that a joke?"

She grabbed the box from his hand and placed it next to the fabrics on the table, all the while keeping her eyes lowered so as to not reveal her flushed cheeks. "Why don't you go catch us some meat for dinner while I get started on our attire?"

She moved around the shed, pulling the sheets until

she found what she was looking for. A spindle. It was just as beautiful as she remembered, even though it was coated with dust.

Killian came to stand next to her, and her body suddenly heated. What was happening to her?

She shook her head, and after grabbing a rag from the table, she focused on wiping down the spindle.

"If that was what you needed, we could've bought you a newer one," Killian said.

"This one used to be my mother's," she replied, brushing the tip of her fingers over the rusted metal as if she could touch the memories that played in her mind. "After my father remarried, my stepmother wanted to get rid of it, so I asked Belle if I could keep it here."

"Your stepmother sounds heartless," Killian said. "Your father, on the other hand, sounds like a man of heart. I don't understand how the two of them ended up together."

Ella's shoulder sagged. "I overheard him say to Belle's father once that he didn't want me to grow up without a mother or a sister. Then, soon after, he married a woman with two daughters. I know he wanted the best for me, but I didn't need another mother. Or sisters. All I needed was him."

"I get it," Killian said with a nod. "I was raised by my mother, and that's all I ever needed."

Ella looked up at him, surprised that he had shared something personal. "What about your father?" she asked. But Killian didn't answer. He just stared at the spindle.

"We've never been close," he said. "You could say he was married to his work and cared very little for his own flesh and blood."

Ella frowned. "I'm sorry."

"Don't be. He's never been missed. Anyway, you better get started on your dress. We should be on our way first thing in the morning."

Kilian's head snapped toward the open door behind them, and Ella followed his gaze.

"Something wrong?" she asked, wondering why the sudden alarm. There was no one there. "Killian?"

He returned his eyes to her, but there was distance in them. "Any preference for dinner?" he asked, forcing an easy smile. "Seems like these woods have quite the variety."

Ella narrowed her eyes, wondering if that was really what he'd heard outside. She knew those woods were filled with wolves. Perhaps he'd sensed it and just didn't want her to worry. "Whatever you catch will be fine," she said.

"All right then." Killian leaned forward to grab the spindle, but Ella touched his arm.

"Wait. What are you doing?"

He gave her a side glance as if it was obvious. "I'm taking this into the house so you can work inside."

"Why?" She motioned around her. "This is a perfectly good working area."

"Not perfect enough," Killian muttered.

"Why not?"

His eyes locked with hers. "You need to be where I can see you."

Ella's skin prickled with heat at the thought of Killian wanting to watch her as she worked, even though she knew that wasn't at all what he'd meant.

She cleared the nervousness from her throat and crossed her arms. "What, are you afraid I'm going to run away again?"

His jaw tightened as if the mere thought of her wanting to get away from him caused him physical pain. And to have that effect on a man like him was strangely arousing.

The corner of her lips curved. "You're concerned for me," she said, not bothering to hide the amusement in her voice. "The fearless warrior from the Underworld who claims souls without remorse cares if I'm snatched up by a wolf."

Killian rolled his eyes, then lifted the spindle over his head with one arm. "For someone with a death sentence, you seem quite playful."

His tone was light and not at all threatening. He was teasing back in his own Killian way.

"For a killer, you seem quite protective," she retorted, noticing that the corner of his lips twitched upward as he turned toward the door.

"I'll let you know when dinner is ready."

By the time Ella looked up from the last stitch, not only was the room a disaster with loose pieces of fabric scattered everywhere, but the sky had darkened, and the smell of beef stew still lingered in the air. She could hear Killian washing the pans in the kitchen, but it was the sound of flames crackling behind her that caught her attention.

She hadn't even noticed when Killian lit up the fireplace. Perhaps after they had finished eating, or while she had gone to bathe. Or it could've been while she worked. It wasn't surprising because she hadn't even noticed when he'd gone to gather wood. The maids at the castle used to say that when she worked on her dresses, she always seemed to go into a trance, as if the world disappeared around her. Ella thought they were exaggerating, but it seemed to have been true.

The room was warm and dim, and she pulled back to take in her masterpiece that hung on wooden mannequins in the center of the room. A wave of pride bubbled inside her. The dress stood stunningly next to a gentleman's suit. They were elegant and beautiful. The light blue fabric of her dress shimmered in the reflection of the flames, as did his matching tie and handkerchief.

She cracked her knuckles to release the tension from her stiff hands, then flashed a pleased smile. "Perfect."

Killian let out a low whistle as he entered the room. "Perfect, indeed."

She stood from her wooden stool and stepped back to take in the outfits from a different angle. "You really think so?"

"I never say what I don't mean," he said curtly, coming to stand next to her, holding two glasses of wine. "Here. To celebrate your talent."

Her cheeks warmed at his compliment. Even though she knew her work was impeccable, it wasn't often she was praised for it. "Thank you."

As she took the wine, his eyes returned to the suit she'd made for him. "I'm surprised you finished so quickly," he said. "I thought it was going to take you all night."

"It's not done yet," she confessed.

Killian studied the outfits more carefully, looking puzzled. "Looks done to me."

"We need to try them on so I can adjust to the exact size."

"Oh, right. Well, I'll leave you to it then."

"Actually, I'm going to need your help," she said, keeping her eyes on the dress. From her peripheral vision, she could see his puzzled look.

"My help?"

When she pointed to the dress, Killian froze. His Adam's apple bobbed as he swallowed hard. "Oh..." His mouth hung open for several seconds. "You need help getting *into* the dress."

"Yes." She downed her entire glass of wine in one gulp, hoping to drown the butterflies that fluttered inside her stomach. "Can you close your eyes, please?"

Killian stared at her as if trying to register her words.

"Killian."

"Yeah?"

She took the wine glass from his hand. "Close your eyes."

"Right." He shook his head as if shaking off a spell, then pressed his eyes shut.

Ella placed the wine glasses aside, then removed the dress from its stand. "Here, hold it like this." She guided Killian's hands, and he held the dress in place, all the while keeping his eyes closed. "Now, lower yourself to your knees," she said in a soft tone.

Killian slowly got to his knees, lowering the dress just enough that she could step into it. "There. That's good." She stepped back and let out a shuddering breath. "I'm going to undress now."

Killian's whole body stiffened. The veins in his neck bulged as if he was holding back a carriage of horses from running wild. She swallowed hard, pushing through the lump in her throat, then she let her outer garment fall to her feet.

Her shoulders were bare, as were her thighs. And even though Killian's eyes were shut, she was still standing in front of him, *over him*, in only a bodice. Her heart raced as she reached for his shoulders. His muscles were as hard as iron as she balanced herself before stepping into the dress.

"You can stand now," she said softly, keeping her hands on his shoulders.

Killian stood slowly, bringing the dress up with him. But as his thumbs brushed against her thighs, a gasp got caught in her throat. When he stopped, she realized she had dug her nails into his shoulders.

A low grunt ripped through his throat, and Ella knew it wasn't because of her nails against his skin. His skin was impenetrable. His skin was also hot against her outer thighs, and she wondered if he could sense the sudden wave of desire that was rising within her.

She leaned into his ear. "Keep going," she whispered.

Killian gulped loudly as the gentleness of his touch resumed. Ella bit her lip, reveling in the sensation that traveled up her body. She closed her eyes, imagining how it would feel to slide her hands to the nape of his neck, to tangle her fingers in his hair. She fought against the urge to pull him into her, to guide his lips to her neck, to beg for his tongue to taste her skin.

And when the dress reached her chest, her breath caught in her throat as Killian pulled it over her bosom. An electric shock shot down her spine. Every muscle in his body hardened as he pressed her against his chest to reach for the back of her dress.

As he began tying the dress over her bodice, she looked up at him, his skin glistening with the reflection of the fire. The heat between them was tantalizing.

"Tighter," she whispered, and he obliged.

Her chest pressed even tighter against him as he worked his way up her back. With every button, the sensation of his strokes filled her with pleasure.

"I never knew you could be so gentle," she whispered.

Killian jolted backward and shot his eyes open. Ella cleared her throat, then averted her eyes toward the suit. "Go on and try yours on. Let me know how it fits," she said breathlessly.

But he didn't move. He just stood there, staring at her. But he wasn't looking at her dress. He was looking at her face. At her lips.

Something inside her flared, and with it came the memory of them at the top of the tower in the dream world. Him calling out her name, cupping her face, pressing her palm to his chest. Then his kiss, hard and urgent. She knew he was only trying to pull her out of a trance, which was why it ended so abruptly, but the memory was enough to make her want that again.

Killian pressed his eyes shut and shook his head as if reprimanding himself. "I should..." He motioned toward the suit, then took it from the mannequin. "I'll be right back." He walked past her and went to change in the other room.

Ella let out a shaky breath, then took a seat to steady her wobbly knees. Something pinched her inner thigh. The glass knife Killian had given her was still strapped to the fabric around her upper leg. As she tried reaching for it, the smoothness of the glass brushed the tip of her fingers, but she couldn't grab hold of the handle. Not while wearing that dress. She needed to find a better place for her weapon. A place with easier access in case of an emergency.

Killian returned, and Ella did a double take. His hair was pulled back in a neat bun, and he looked as royal as a prince. She could suddenly see how royal he would look if he claimed the throne in the Underworld.

"Something wrong?" he asked, looking at her leg. That was when Ella realized she still had her foot propped on the stool and a hand under her dress.

"The knife," she said. "I can't reach it."

"It probably got tangled with the fabric," he said, kneeling in front of her. "May I?"

Before Ella could tell him that was a bad idea, Killian's hand was already at her knee. Her mouth hung open, the words at the tip of her tongue, but she couldn't bring herself to stop him. His touch was just as tantalizing as before, except this time his eyes were locked with hers. And the intensity of his gaze, along with the roughness of his touch trailing up her bare thighs, set her insides ablaze.

When his hand reached the knife, she bit down on her tongue to keep herself from demanding that he keep going.

He untangled the knife and pulled it free but kept his hand on her thigh. His piercing blue eyes peered into hers with such intensity, she wondered if he could sense her pulsing at her core.

When the knife came into view, Killian rose back to his feet. "Here you go." He flipped the knife and caught it by its blade so Ella could take the handle.

"Thank you," she said, taking it but not quite sure where to put it. "So, how does the suit feel?"

Killian looked himself over. "Not bad. What do you think?"

Ella thought he looked impeccably charming, but she didn't want to use those exact words. He was smug enough as it was. "Not bad," she said instead.

The smug smile made an appearance anyway. Perhaps he could see the truth in her eyes. "I have something for you," he said, lifting a finger to signal she should wait. He disappeared into the kitchen for several seconds, then returned with a piece of glass in his hand.

He stopped in front of her, and when he lifted the object, Ella's hand flew to her open mouth. It wasn't just any glass. It was the same glass material as her knife. As his sword. But it wasn't a weapon. It was a pair of shoes. A pair of glass slippers.

"I figured they would go well with any dress," Killian said, handing her the slippers.

Ella stared at it in amazement, tracing the smooth edges with the tip of her fingers. "They're absolutely beautiful," she breathed.

"They're not the most beautiful thing in this room, though."

Ella looked up to meet his eyes, but before she

could respond, he placed the slippers on the floor. "Put them on."

Ella slipped her feet into them. They were a lot more comfortable than she'd expected. The glass from the Underworld was, without a doubt, unlike anything she'd ever seen.

But what surprised her the most was the gesture. She never thought Killian was even capable of such thoughtfulness, yet he kept surprising her. There were so many layers to him, and she found herself captivated by every single one. His strength. His loyalty. His justice.

Ella stood in front of the mirror. The slippers matched the dress perfectly. "Thank you so much," she beamed, catching his eyes through the reflection of the mirror as he stood behind her.

He held her gaze for a long moment, his blue eyes bright with the reflection of the fire. "Stunning," he said softly.

A sudden wave of heat swept through the room, and a rush of horrifying flames grew next to them. Ella screamed and covered her eyes. Killian jumped in front of her, shielding her from the flames that licked at his back.

Ella's feet suddenly left the ground as Killian threw her over his shoulder. The fire from the fireplace grew even wilder, and within seconds, it caught onto the scattered fabrics from the floor.

"Killian!" Ella screamed, coughing as the smoke choked her.

Killian darted toward the window and shattered it with his fist. He then climbed out, taking Ella with him. Outside, the air was fresh and cold, and Ella could breathe again.

Killian placed her back on the ground, the grass soft under her heel.

"What happened?" she asked, feeling like she was coughing her lungs out.

Killian was about to answer when the sound of hyenas laughing echoed from the woods. He turned toward the sound with his chest puffed out and his fists balled, bracing for a fight. But no one appeared. And eventually, the laughter faded.

"What was that?" Ella asked, but this time her eyes stared in horror at Belle's cottage in flames. Thick smoke bellowed into the dark skies. "How did that…?"

"This wasn't an accident," Killian hissed, turning away from the woods with a glare. "It was a message."

"A message?" Ella echoed, horrified. "What kind of message is *that*?"

But by the anger on Killian's face, Ella knew the answer. "It was the bounty hunters from the Underworld, wasn't it?" she asked. "They'll be coming for me after the blood moon. That's the message."

Killian cupped Ella's face with his strong hands as if trying to steady her thoughts. "They will have to go through me. And they cannot. So, you are safe, do you hear me?"

When Ella nodded, he pulled her into him and wrapped his protective arms around her. "They will not touch you," Killian whispered in her ear as she buried her face in his chest. "You have my word. Now, wait here."

The last thing Ella wanted was for Killian to let her go, but he didn't go far. He took a few steps toward the flaming cottage and stretched out his arms. The red and yellow flames suddenly turned blue and white, and a moment later, they vanished. The fire disappeared.

Killian dropped his hands, then turned to make sure Ella was all right. She ran into him again, and he tightened his arms around her. "Let's get you out of that dress before it gets ruined."

Ella looked over her dress, surprised it hadn't caught any of the mud from the grass. And neither had his suit pants. Perhaps the smell of smoke would fade before the ball.

"Do you really think it will work?" Ella asked. "Going to the ball, I mean."

"It has to," Killian said firmly. "We will find the

King's killer, and when we do, your soul will be absolved. I'm sure of it."

"It's not my soul I'm worried about," she confessed. "It's the trigger."

"One thing at a time," Killian said. "For now, we need to dye your hair a different color. I'm fairly certain the Prince will be skeptical of all blondes."

Ella touched her curls. "I hadn't thought about that."

"Come on." Killian offered her his hand. "I know just the plant mixture to make that happen. He will never see us coming."

13

KILLIAN

Ella was fidgeting in her seat next to Killian as they joined the long line of carriages leading to the castle on the Shores. The air was thick with nerves, and Killian could taste the salty sweat every time he opened his mouth. But when he tuned into Ella's delightful scent, it drowned out all others. Even the potent smell of horse manure.

As their stolen carriage stopped outside the front, a guard opened the door and stepped aside.

Killian heard Ella's breath catch in the back of her throat, and when he climbed out of the carriage, he made a mental note to hold Ella extra tight. He hated that they had to be so close to the Prince. What if he recognized her? What if the plan didn't work, and she never got her memory triggered? All of that risk would have been for nothing.

But as she and her extravagant gown came into view, and her mask glittered in the golden castle lights, Killian momentarily forgot about his concerns. He offered his arm, and she took it, squeezing his bicep as she linked her arm with his. He offered her a smile, and her mouth picked up into an anxious smile for a flicker of a moment.

"Thank you," she said to the guard. The warmth in her tone made Killian wonder if she knew the man. Seeing as she used to work at the palace, he thought that might have been true. Ella was the type of lady to know everyone's name and show them kindness no matter their social class.

Killian held his breath, keenly watching the guard for any sign of recognition on his face. But he kept his expression impassive as he bowed to Ella. "You're very welcome, my lady. I hope you both have a pleasant evening."

Killian inclined his head and rested his hand over Ella's at the crook of his arm. Then he took one last look at Ella's soft red hair, swept up into a tight bun at the back of her head. Personally, he preferred her golden curls, but it was important that no one recognized her.

Still, she was exquisite. The soft curve of her neck was perfectly visible, and Killian found himself wondering how her smooth, milky skin would taste against his lips. But then they reached the castle doors and Ella's nervous squeeze on his arm brought him back into the moment.

String music flooded the air, and it was not nearly as grating as it was the last time he had been to a ball. Usually, Killian found human music to be like two toddlers beating on wooden crates. Or dragging rusty saws on the stone floor. But tonight, with Ella's heart-beat to add to the symphony, it was quite pleasing.

The distinguished guests were dressed in their finest silks while villagers starved in the streets. In all the centuries Killian had been alive, that was one thing that never seemed to change. At the palace, the wealthy wined and dined, worrying about what Lord What's-His-Name thought of Miss Cares-Too-Much's red gown.

Killian scanned the sea of faces as the ladies and gentlemen danced in the center of the ballroom. The vast golden chandeliers glowed like warm embers above their heads. There must have been more than a hundred candles on each one. The smoke stung Killian's nostrils.

But then he found the Prince standing beside one of the banquet tables, dressed in his royal attire, and Killian's blood boiled.

That was the man who wanted Ella dead.

To Killian's utter annoyance, he couldn't sense a

drop of guilt from his aura. Just the heady scent of sadness and grief, like damp driftwood with wet grass. And if the scent of his aura was not enough of a give-away, the dark circles under his eyes were.

Killian cleared his throat. "To the left, by the drinks," he muttered with a nudge. Ella followed his line of sight and her heart quickened like a deer caught in a crossfire. But Killian squeezed her hand. "I won't let him harm you. I promise."

Her breaths eased at his touch, and he liked being able to soothe her.

"What do I do?" she asked in a whisper as they made their way casually around the dancefloor.

Killian watched the Prince, wondering what it would take to trigger the rest of her memory. He had hoped just being within the vicinity of the man would be enough, but so far, nothing had changed.

Ella's aura grew excited, and the scent was like standing in a field of flowers on a hot June afternoon. "Wendy!" She grabbed the arm of a young woman with a matching silver mask and gown. The young woman seemed startled at first, but then Ella began signing with her hands, and a wide smile grew on the young woman's face. They embraced for a moment, then broke apart.

"What are you doing?" Killian asked, leaning into

Ella as discreetly as he could manage. "I thought we agreed that no one should recognize you."

"But this is Wendy," Ella said with an easy smile. "We can trust her."

Killian trusted no one.

After the young woman curtseyed to Killian, she turned to Ella and began signing. Perks of having lived for centuries, there wasn't a language on Earth Killian didn't understand, but he didn't pay much attention to what was being said. Instead, he took the opportunity to sense her aura. She seemed honest and pure, but that didn't make her any less of a threat.

Anyone who recognized Ella was a threat. And Killian was not about to lower his guard for anyone. Not until they were miles away from that kingdom.

"Lexa and Ryke are on a ship, sailing the seas," Wendy signed to Ella. Killian remembered meeting Lexa at her wedding. She was the one responsible for singing the forbidden song, and for Ella being marked. "They're trying to make a peace treaty between the mermaids and pirates. But so far, neither party is having any of it."

Killian smirked. The feud between pirates and mermaids had gone on for hundreds of years, and just because two of them decided to marry, that would not be enough to undo centuries of deaths.

Wendy motioned to Ella's hair, and she tucked a

stray strand behind her ear. But then she signed with more urgency, telling Wendy that no one could know she was there.

"The Prince has ordered my capture. He says I killed the King," Ella signed, and Wendy's eyes grew big. "It's not true. And I'm here tonight to find a way to prove my innocence."

As the ladies continued, Killian shifted his attention to the Prince. He stood like a statue by his throne, watching the guests on the dancefloor. He reeked with grief, and his stonelike demeanor made it clear he'd been forced to attend the event.

"All right, enough chitchat," Killian said, turning to Ella. "I don't want to spend all night here."

Ella's brows pinched together, and she gave Wendy a hug. After Wendy walked away, she turned to Killian with an irritated frown. "Well, that was rude."

"We are not here to socialize," he reminded her. "The sooner you tell me who the killer is, the sooner I can remove the mark from you."

"Fine." She let out an exasperated sigh, then turned toward the Prince. "Still no trigger."

Killian held back a grunt. He hated the idea of Ella getting anywhere near the man who wanted her dead, but if nothing else was working, they didn't have a choice.

"We need to get him to notice you."

Ella's eyes grew big. "Are you insane?"

Killian turned to face her, then took her hand. "Do you trust me?"

When she nodded, he pulled her to the dance floor. He took Ella in his arms and pressed her up against him. She fit so snugly against his body, and he held her like he was cradling the rarest jewel in all the realms.

Ella's eyes sparkled at him, and he sensed her nerves were settling too.

"How is charming me going to help our plan?" she asked as they waltzed.

He raised a cocky brow. "You think I'm charming?"

Her cheeks reddened, but instead of looking away, she smiled. "This reminds me of the day we met on that boat. Remember?"

"Ah, yes. We danced then, too." Killian dipped her over his arm, and her chest heaved as he hovered over her. "Although, I must say, I prefer this dress much better." He stole a not-so-discreet glance at her bosom before he righted her and continued the waltz.

Ella's breaths quickened, but she remained composed. "Where did you learn how to dance like this?" she asked.

"When you live for centuries, you learn a thing or two."

The chemistry between them swirled like a pink mist around them, and Ella's heart drummed against her ribcage. It was literal music to Killian's ears. And the heat that radiated from her body burned like an ember inside him.

As they danced, the fire within Killian willed him to ignore all the barriers he'd put in place to keep them apart. He wasn't good for her, and he knew that, but her scent was so intoxicating, the only thoughts that took hold were of him doing all manner of indecent things to her. He decided that Ella must have been able to read auras too, because her eyes softened with desire as she held his gaze.

"May I cut in?" a familiar voice asked, and Ella stiffened in Killian's arms.

The Prince stood next to them, watching Ella with wandering eyes. Killian's plan worked. Even so, it took all of his resolve to pull away. They needed that trigger if he was to save Ella's soul.

Killian gave her a reassuring nod, then stepped back to turn to the Prince.

"Good evening, my lady." The Prince smiled at Ella. There was no sign of recognition in his eyes. "I don't think we have met."

Ella swallowed so hard that Killian heard it. But she recovered herself elegantly. "Giselle of Nottingham, Your Majesty," she said in a breathy voice. She let go of Killian's hand and curtseyed. "This is Lord Smith."

The Prince's eyes hovered in Killian's direction. "Good evening, sir."

Killian gave a slight bow, but then the Prince's eyes were back on Ella as if Killian was nothing but a mere nuance.

"May I have this dance?" he asked, offering Ella his hand.

Ella's eyes glanced in Killian's direction as though looking for his permission. And then Killian remembered that the man responsible for a lady in such situations would indeed need to give permission for another man to dance with her.

More than anything he wanted to snap the Prince's neck for just having put out those wanted signs all over the kingdom with Ella's face on them. As though Ella could hear his thoughts, her eyes hardened in his direction before she smiled at the Prince again.

She didn't need to say it. Killian knew she was reminding him of her *no violence* rule. Although he wasn't a fan of that rule, he couldn't ignore that, in this instance, it was the opportunity they had been looking for. The closer she got to the Prince, the more likely she would trigger the memory they needed.

Killian inclined his head, and the Prince took Ella's fingertips and walked away with her. The other guests parted, making a clear path for them as they walked to the center of the dance floor. Then the musicians started the next song. A slow, stirring song much better suited for a funeral, which Killian thought would be fitting because if the Prince so much as touched a strand of hair on her head, he would die.

The thought made Killian smile.

But then the Prince's pale hand rested on the small of Ella's back, and Killian's amusement vanished. The Prince was clearly attracted to Ella, which shouldn't have been surprising as she was the most beautiful woman there.

Killian forced himself to look away in an attempt to ignore it, but the pull toward her was too strong. The Prince's aura flashed a joyful yellow, and a fire broke out inside of Killian. The longer he watched the Prince's delighted face staring down at Ella while in his arms, an enraged feeling ripped through Killian like a fiery inferno.

The Prince took her other hand and stretched it out to the side as they twirled on the spot. Her gown swooshed, and it was the most beautiful sight of her Killian had ever seen. Some of the guests stopped dancing to stare, and the ladies sighed.

Any moment now, Ella's memory would surely return, and then he could swoop in and take her far away from that place. From that fool.

But the moment never came. Instead, the Prince's hand flexed on the small of Ella's back, and she giggled. Killian wanted to burst into flames and burn the whole castle down. But instead, he curled his hands into tight fists and clenched his jaw.

Watching her laugh in the Prince's arms was torture. And Killian knew torture. He had hundreds of scars to prove it, but yet, the sight of her in another man's arms by far surpassed any agony he'd ever experienced.

He wasn't sure how much more of that he could take, but at least now he understood why some murderers would say that all they saw was red.

When the Prince leaned in to whisper in Ella's ear, Killian charged forward, ready to throw his fist and knock the Prince back. But Ella's eyes flashed him a warning, and he stopped just short of doing something foolish.

"Lady Giselle," he said through his clenched jaw, "your presence had been requested outside."

The Prince's face remained perfectly composed, but there was a rush of annoyance in his aura for a split second. "It was lovely meeting you." He inclined his head, and as he offered Ella a slight bow, he pressed his lips to her knuckles. "I hope to see you again, Giselle."

Killian fought back the urge to glower at the Prince as he stepped aside. Then he motioned for Ella to walk ahead of him.

Once they stepped outside, Killian took her by the hand and marched down the steps toward the gardens.

"Killian, wait." She staggered next to him, her heels making it hard to keep up with his strides. But getting her as far away from that dance floor as possible was all Killian could think about. "Killian, stop!" When he still didn't listen, she yanked her hand from his grasp. "I said stop! What is wrong with you?"

He pressed his eyes shut and sucked in a deep breath. The salty sea breeze cleansed the air as they walked past the gardens that led to the shores. The rolling waves crashed against the beach, and the sound soothed his nerves just enough to gather his thoughts.

"We didn't come here for you to flirt with the Prince," Killian said harshly. "We came for you to get a trigger. And since the Prince isn't being much help in that department, we need to start thinking of an alternate plan before the night is over."

Ella crossed her arms. "Who says I was flirting with the Prince?"

Killian swung around and leaned into her. "I can sense you, remember?"

Her eyes locked with his, and they shone an indigo blue in the reflection of the moonlight. "Then you should've been able to tell that during that entire dance I was thinking of *you*."

Her words knocked the air out of his lungs, and

Killian took in a breath.

"For someone who can sense other people's feelings, you are terrible at understanding your own," she said, her voice soft in the night. "What you sensed in there… that wasn't me flirting with the Prince. That was you being *jealous* of me."

Killian let out a dark chuckle. "Jealousy is for the insecure. I don't feel jealousy."

Ella gave him a lopsided grin. "Is that so?"

"Very much so."

"Then I don't believe you would mind if I went back to finish my dance with the Prince?" She picked up her skirt and turned around, but Killian grabbed her arm and swung her back to face him.

"Don't even think about it."

A pleased smile spread across her face, and she leaned into him, her lips mere inches from his. "Then admit it," she whispered, her sweet breath brushing against his lips. "You were jealous."

With a grunt, Killian clutched Ella's waist and pulled her close until her hips bumped his. An agonized groan ripped from his mouth at the contact, and he walked her backward until she was pressed up against an oak tree. Without a word, he took her hands and raised them above her head, holding them against the tree. Her neck pulsed rapidly, but the heat in her eyes beckoned for more.

"What do you want me to say?" he hissed. "That I wanted to break every finger in his hands for touching you? That the entire time he was dancing with you, all I wanted was to take you back in my arms and burn that whole castle down?"

Ella watched him in wonderment. "You *were* jealous," she whispered in disbelief.

Killian leaned in but paused near her mouth, inhaling the decadent scent of her warmth with each breath. Then he looked her hard in the eyes. "Tell me you don't feel the same way, and I'll stop."

"I don't…" Ella said, eyeing him closely. Killian froze, furrowing his brows. But then her eyes darkened, and a permissive grin curved her lips. "I don't want you to stop."

Heartened, Killian secured his grip on her wrists with one hand and reached down to pick up her leg. He wrapped it around his waist and kissed the hollow of her neck. Ella let out a shuddering sigh, arching her back, pushing her body against his.

Every brazen touch set off a chain reaction in Killian's body. Her entire being heated under him, and as he left a trail of kisses up her neck, her breaths came out raspy. "Oh, Killian," she said through a gasp.

He nipped her earlobe, then pulled back to look into her eyes as they sparkled through her mask. Her rich, sweet scent intoxicated him, and every part of her body told him what she wanted. But he wanted her to say it.

"What do you want?" he asked gruffly against her ear.

Her body quivered against him. "Not want… *need*," she whispered back.

If anyone were to walk out into the gardens and follow the path to the sea, they would first hear the moans, then in the deepest shadows of the trees, they would see a most improper sight.

But to Killian, nothing felt more natural than capturing Ella's lips with his hot mouth. He squeezed her thigh and tasted her tongue before sucking on her bottom lip. She tasted just as good as he thought she would. Like warm honey. Sweeter than anything he'd ever tasted.

Her wrists wrestled against his hold, and he let her go. Her hands flew to his shirt and unfastened the buttons. It was the most unusual time and place for that, but as Ella's nails grazed his bare chest, his worries scattered.

Forget the throne to the Underworld. Ella was his prize. All of her. Right then on the beach. Something about claiming her on the palace grounds sent a flood of satisfaction through Killian, like an alpha marking his territory so the likes of the Prince could never again lay hands on her.

But just as he deepened their kiss and his hands began to wander under her dress, a soft voice broke them apart.

Killian ripped his body from Ella's, and the two looked around at the childlike singing that had interrupted them. Near the shoreline, a young girl with golden curls skipped about, picking up shells. She sang an old folk song, completely oblivious to the fact that Killian and Ella were there.

Then more young maidens came into view, running around the beach, their dresses billowing out behind them. A wave of sadness hit Killian, but it wasn't his own. He looked at Ella. Her face had paled, and even behind the mask, he could see the look of devastation in her eyes.

"Who is that?" Killian asked.

"That's Lily," Ella replied with a sad smile. "I used to look after her. Everything happened so fast, I never got to say goodbye."

Killian put a comforting hand on her shoulder and gave it a light squeeze. "You know that she can't know that you're here, right?"

Ella nodded. "I know."

She watched Lily for a bit longer while Killian buttoned up his shirt, then he took her hand and tugged on it lightly. "Come on, we should go back," he said in a whisper. "We still need that trigger."

As they re-entered the ballroom, the Prince was standing beside the resting musicians. He was holding up a glass of champagne and was in the middle of a speech. Ella and Killian edged around the people to get a better look.

"To my dear friends and esteemed alliances, may the coming year be full of promise and good health to all."

The guests murmured their agreement, and everyone took a sip of their champagne.

"And lastly, to my late father, the King. May he rest in peace and we never forget the legacy he left behind."

As he raised his glass again, Ella gasped, her hand flying to her open mouth.

Before Killian could stop her, she flew up the staircase, her heart hammering in her chest. But halfway up, she stumbled and fell. The guests gasped and all eyes were on her as she struggled to her feet. Killian inwardly groaned as her curly locks fell from their updo and her mask slipped from her face.

Her mouth was the perfect shape of an 'O' as she locked eyes with the Prince, who stared at her like he was seeing a ghost.

That was when Killian had two realizations. The Prince recognized Ella. And Ella's memory was finally triggered.

14

ELLA

Memories flooded Ella's mind as the Prince's eyes locked with hers. Flashes of that night jolted inside her brain like shockwaves. The King's blood on her hands and arms. The strong smell of iron and rust on her cloak. The Prince's voice yelling, "Seize her!" as she towered over the King's lifeless body.

But most importantly, the face of the killer holding the bloody knife.

It took Ella's brain several seconds to register that the Prince's voice was no longer inside her head. His voice was echoing in the ballroom.

"I said *seize her*!"

Guards ran toward the staircase with hands on the hilt of their swords. Ella's stomach churned, and she clutched the red carpeted floor covering the steps.

Killian's strong hand grabbed her arm and pulled her to her feet. She staggered forward as one of her glass heels slipped off.

"My shoe!" she shrieked.

"Leave it!" Killian demanded, pulling her with him toward the exit at the top of the stairs.

Killian swung his arm, hitting a guard on the jaw and flipping him over the railing. Screams filled the ballroom. The rest of the guards came in waves but were thrown about in every direction like rag dolls until she and Killian finally made it out the double doors.

The fresh air hit Ella's burning skin, and she sucked in a breath. Her mind cleared and the flashes of memory came more quickly. She remembered everything. But then she lowered her eyes to the ground floor and spotted an army of soldiers approaching at the bottom of the steps. They moved slowly, clutching their weapons as if approaching a wild animal.

Ella reached for Killian behind her and touched his back. He was shoving his sword between the handles of the doors to keep the inside guards from coming after them, but Ella was fairly certain he was going to need that weapon if they were to face the guards outside.

"Killian," she called out. He appeared at her side, breathing heavily. She backed away but felt his hand on her lower back. His touch was firm and confident, and her fear vanished because she remembered who he was. *What* he was.

"Climb on my back," he ordered. "And don't touch the ground."

Ella hopped on Killian's back without a second thought and laced her legs around his waist. The strength of his back muscles against her chest as he turned to retrieve his sword from the door sent a sizzling sensation to her core. The pressure of their bodies together filled her with heat. The places where his lips had touched burned on her skin with an untamable yearning she couldn't control. They needed to make it out alive because she needed to feel his lips on her again. His tongue. She needed to taste him, even if just one last time.

A group of guards barged through the double doors, and Killian jumped to the middle of the stone steps. Guards approached from every direction. They were surrounded.

"Hold tight," Killian said in a low rumble as he lifted his sword over his head. The spark of electricity crackled in the air like lightning as a blue flame consumed his blade. He struck the ground with the tip of his flaming blade with as much force as he could muster. The ground shook from the thunder his sword expelled, sending a shockwave that flung the guards into the air before they hit the ground with a thud.

Killian let out a loud whistle, then ran past the few whimpering guards while the rest were unconscious. A white horse with large wings and captivating electric blue eyes flew down from the night sky and landed in front of them.

"What is this?" Ella asked, staring agape at the supernatural creature.

"I told you I had a horse," Killian said. In one swift motion, he placed Ella astride the mystical creature, then hopped on behind her. When the horse took flight, Killian pressed Ella's back against his chest, securing her in place. The cold wind brushed her face, and the loose strands of her hair flapped in the wind. The forest below became a dizzying blur of brown and green, and they disappeared into the darkness, leaving their enemies far behind.

Ella had no idea how much time had passed before Killian guided his horse to descend and land by a lake. By the slow rhythm of his heartbeat against her back, she knew they were no longer in danger. Still, she couldn't bear to close her eyes. The true danger lived inside her mind in vivid detail. The silvery reflection of the moon on the knife that killed the King. The crimson liquid that dripped from the blade.

The truth was horrific.

She lifted her eyes to the moon as it peeked through

the trees, searching for guidance. What was she to do with what she had discovered?

Killian nuzzled the top of her head, and she snuggled into him. "What happened back there?" he asked, his breath hot in her ear. "What did you remember?"

Ella wanted to tell him, but she couldn't. Killian wouldn't understand.

"It didn't work," she said, trying hard to keep her voice from shaking. "I couldn't trigger the memory."

Killian stiffened behind her, then when he jumped down, she noticed his jaw was clenched.

"Killian," she called after him, but he didn't answer. He simply guided the horse to the water and waited for him to start drinking.

Ella kicked off the remaining glass slipper, then jumped down from the horse. "Look, it's not my fault that it didn't work."

Killian didn't respond. He didn't even bother turning around to face her.

"Say something," she demanded.

"I don't know what to say to you," he spoke through clenched teeth, and she had no idea where such hostility was coming from. But it didn't matter. They were running out of time. The silvery glow of the moon above them was dimming, which meant the blood moon would soon take its place.

She sucked in a breath as the words formed inside

her turmoiled mind. "I'll start, then," she said, her voice soft. "I'm in love with you."

Killian swung around, a spark of longing in his eyes.

"I'm in love with you, Killian."

His gaze hardened and his brows furrowed. "How do you do that?"

"Do what?" she asked.

"Be genuine and honest, but a liar all at the same time?"

She pulled back as if he'd splashed cold water on her face. "Are you implying that my feelings are a lie?"

"No. I can sense they are true." He pressed his eyes shut with a grimace. "But you're only saying them because you want to distract me from the matter at hand."

Ella frowned. He was right, but it didn't make her feelings any less true. She stepped into the water and cupped his face with her small hands. "The matter at hand is that I'm in love with you."

His gaze was sharp as he peered into her eyes. "Then why won't you tell me the truth?" He cocked his head, studying her. "You know who killed the King."

"Yes," she admitted. "But I can't say."

He grabbed her wrists with his strong hands. "Who are you protecting?"

When she lowered her eyes to the water, Killian's

shoulders sagged. "Ella, please…" His voice was soft as his grip loosened. The roughness of his thumb brushed against her skin, and the sensation of his touch filled her with warmth. "Please tell me…" he begged. "Who are you protecting?"

Tears stung her eyes as she looked up at him again. "The kingdom."

He shook his head. "What does that mean?"

Ella tried pulling away from him, but he didn't let her. He grabbed her hands and pressed them to his chest. His heart was thumping hard.

"Give me a reason." His voice shook, and she wasn't sure if it was anger or unbearable sadness.

"I cannot, in good conscience, hand an innocent person over to death. I will not," she said.

"If they killed the King, they are not innocent, Ella."

"They did not know what they were doing—"

"Don't you understand?" Killian cupped her face with his rough palms, the gentleness in his eyes replaced by desperation. "If I don't find a soul to claim, it will have to be yours."

It wasn't a threat. It was a fact. A simple fact that seemed to be causing him an insurmountable amount of pain.

A pain she wanted to desperately soothe.

She leaned closer, her lips inches from his. "Kiss me," she begged. "Kiss me like it's the last time."

His eyes dropped to her lips, and the hunger in his gaze just about set her body ablaze.

"Kiss me, Killian—"

Her words died on a squeak as his mouth covered hers. His arms slid around her waist and urged her against him. The heat from his body poured into hers, warming her wherever he touched, her back, her bottom, the backs of her legs.

Ella's eyelids drooped closed as her body responded to the delightful way his calloused fingers grazed her bare skin. When he squeezed her, she moaned against his mouth.

Killian traced her neckline, sliding her dress off her shoulder. Ella tore her lips from his, throwing her head back in pleasing agony. "Oh, Killian—" This time her words ended on a gasp as his other hand slid over her inner thigh.

She was on fire as the combination of his hands on her body and his mouth at her throat stirred her into a frenzy.

"Make me yours," she pleaded as he kissed the most sensitive part of her neck.

"Ella…" His voice was breathy in her ear. "You already are."

She grabbed two fistfuls of his hair, urging him on. Daring him further. She wanted to feel all of him, in the deepest parts of her being. She didn't want to die without knowing what it would feel like to belong entirely to him.

Killian tore himself away, then gave her an incredulous look. "I can sense you…" he said.

"Then why did you stop?" Ella asked between breaths.

He narrowed his eyes as if trying to isolate her feelings from her desires. "Is that what this is? Goodbye?"

"I want you to have everything you ever wanted," she said, brushing the tip of her fingers over his stubble. "So, take me. Take my soul. Claim it so you can win the throne. I want that for you."

"No." He let her go and backed away. "This is not how your story ends."

Ella looked up at the moon. It had already lost its glow. Even if Killian didn't claim her soul, the other bounty hunters would. Their time together was coming to an end, and all she wanted was to spend the time she had left in his arms.

"You won't have a choice," she said with a soft smile as the tips of her fingers continued to caress his face. "If you don't claim my soul, someone else will. I'm marked, remember?"

His expression hardened. "For the love of all that is sacred, Ella. Who are you protecting?" he hissed.

She frowned. "I cannot let you kill anyone else."

Killian gave her a hard look. "I will kill every person on this Earth if it means saving you."

And without another word, he turned around and stormed into the darkened woods, leaving Ella with her fervent body, longing for his embrace.

She sighed, then went to sit by a tree. Her heavy eyelids drooped from the exhaustion of the day.

Then suddenly a cloth was thrown over her head as a strong rush of wind and sand hit her face, like wings flapping overhead. A screech of a flying creature came from a few feet away, then a hand covered her mouth, muffling her scream.

15

KILLIAN

Ella's scent was all over Killian as he paced the dark forest. His breaths came out in short, fast puffs and stung his nostrils. He couldn't understand how a woman could be so infuriating, and at the same time, utterly seductive.

He dragged his fingers across his lips, wiping his mouth, but it did nothing to erase the taste of her sweetness. His body longed to go back to her and finish what they started. He could still sense her arousal. She wanted him. She needed him. And he had been more than willing to oblige. Until he realized that it was only for one night.

The thought of losing Ella splintered Killian's heart, and his chest tightened. She made him feel more alive than he'd ever been. More complete. More satisfied. But equally infuriated.

When she wasn't flooding his soul with her warmth and tenderness, she was dipping him into a cold bath of frustration as she stood her ground against him. She was the only woman to ever challenge him. How could a feeble human possess a spirit so strong? She was kind and pure even though deep down she was tormented and defiant. She was an intriguing puzzle he wanted to spend the rest of her days trying to solve. He was certain it would take that long. The more he got to know her, the more layers she seemed to have, and he wanted nothing more than to peel back each one until he got to see the core of who she really was.

He knelt beside a river and thrust water over his face, washing away her scent and flooding his senses with the earth instead. His heart calmed as he grounded himself again. He tuned into the soft trickling water running over the earth, and the fish hidden between the rocks. The soft glow of the moonlight cast a silver light, and the tree-shaped shadows danced across the forest floor. The air was cool and moved as a gentle breeze.

He stood up and filled his lungs with the musty scent of the earth, compelling every atom in his body to become still and calm. But the absence of Ella's scent made him feel empty. He turned around and marched back, taking a deep breath every few steps, waiting for her delicious scent to flood him again.

But it never came.

"Ella!" he shouted, picking up his pace to a jog. Leaves crunched under his boots, and squirrels scurried away upon sight of him as he hurried by. When he returned to the place he left Ella, she was gone.

He whipped around, trying to pick up her scent. But there was nothing. His heart thrummed against his ribcage as his mind concocted all of the worst possible scenarios. Had another bounty hunter gotten to her? Had the Prince's guards caught up to them?

Killian pulled out his sword and dragged his palm across it, coating the blade in blue flame. It lit up like a torch, and he studied the ground, looking for her tracks.

He found his own footprints, as well as the dainty outline of Ella's feet. But there was a third set. Small, stubby shoes. There was a struggle. The ground was deeply trodden beside the ash tree. That was when he noticed the massive footprints by the water's edge. The trail abruptly ended, which meant it had to be a flying creature of sorts.

Killian raced forward until he reached the dirt road. Ella's scent reached him, though it was faint. He sheathed his sword and ran back to his horse. On mounting Azul, Killian grabbed the reins and focused on transmitting his energy. Azul's wings stretched wide, and his eyes flashed an electric blue, as did his mane and tail. Once his glowing hooves left the ground, Killian charged in the direction of Ella's scent.

His panic faded and gave way to raging fury. Ella had not been taken by a bounty hunter, that much he was sure. And her scent was coming from the opposite direction of the palace, so the Prince's guards hadn't gotten to her either.

When Killian reached the large stately home, Ella's fearful scent flooded his nostrils, setting his body on fire. Every fiber of his being shook in an endless rage, he was surprised that he himself had not burst into flames.

He took short breaths as he marched toward the house of Rumpelstiltskin.

Killian disliked the man before, but now that he had taken Ella for his collection, he loathed him. Deal or no deal with Hades, Killian was going to rip the man limb from limb.

He forced his way into the back door and hurried down the stone steps, deep underground. A large wooden door with a cast iron lock was his only obstacle, and all it took was a hard shove with his shoulder for the door to break from its hinges and fall to the stone floor with an earth-shattering bang.

If Rumple didn't know Killian was there, he did now. But Killian didn't care to be quiet. Ella's scent urged him forward, but all he found were iron cages lining the underground dungeon.

Pale, sad faces looked in his direction as he walked by. He cast his eyes about the place, searching for Ella. But as he looked at the occupants of the cells, Killian frowned deeply and wondered what Rumple's devious plan could possibly be.

A mermaid with a long silver tail lay on the dirty floor, her hair in tatters over her bony shoulders. Next to her lay an elf with dark circles under his eyes as though he had not slept a wink for a hundred years.

There was also a wolf, curled up in a corner like a dog, whimpering.

Killian looked about, seeing that there was possibly one of every creature in here. He knew that Rumple enjoyed collecting things. Even creatures. But what did he want with Ella? Was this Hades' doing? Was he somehow trying to sabotage Killian's final claim?

It would make perfect sense. Hades lusted for power. Perhaps he was reluctant to give up control. Though he was bound to the laws of the Underworld and could not stop Killian from retrieving souls, he would no doubt find a loophole. And working with Rumple to make sure Killian failed his mission was not out of the question.

Killian reached the end of the dungeon, but there was still no sign of Ella. His heart sank while his mind spun as he kept trying to catch her floral scent. But it had grown faint, and the rustic smell of iron bars masked his tracks.

That was when he heard her voice.

"Thank you," she said, shaken but her tone formal as though she was at a dinner party that she did not want to attend.

Killian ignored the pleading cries of the prisoners in the dungeon and raced up the steps to the upper floor. He strode through the halls of the mansion until he found a soft glow of candlelight under one of the doors.

Muffled voices could be heard from the other side. Killian balled his hands into tight fists and kicked the door down. It fell on the hardwood floor, and he stormed into the dining room with his blue eyes blazing with fury.

"Get your greasy hands off her," he roared.

Rumple drew his hand away from Ella's arm and looked up at Killian from the dinner table. "Finally,' he said calmly. "We've been waiting for you."

The sound of chair legs scraping across the floor filled the air as Ella got to her feet and ran into his arms. "Killian!" She buried her face in his chest.

"Ella." His heart soared at having her in his arms again. He made a silent vow to never let go, and to burn down the entire world if she was ever taken from him. "Are you hurt?"

Killian pulled back to get a better look at her. Her hair was wet and back to its original golden. She had bathed. And when he saw no bruises or blood stains, a wave of relief washed over him.

"She's fine," Rumple said, waving off Killian's concern. "She bathed, ate a tasty meal. After all, she did grow up with my daughter. I'm not a complete monster."

Killian wrapped an arm around Ella, keeping her snug to his body. Then he withdrew his sword and aimed it at Rumple.

"Why did you take her?" he growled. "Why bring her here?"

Rumple's palm rose in the air, and his thin mouth turned upward into a delighted grin. "Would you have come otherwise?"

"I've had enough of your games. Just tell me why we're here," Killian demanded.

"To reveal the truth that your beloved has been hiding from you." Rumple's eyes shifted to Ella briefly before returning to Killian.

"The truth about what?" Killian asked.

"The King's slayer."

Killian blinked several times, and Ella squirmed against his chest, shaking her head. "No. Please. Don't." Her eyes were wide with horror. "He's innocent!"

Rumple's dark laugh had Killian aiming his sword at his neck. "If you know who killed the King, tell me at once!"

Rumple grinned. "I am certain it will give you great satisfaction to find out who did it."

Killian swallowed hard. A mixture of emotions flooded his body. If he could just get the true killer's soul in time, Ella would be free. "Give me the name," he said, glaring at Rumple. The man lifted his chin and gave him a satisfied look. Killian hated that Rumple had so much control.

"The Prince," Rumple said with a devilish smirk. "He killed his own father."

Killian frowned, then looked down at Ella. Upon seeing her devastated eyes, he knew it was true. "But he's been hunting Ella down. Insisting that she…"

"Of course he has," Rumple interrupted, rising to a stand now. "The new king needed a scapegoat. He couldn't very well come out and confess his crime to the kingdom."

Killian's mind set on a new mission. He withdrew his blade from Rumple's neck and looked at Ella. "You know what this means," he said.

Ella shook her head. "Killian, please. Don't kill him. I beg of you. Don't take his soul."

Killian stared at her indignantly. "Why are you protecting him after all he has put you through?"

"It's not what you think. And he's all that Lily has," Ella added. "If you kill him, she will be forced to live on a ship with Ryke and Lexa. In a warzone between mermaids and pirates. What will happen to her? What will be of her life? Killian, please. Don't do this."

Killian leaned in and kissed her, tangling his hands through her curls and soaking in her gorgeous aura. When he pulled back, he gave Rumple a hard look.

He didn't know what game he was playing, but when the man held his gaze, there was not a hint of guilt or malice in his aura. For a reason beyond his scope, Rumple truly was protecting Ella.

"Will you keep her safe until my return?" Killian asked.

Rumple nodded, and as though he had read Killian's mind, he added, "Believe it or not, we both want the same outcome."

"And what is that?" Killian asked.

Rumple stepped closer, his smile widening. "Our new King of the Shores removed from the throne. And to keep Ella safe."

Torn, Killian looked at Ella, then at Rumple again. He could not bring her with him. She would only try to stop him. But he did not entirely trust Rumple.

"She will not come to any harm. You have my word," Rumple said with a slight dip of his head.

Killian turned to Ella and grasped her arms. "Look at me."

Ella blinked her pleading eyes. "Killian, don't do this. I'm begging you."

Killian held her firm. "This is how I save you," he said, then he pressed his lips to hers. "I will come back for you when it's done."

With one final kiss, Killian tore himself from Ella and charged out of the room, his mind set on what he must do.

16

ELLA

"Killian, please!" Ella ran toward him as he mounted his horse. But before she made it to the door, it slammed shut as though by a gust of wind. She reached for the handle, but despite yanking with all her strength, it didn't budge. "Killian!"

"Now, now," Rumple's calm voice came from behind her. "You know there's no stopping a warrior from the Underworld."

Ella ran to the closed window and banged on the glass with tight fists. But Killian galloped away without looking back.

Once he disappeared from sight, Ella swung around to catch Rumple finishing his dinner. "Why would you do that?" she demanded, stomping toward him.

"You should be thanking me, dear. If he takes the

Prince's soul, you get to survive. And perhaps even be with your beloved—that is, if he gives up the throne for you."

"That is no excuse for taking a life and leaving a precious little girl without a home." Ella's eyes pricked with tears, but her anger forbade them from spilling from her eyes.

"Oh, please." Rumple brushed it off without even looking up from his plate. "You lost both your parents at a young age and look how well you turned out. She'll survive. Now, please, take a seat and finish your dinner, dear."

She took a seat across from him reluctantly and reached for a piece of bread. Hunger was the furthest thing from her mind, but her empty stomach demanded she swallow more than her pride.

"I am quite baffled at just how much he's in love with you," Rumple said with his mouth full. "His father would be deeply ashamed."

"Killian's father?" Ella leaned forward, her curiosity piqued. Killian had briefly mentioned his mother, but never his father. "Why would he be ashamed?"

"It's not uncommon for men from the Underworld to get, shall we say, *entangled* with human women. However, falling in love comes with a price."

If Ella could reach Rumple and shake him, she would. Her entire upper body was practically on the table as she hung on his every word. "What kind of price? Tell me."

His eyes rose from his food and landed on her with amusement. "Worry not, dear. That man would move the Earth's core to keep you safe."

Ella's heart soared at the thought that Killian loved her that much, but still, she frowned. "Why would his father be ashamed of that?"

"You must understand..." Rumple put his spoon down, then dabbed his lips with a napkin. "Killian's father, my dear, is none other than Hades. And he takes his payments very seriously. He makes no exceptions. Not even for his sons."

"Hades?" Ella echoed. At merely hearing his name, her bones turned cold. "Killian's father is the Ruler of the Underworld?"

Rumple filled a glass with wine, then slid it across the table. "Here. Have a drink. It'll help you digest the news."

Without much thought, Ella grabbed the glass and chugged it down. "What price must he pay to be with me?"

Rumple took a sip from his own wine. "I don't know much of the workings of the Underworld. I try to keep my business above ground." As if on cue, a bright twinkle shined from the window, catching Ella's attention. "Ah, speaking of business. My client is just in time."

He flicked a finger and the window rolled open. A fairy the size of Tinkerbell flew in holding a velvet bag twice her size.

Ella thought fairies didn't travel, so what could possibly have brought that fairy to visit Rumpelstiltskin?

"I was beginning to think you changed your mind, dear." Rumple leaned back in his seat and laced his fingers over his stomach. "Come, come. Present me your gift."

When the fairy flew by Ella's face, she noticed a glare on the fairy's expression. She was not happy to be presenting this so-called gift.

The fairy dropped the velvet bag on the table, and the clang of metal on wood echoed in the room. Rumple gave her a stern look, then reached for the bag to inspect the item.

A doorknob made of copper came into view, and Ella didn't have to touch it to know it was made of elven metal. It had the same etchings as her father's box. The box she handed to Finn before he leaped into the rapids.

"You have done well," Rumple said, running a finger over the smooth metal. "Very well."

"May I have my sister now?" the fairy asked, her voice shaky but firm.

"Of course." Rumple looked up at the fairy whose wings batted like that of a hummingbird as she hovered above the table. "I'm a man of my word."

He stood and started toward the door Killian had dismantled. "Ella, love..." He motioned toward the hall. "Accompany us."

Ella didn't want to, but he hadn't phrased it as a question. When she stood, he offered her his arm. She hesitated for a moment, remembering how he had promised Killian that she would come to no harm. If he'd been lying, Killian would've sensed it. If she wasn't safe with Rumple, Killian would never have left her there.

Taking his arm, she followed his lead down a narrow corridor, then down some stone steps. The fairy hovered just above Ella's shoulder, and although her wings moved swiftly, she held back. Perhaps she was hesitant to charge ahead. Ella would too, considering she had no idea what she would find beyond the darkness.

As soon as they reached the underground floor, fire lit up every torch on the wall, casting a golden glow on yet another wooden door broken on the floor.

A smile tugged on Ella's lips at the thought of Killian kicking every door down in search of her. That man really would move the Earth's core for her.

Her smile fell when she spotted prisoners in the

dungeon. Sunken faces and pale skin stared back at her.

The fairy gasped, and Ella followed her line of sight to a rusted birdcage hanging from the ceiling at the end of the dungeon. The fairy darted toward the cage, buzzing like a bee. Another pixie came into view and stretched out her arms through the bars. They embraced tenderly, then went on to buzz again.

With a flick of Rumple's finger, the cage's door squeaked open, and the captive fairy flew out to meet her sister on the outside, the buzzing much more high-pitched than before. Then without saying anything else, they flew down the hall, back where they had come from, leaving Ella alone with Rumple.

Fear began forming within Ella. Why had he brought her there? Was he going to throw her in one of those cells like he had done to the mermaid with chapped lips? Or was he going to feed her to the wolf, shivering in the corner?

Ella gulped loudly as he continued leading her down a tunnel. As they rounded the corner, an old wooden door appeared to their left. Rumple stopped in front of it and grinned.

"Would you like to see a trick?" he asked, turning toward the door with darkened eyes.

The bubble of fear that had been lodged in the pit of Ella's stomach spread through her entire body, and an urge to run overtook her senses. But she knew that, without Killian, she wouldn't make it far running from Rumple.

He pushed the door open, and the smell of mildew hit Ella in the face like a horse's hot breath. Once her eyes adjusted to the darkness, she noticed it was a small closet. Until she spotted chains latched to the wall and floor. It was solitary confinement.

"Isn't this marvelous?" he said, admiring the space as though it were a room full of gold.

Ella gulped loudly. Was he going to torture her in there?

"Belle," Ella said in a desperate attempt to appeal to Rumple's weakness. "How is she doing?"

Rumple moved toward the door, then began to tug on the broken doorknob. "She's happy," he said as he removed the old handle and tossed it aside. "She has made a beautiful queen, hasn't she?"

"Does she know what you've become?"

Rumple hesitated, but only for a moment. "She has a father when she needs it. That will never change."

"What about me?" she asked as she watched him fit the new copper handle where the old doorknob used to be. "You promised my father you would look after me. Does that still hold true?"

Once the handle clicked in place, Rumple closed the door and turned to look at Ella, his face half cast in shadow from the glow of the flames. "Even though I have very little space in my heart these days, and my Belle occupies most of it, I assure you, your father takes a portion. No man as good as him has ever existed."

Ella stared at Rumple, wondering what all of that meant for her life. He must've discerned the question in her eyes because a grin formed on his lips.

"I assure you, my dear." He offered her his hand as if inviting her to dance. "You have nothing to worry about. I have everything under control."

Ella still didn't know what that meant for her, but she took his hand anyway. He then reached for the door and turned the handle.

The door opened with a rusted squeak, revealing a different room entirely. Instead of the solitary confinement as before, the room had transformed into a large study. Hundreds of books lined up the walls. And as they stepped inside, the mildew smell was gone, the scent of vanilla taking its place. A fire burned near a sofa across the room, and the reflection of the flames danced on the walls.

Ella had seen that study before, but she couldn't quite remember where.

"Fascinating," Rumple said, admiring the door which was left ajar behind them.

"What just happened?" Ella asked.

"The doorknob," Rumple explained, brushing a

gentle finger over the elven markings on it. "You put it on any door, and it becomes… sort of a portal."

Ella's eyes stretched wide. "A portal? To where?"

"Anywhere in the kingdom," he said, turning to her with a wolf-like grin. The image of a wolf flashed inside Ella's mind. The wolf that protected her from the guards in her nightmare.

Her nightmare.

Ella gasped, suddenly remembering where she had seen that library before. And who it belonged to.

Rumple's grin grew wider as he slammed the door closed. The sound vibrated the bookshelves, and a startled yelp came from the sofa across the room.

Ella swung around to find the Prince jolting upward, his brown hair thrown to all sides as though he'd been sleeping.

"What is the meaning of this?" the Prince asked, rubbing his puffy eyes. He was still wearing his tuxedo from the ball earlier that evening.

"This…" Rumple motioned toward Ella. "Is my end of the deal."

It took the Prince several seconds to register who Ella was, but as soon as he did, he jumped to his feet with a growl. "You!"

Ella stepped back, and Rumple shielded her from the Prince's glare. "Not until you meet your end of the deal, Your Highness." Rumple bowed his head in feigned reverence, then reached out his hand. "My document, please?"

As the Prince moved toward his desk, Ella stepped toward the door discreetly. He rummaged through the drawer until he pulled out a rolled-up paper. Rumple snatched it from his hands and unrolled it like a treasure map.

"As per your request," the Prince said, closing the drawer, "in the event of my passing without an offspring, the kingdom shall be yours."

"Perfect." Rumple's lips curved into a smile. "She is all yours."

As soon as the Prince's eyes locked with Ella, she ran toward the door. She yanked it open, but instead of returning to Rumple's dungeon, she found herself in the hallway outside the Prince's study.

"Guards!" the Prince yelled from behind her. "Seize her!"

Ella ran to her left only to spot a group of guards rounding the corner. She turned on her heel and ran back the other way, but even more guards crowded the hallway. She tried fighting off the two guards who grabbed her arms at each side but to no avail. They easily overpowered her and dragged her back into the study.

Upon seeing that Rumple was gone, she looked at

the Prince with pleading eyes. "Listen to me, he's playing you."

The Prince charged toward her and pulled something shiny from his pocket, pressing it to her throat. It was a knife.

"Remember this?" he hissed, scraping the blade against her skin.

Ella gulped. "That document is a trick," she said, her voice shaking. "Someone is coming to kill you. Tonight."

"You killed my father with this knife," he continued as though she hadn't spoken at all. "And you had the audacity to dance with me at my ball. Give me one good reason I shouldn't kill you in the same manner. Right here. Right now."

"Your father was good to me. He gave me work. He gave me a home," she said, her eyes blurring with tears. "I would never have taken his life."

She could've told him the truth in the moment—that he was the one who killed his father—but he wouldn't have believed her. Mainly because she knew he had no recollection of it. And the accusation would no doubt make him even angrier. Perhaps angry enough to slit her throat without another thought.

"I know what I saw," he hissed. "You were standing over him. Your hands were dripping with his blood."

His breath smelled like alcohol, and panic rose

within Ella. If her chances at reasoning with him sober were already slim to none, now she was truly done for.

"Please..." she begged. "Don't let Lily see me bleed. She's only a child."

At the mention of his niece, he pulled back and dropped the knife. He wobbled backward, then stumbled onto the sofa.

When his head fell into his hands, hope rose within Ella. Perhaps the Prince would show her mercy for all the years she'd spent caring for Lily. Perhaps—

The Prince looked up with his droopy eyes, and for the first time, there was no hatred or anger in them. Only sorrow.

Still, when he opened his mouth, Ella's blood turned cold.

"Take her to the gallows," he said to the guards. "She dies tonight."

IN THE PRINCE'S DUNGEON, ELLA PACED NERVOUSLY inside her cell. The sound of footsteps came from the darkened tunnel, making Ella step away from the metal bars. But then a familiar face came into view with the reflection of the flames and a wave of relief washed over her.

Wendy!

Ella ran to embrace Wendy through the bars. "How did you know I was here?" she signed.

"The Prince asked for the gallows to be prepared," she replied, her hands trembling as she signed back. "Then I read their lips. They said it was for you."

"It's going to be okay," Ella assured her. "But I need your help."

Wendy nodded, then pulled out a bundle of keys on a ring and held them up. "I took it from one of the guards. I can get you out of here."

"No." Ella grabbed Wendy's hand and gave it a hard squeeze. "If you free me, you will be committing treason. That means you will have to live on the run from the Prince for the rest of your life. I do not want that life for you."

"Then what can I do to help?" Wendy asked.

"We need to prove I'm innocent," Ella said.

"How?"

Ella peered into Wendy's eyes, knowing this was her very last option. "You'll need to do exactly what I tell you."

Ella couldn't bring herself to sit. She wasn't sure how long it had been since Wendy had left, or how long it would take her to find the proof they needed, but Ella was running out of time.

As if on cue, guards rounded the corner and began to open her cell. She hurried to grab the chains latched to the wall, but they pulled her with ease and dragged her out of the cell.

"Please, you have to listen to me. This is a mistake," she said. "Your prince is the one who will be killed tonight. Rumpelstiltskin has a bounty out for the Prince's head. Listen to me!"

But they didn't.

They held her in silence. The night was dark and cold as they dragged her to the empty courtyard. The ball was over, and all the guests were gone. At least there would be no audience for this. Although Ella wasn't entirely sure if that made her feel worse. Being killed alone made her feel like she never mattered to anyone. Like she wouldn't be missed, and the thought that her existence meant nothing made her feel like those who sacrificed their lives for her had done it in vain.

At the sight of the gallows, Ella's eyes filled with tears. But it wasn't the thought of her death that filled her with dread. It was the memory of the last time she'd seen that deadly rope dangling from above the wooden stool.

Her father's face surfaced from the back of her mind. His calm. His courage. His strength.

If nothing else, at least she found comfort in dying in the same manner he did. Or perhaps the universe was simply balancing justice since she was the one who was supposed to have been hung years ago. Not him. He died in place of her.

The guards led her to the top of the gallows. One of them roughly tied her hands behind her back before propping her up on the wooden stool. Another one wrapped the noose around her neck.

Ella pressed her eyes shut, and a torrent of tears slid down her face. The guilt over her family's death was so strong, she wondered if Killian could sense her despair wherever he was. The potency of her pain. The intensity of her feelings. Could he hear if she whispered to the wind?

"Killian…" she whispered with trembling lips. "I love you."

17

KILLIAN

Killian raced through the woods on his horse, barely taking breaths, his body pumping with adrenaline. The soft peaks of the castle were within his sights, and his heart jolted. After so many years, his time had finally come to claim his final soul and take his victory.

He was not sure what gave him more of a thrill. The idea that he would be dethroning Hades, or the fact that he would become the new Ruler of the Underworld, giving him the authority to carve out his own laws. He would finally be able to free his mother from that wretched world, and from the clutches of that maniac.

After all, Hades kidnapped and married his mother, Persephone, while she was still a human. She had hopes and dreams that did not involve being confined in the

Underworld. She had a happy life ahead of her, but he took that away when he dragged her below to be with him. All Killian ever wanted to do was to return his mother's freedom to her. That was the driving force behind the tens of thousands of souls he spent centuries collecting to win the throne.

And for his prize to come at the expense of the Prince's soul gave Killian great satisfaction. The man who'd been hunting down Ella would finally pay for his sins. And through his death, not only would Killian gain his throne, but he would be freeing Ella from danger. She would no longer have to spend her life running and hiding, or afraid to be recognized because of those wretched flyers.

Azul's flaming hooves lit up the dark forest in blue light, and soon the trees thinned out until he reached the outer wall.

Killian jumped down, then turned to Azul. "Stay hidden," he muttered, briefly pressing his forehead to the horse, then he ran to the wall and scaled it like a cat climbing a tree.

"Killian… I love you."

It was Ella's voice, and Killian's blood grew cold as he jumped down and landed in the royal courtyard.

"Hang the traitor, now!" one of the Prince's guards called out.

Unable to scramble any thought to explain why

Ella was at the castle, or how she got there before him, Killian took his knife and flung it through the air. The glass blade sliced through the rope like butter, then landed on the ground with a thud.

Outcries of anger echoed through the courtyard, flooding Killian's nostrils with a most bitter scent. Ella stumbled forward and fell to her knees, but a guard quickly wrenched her back to her feet.

"Get your hands off her," Killian roared, hurling his sword. It pierced the guard straight through the heart, and he crumpled at Ella's feet.

Four guards stepped in front of the Prince and all of them drew their swords. But Killian paid them no attention. He watched with bated breath as Ella wrestled out of her bonds beneath the gallows.

Once she freed her hands and pushed the noose over her neck, she retrieved Killian's sword. The two of them locked eyes for the briefest moment, just long enough for Killian to give her a nod.

She raised his sword over her head, and he reached out his hand. The sword flew back into Killian's grasp with a gravitational pull as though it was part of him. Then he squared his shoulders and scowled at the palace guards who had dared to harm Ella.

When the first guard lunged at him and raised his sword to strike, Killian caught it between his palms and bent the sword like a metal spoon. He wrenched it forward and buried the tip through the guard's armor, sinking it into his chest. The man cried out and collapsed to his knees. But Killian was already fighting the next guard.

This one ducked, missing Killian's hands by a hair's width. But when he went for his legs, Killian snapped the guard's arms like matchsticks. His high-pitched scream splintered Killian's ears, but only for a moment. He kicked him to the ground, then turned to face whoever was left.

The last two guards looked at each other. Their faces paled, and without a word, they ran away.

"Come back!" the Prince shouted. "Stand your ground and defend your prince!"

But the men were gone.

Killian turned to the Prince, smiling now. The Prince raised his sword, but the blade wobbled in the air. Killian caught a whiff of alcohol and realized the Prince had been drinking.

"Of all the souls I've had to take, yours will by far bring me the most satisfaction," Killian said tauntingly as he approached.

"No, Killian, wait." Ella jumped down from the platform and ran to block his path. "He's innocent."

Killian gave her a hard look. "It's either him or you. Not a tough choice for me."

He marched past her. "Killian, wait! Stop!" But he

was done listening. Done wasting time. He reached to grab the Prince's neck. "If you take his soul, you will lose your streak!"

The authority in her voice made Killian pause, and Ella was once again standing between him and the Prince. "Look at his aura," she said. "I can't see it, but I know it's not dark."

Killian's face hardened. "What kind of person doesn't feel guilty for killing his own father?" Killian looked at the Prince, waiting for his aura to darken at the accusation. For the guilt to set in now that his secret was discovered and take over his soul like dark clouds in a storm.

But all he sensed was confusion, puzzlement, and disbelief. The Prince shook his head. "I… I didn't."

"Oh, but you did," Killian hissed. "Your greed for the throne drove you to stab your father in the heart with his own knife."

"No!" The Prince stumbled back as though Killian's words had physically shoved him. "That's impossible. I would never have…"

"Confess to your crime!"

"Killian, stop!" Ella demanded. But before either of them said anything else, Killian caught a strange new scent.

He looked up as the air whooshed above his head, and to his surprise, a young man with a mop of ginger hair flew down from the skies. "Peter!" Ella shrieked. He thrust a bag to Ella, who caught it in midair and quickly opened it up. She took a handful of whatever was inside and held it out for Prince to see.

"Do you recognize this?" she asked.

The Prince stepped forward, staring at the glittery powder in her hand. "My father..." he said, his voice barely audible. "He had a bag full of those."

"It's pixie dust," she told him. "It has mind control capabilities."

The Prince looked at Ella as though she was speaking a different language. But Killian knew the effects of pixie dust. It would never work on an immortal, but on humans, it was a powerful weapon.

"Do you remember anyone giving you this?" Ella asked the Prince. "Or putting it on you?"

The Prince's eyes stretched wide, and Killian could tell he was shuffling through his feeble mind for the memory. "My father threw it at my cousin. I thought it was going to harm him, so I jumped in the way."

Ella moved closer to the Prince, and Killian had to fight back the urge to step between them. After all, the man was still holding a sword.

"What happened after that?" Ella asked, her voice soft, almost careful.

"I..." The Prince shook his head as though the motion itself could somehow will the memory to appear. But Killian knew it wouldn't. He had seen it with Ella. "I woke up on the upper deck next to my father's bleeding body. But I… I have no idea how I got up there."

"The pixie dust causes you to blackout," Peter said as he stood next to Wendy a few feet away. "And for that window of time, your mind can be controlled. I know because it was used on me many times."

The Prince paced back and forth in a daze. "But it doesn't make any sense. My father threw the pixie dust on me, but if he was the one controlling me, he wouldn't have killed himself."

"Then someone else had to be controlling you," Ella said. "Do you know anyone that would want your father dead?"

"He was a greedy king," Killian cut in. "I'm sure the list is long."

Ella gave Killian a pleading look, but he couldn't care less about the Prince's feelings if that was what she was worried about.

"It could've been Neri," Peter said, stepping closer. "She controlled a lot of us at Neverland. And she was there that night."

The Prince nodded. "That would make sense. My father had dealings with her, and I told him many times she couldn't be trusted."

Ella's eyes sparkled with hope, and she turned to

Killian. "Then all you have to do is find Neri and take *her* soul."

Killian clenched his jaw. "That won't work."

"Why not?" Ella asked.

"Because Neri is already dead," Killian said. "There is no soul to claim."

A wave of disappointment rose within Ella, and the sickly feeling lodged in the pit of Killian's stomach.

"What is happening right now?" the Prince asked, looking from Ella to Killian.

Ella sighed. "We've been trying to find the person responsible for your father's death. We thought it was you, but now we know it was Neri."

"Why did you think it was me?" the Prince asked.

Ella frowned. "I was there. I saw everything." Her voice was barely above a whisper, and the Prince seemed to have stopped breathing. "I didn't understand why you were fighting with your cousin, but when you stabbed your father, I knew at that moment that you weren't yourself."

"But I saw you." The Prince's eyes darted to Ella. "You were kneeling over him. His blood was all over your hands."

"I was trying to save him."

The Prince was silent for a long time, then he ran a hand through his hair. "Ella, I am so sorry. For everything…" He staggered backward at the realization that he had indeed killed his father. Killian watched his aura darken like a storm cloud, and for a moment, he felt hope for Ella. If his soul became consumed with guilt, that was all Killian needed to drag him to the Underworld.

But to Killian's dismay, the Prince's aura didn't darken with guilt. It darkened with grief. And he wanted to curse under his breath because he knew that a grief-stricken soul wouldn't absolve Ella of her mark.

The Prince's eyes filled with tears. "Ella…I am so sorry. I am so, *so* sorry."

Killian stepped toward the Prince with balled fists. "No apology in the world is going to make up for the fact that she's had to live with a bounty on her head because of you!" Killian's voice ripped with rage. "So, if you want your apology to mean something, then you will call off her execution and waste no time absolving her of this crime. And if I so much as see one more flyer with her face on it, I will set your entire castle ablaze. Understood?"

The Prince stood tall in front of Killian. "No threats needed," he said calmly, then he turned to look at Ella. "I will remove the bounty first thing in the morning, and I will have all the flyers burned. If there is anything else you need—"

"She needs nothing from you," Killian said. "Now,

get back into your castle before I change my mind and snap your neck anyway."

The Prince puffed out his chest as though to appear unafraid, but Killian could sense his nerves buzzing inside him.

A new flood of royal guards came running out to the courtyard with their swords drawn, but the Prince held up his palm and they stopped in their tracks.

"There will be no execution today," he said with a booming voice. "Ella is innocent of all crimes. A formal announcement will be made in the morning and sent out to all kingdoms. Now return to your posts."

The guards looked at one another in confusion, but eventually, did as they were commanded and marched away.

The Prince gave Killian a courtesy bow, then turned around and disappeared into the castle. Killian scanned the premises for any additional danger while Ella went to give Peter and Wendy a hug.

"Thank you so much for your help," she signed to Wendy, then gave Peter the bag of pixie dust. As powerful of a weapon as that was, Killian could understand why she wouldn't want anything to do with it.

After saying their goodbyes, Peter wrapped Wendy up in his arms and flew her away. Ella watched them head for the forest until they became nothing more than a twinkle in the night's sky. Once they were gone, she let out a sigh.

"Thank you," she said, reaching for Killian's arm. "For sparing his life."

But Killian moved away from her touch. "Don't thank me for that."

She looked up at him, surprised. "You could have killed him, but you didn't."

"I would have!" he said, peering into her eyes. "If his aura so much as *flickered* with guilt, or his will to live dropped by a mere fraction, I would have gladly dragged him to the Underworld and claimed his soul in a heartbeat."

When she frowned, her sadness rose within him, and the wave was nauseating. Her aura was darker than ever, and she reeked of guilt. At one time, he would have found the scent to be alluring, but now it made his stomach churn.

"You know what I don't understand?" Killian said, turning to face her. "If you didn't kill the King, and you just saved the Prince's life, why is guilt still seeping from your pores? Why is it burning so hot inside your heart? Where is all that darkness coming from, Ella?"

Ella hugged herself with a shiver, and Killian knew that whatever it was she was hiding from him was the darkest secret she possessed.

He pulled her close and wrapped her in a tight embrace. "You can tell me anything. You know that."

Ella sucked in a breath as Killian stroked her soft curls, pulling them away from her neck. "My guilt isn't just about my parents' death," she said.

Killian frowned but didn't speak, waiting for her to continue. Ella broke from his embrace and turned toward Azul, who was still waiting by the trees. When she said nothing else, Killian took her by the hand. "Come on."

They walked from the gallows to the dark forest until they had returned to his horse. Perhaps the shelter of the trees would offer Ella more courage.

Killian rubbed her back. "Talk to me."

Ella turned her back to him for a moment, her aura flooded with guilt and shame. "Remember when I told you about my sister?"

Killian nodded, and she turned to look at him again, her blue eyes glistening with tears, like two diamonds in the moonlight.

"Have you heard of King Midas?" she asked.

Killian lifted his brows and gave her a nod. "I've had the displeasure of meeting him once," he said. There was not a reflection the old man did not like. He could have given Narcissus a run for his money when it came to self-love. But the thing he worshiped the most was gold. "What has he got to do with…"

"He's the one who took my sister," Ella said. "He locked her in a golden tower."

That explained why Ella's memory was inside a golden tower in the dream world. But Killian didn't bother stating the obvious. Instead, he kept silent, prompting her to go on.

"My father worked in his gardens. My sister and I would wait up for him to come home each night, and sometimes, he would bring two golden sunflowers for us. They were so beautiful." She smiled for the first time, but it lasted only a heartbeat. "He did it for many months, and we started to grow sunflowers in our garden. They grew so tall that someone must have noticed."

Her voice was strained now, as if there were invisible hands encircling her throat, constricting it. "King Midas was furious. He forbade anyone in the kingdom from taking his sunflowers. Seems there's something special about them. He called our father a thief and demanded to have something of his in return."

Killian couldn't believe his ears. "Your sister?" he asked. "The King demanded to have your sister because your dad plucked some flowers… that is ridiculous."

Ella lowered her eyes to the ground, and he shook his head. None of that made sense, nor did it explain why Ella possessed so much guilt.

"It was not your fault." He reached for her hands, but she pulled away, shaking her head. Tears fell down her cheeks.

"He didn't ask for my sister," Ella said. "He asked for one of us. The King threatened to kill us both if our father did not willingly offer one of us up. But he was unable to choose between us." She bit her lip and looked away. "We drew lots and I was the one chosen."

Killian raked a hand through his head with a sigh. "Oh, Ella…"

"My sister took my place," Ella said, her breaths growing short and rapid. "I should've stopped her, but I was so scared. When she told me to hide, I did. And I let them take her instead of me."

Killian took her hands again, and this time, she didn't pull away. Slowly, her misty eyes met his gaze. "You were only a child," he said.

"So was she." Ella's turmoil ached in his heart. "I should've fought for her, not hid like a coward."

"Is that the source of your guilt?" he asked, brushing her hair from her face. "That you didn't fight hard enough to save your sister?"

Ella nodded as she wiped her wet cheeks.

"Ella…" Killian's mind spun as he formed an idea, then he locked eyes with her again. "I think we can fix this."

Ella narrowed her eyes. "What do you mean?"

Killian paced around as his mind swirled with a million thoughts. "If we save your sister now and set matters right, your guilt will be gone. Without guilt, your soul will no longer qualify. And if you reunite with your sister, your will to live will be stronger than ever. Ella..." He turned to face her with hopeful eyes. "Your mark may even dissolve on its own."

Ella's eyes sparkled with hope. "Has that ever been done before?"

"Not that I know of. But I don't think anyone has ever tried it." And Killian never backed down from a challenge. "So, what do you say? Should we go save your sister?"

Ella hitched a breath with a squeak. "You'll help me save my sister?" she asked.

Killian cradled her face in his hands and kissed her velvety lips. Then he drew back with a smile. "I would do anything for you, my love," he said. "But we'll need to be quick. We have less than a day before the blood moon appears."

He glanced up at the moon. It already had a pink aura around it.

"All right, then," Ella said, sniffing. She jumped up on Azul and took the reins, then gestured for Killian to join her. "No more hiding."

18

ELLA

Ella never thought she would ever set eyes on the Tower of Gold ever again. The tower looked the exact same as it did the night she was caught trespassing years ago. The night she was dragged to King Midas, pleading for her sister's release.

But all she got in return was a death sentence. Had it not been for her father pleading in her favor and offering to take her place, she would've been the one put to death.

She wrapped her arms tightly around Killian's waist as he urged his horse to gallop faster. Thankfully, Azul never got tired, seeing as he ran on supernatural energy. Once they reached the edge of the property, Ella caught sight of the sunflower field. All of the flowers faced away from the moon and were hunched over like they were sleeping. She wondered if her sister was also sleeping.

Or if she was even alive.

That thought had not crossed Ella's mind, and panic rose within her as a trembled breath lodged in her throat. "Stop! Killian, stop!"

Before Azul came to a complete halt, Ella was already jumping to the ground.

"What's the matter?" Killian joined her, dropping from his horse.

Ella buried her face in her hands, feeling the wetness from tears she hadn't even realized had spilled from her eyes. "I can't," she sobbed. "I can't…"

"Of course you can. I'll be with you the whole time—"

"What if she isn't there?"

"Then at least you'll know."

"What if she's dead?" Ella swung around with a glare, but her anger wasn't towards Killian. It was towards herself. And her aura must've darkened because Killian frowned deeply. Ella shook her head. If her sister was dead, she wouldn't be able to bear it. "Killian, I can't."

Killian drew close and cupped her wet face. "Don't you see? The reason your guilt makes your soul so dark is not because of the people you've lost. It's because you didn't get to fight for them. Ella, even if we don't find your sister, at least you tried, and that act alone just might cleanse your soul."

Ella had never thought about that, but it made so much sense. None of the events that had gotten her family killed had been Ella's fault. She didn't ask her father to bring the sunflower home. She didn't penalize him for the act by taking one of his daughters away. And she wasn't responsible for the overwhelming sadness that made her mother sick. Ella's only mistake was not fighting harder to save them. She hid like a coward as King Midas' guards took her sister away. And she never spoke up in the square the day her father was hung.

That was the source of her guilt. Not having fought hard enough.

She grabbed Killian's face and pressed her lips to his. Just in case their plan didn't work. Or even if it did. If she found that her sister was still alive, she was ready to take her place in order to set her sister free.

Of course, Killian wouldn't understand because he was a force of nature that could not be tamed, but he also wasn't going to stick around to protect them forever. He was going to return to the Underworld and leave them to fend for themselves, and the truth was that neither Ella nor her sister had the means to run and hide from a king like Midas.

Killian wrapped his arms around Ella's waist and

pulled her close. As her body molded to his, she reveled in his strength. Never in a million years had Ella thought she would ever have felt safe in his arms. Not too long ago, he was her captor. He had tied her up to a tree and treated her like a prisoner. He wanted to end her life and claim her soul. But now, as his tongue sought hers and his gentleness caressed her skin, the only thing he'd successfully captured was her heart.

And as he deepened the kiss and tightened his embrace, she could feel his heart was also hers. The ache of losing him was going to destroy her from inside out, but there was no time to think about anything with the potential to incapacitate her. Not now. Not when she still had to save her sister.

Ella pulled back and looked into Killian's blue eyes. She wanted to tell him how much she loved him, but if he found out she was planning to take her sister's place, he would probably tie her to a tree and go by himself.

"We should go," she said, caressing his face. "We are running out of time."

The crimson light of the moon reflected on the sunflower field, and Ella didn't have to look up at the sky to know the moon was turning red.

Killian nodded, then lifted her up to saddle onto Azul. He mounted behind her and grabbed the reins. "Let's cleanse your soul once and for all."

When the sunflower field turned blue, Ella realized

the light came from Azul's eyes as he lit up their path. But before she could say anything else, they were galloping across the field, toward the tower. Azul really was from another realm because he never slowed, not even for a breath. He didn't need to. And Ella couldn't have been more thankful to that beast of a man to have come into her life, bringing with him that remarkable creature.

"There!" Ella pointed to the top of the tower. "Those vines lead up to the window."

"We won't need to climb," Killian assured her. Then he urged Azul to run faster. The wind blew back her curls and the speed was exhilarating. As soon as they crossed over the bridge, Azul's hooves left the ground and a pair of wings appeared at each side, gliding them upward.

Ella grabbed onto his mane as the ground was left behind them. Killian pressed his chest to her back as his arms tightened around her. Normally, that would've been enough to soothe her, but the anticipation of seeing her sister again as they got closer and closer to the window at the top of the tower filled her with a buzzing electricity she couldn't control.

As they reached the window and Ella grabbed onto the ledge, a loud, hawk-like shriek came from above her. By the time she even caught sight of the flying creature, a feathered wing rammed into her side, making her lose her footing. She slipped and fell, only to be caught by Killian who was still mounted on Azul.

"What was that?" Ella asked, grimacing as the pain on her side pulsed.

"Get ready to jump," Killian said, guiding Azul to get as close to the tower as possible. She braced herself.

The creature shrieked again, and their eyes locked. It wasn't a bird. It was another flying horse. A black one. And mounted on that horse was a man with hair just as dark and long as Killian's. His chest was bare as he flexed his muscles.

Ella gasped. It was another bounty hunter from the Underworld. They had come for her. And judging by the blood moon shining down on them, she was out of time.

"Found you," the man said in an eerie singsong voice, as if they'd been playing some sort of deadly hide-and-seek. That was when Ella realized he wasn't looking at Killian. He was looking at *her*.

Without another word, the man dove down toward them again. Killian jumped to his feet on top of Azul and drew his sword. The blue flame came to life just as the creature swooped down. Killian sliced its wing as it flew by, and the creature wailed in pain.

Falling from his horse, the bounty hunter plummeted to the ground and slid through the sunflower field, destroying its path. The wound on the horse's wing quickly healed as he rose back to his feet.

"Ella, jump!" Killian yelled.

Ella leaped into the air and grabbed onto one of the vines. It took a few heartbeats to get her footing, but once she planted her feet on the wall, she pulled herself up toward the window.

"You've had your chance, Killian!" the bounty hunter yelled from the ground. "Now, hand her over."

"Over my dead body, Orcus," Killian thundered, his sword still ablaze.

Orcus flashed Killian a wicked grin. "That will be my pleasure."

He remounted his horse and lifted off the ground again. But it wasn't until he sniffed the air, filling his lungs with a pleasant scent which Ella could only imagine might've been hers, that Killian roared to the heavens. His blade grew brighter, and he shot a ball of fire from his sword, grazing Orcus' arm.

He dodged Killian's blow, then flashed a challenging smirk.

Ella's arms grew tired as she pulled herself up toward the window.

"You know the rule, Killian," Orcus said with a growl. "After the blood moon, it's all fair game."

"She is not a game," Killian barked. "And her soul is being cleansed. It will do us no good."

"Her soul is dark enough, and you know it," Orcus said, raising a skeptical brow. "My only question is... why haven't you claimed it already?"

"Leave her be," Killian demanded. "I shall not repeat myself."

But it seemed the more Killian threatened him, the more intrigued Orcus became. He drew a black sword from his sheath, but when he set it ablaze, the flame was a bright red.

Killian charged toward Orcus, and Ella pushed herself to hurry. All she needed was to get to her sister, then her soul could be cleansed from all the guilt, and the bounty hunters would no longer have a reason to take her. When she finally reached the window's ledge, she pulled herself up and stumbled into the tower.

"Rapunzel!" Ella staggered to her feet only to find an empty chamber, an empty bed in the corner, and a cold fireplace with nothing but burned charcoal left behind. "No..." Ella breathed, her lungs deflating with panic. "No, no, no! Rapunzel!"

A loud thud came from the window, making the floor beneath her tremble. She swung around to find another bounty hunter stomping toward her with heavy boots. She knew she needed to run, but her mind was spinning. She grabbed onto the wall to keep herself from falling.

Her sister was gone. But was she dead?

When the bounty hunter grabbed her, Ella didn't fight it. Not that she would even be able to. He threw her over his muscular shoulder just as Killian had done the first time they met, but this hunter's smell was different. He reeked of sweat and mud, and she wanted to recoil. But his grip on her was immobilizing.

He jumped out the window and climbed down with ease. But as soon as his heavy boots hit the ground, Killian's blade pierced through his stomach and came out his back. As his limbs grew weak, Ella fell from his shoulder only to be caught by Killian.

"Are you all right?" he asked, running his eyes through her body, scanning for any sign of injury. But he wasn't going to be able to see it because the injury was deep inside her heart.

"My sister…" Her eyes filled with tears, and Killian frowned with understanding. But before he could speak, a thud of heavy boots hit the ground behind them, and Killian swung around to find Orcus standing on a crouching position.

Killian stepped in front of Ella, shielding her.

"If you think I'm going to let you claim your last soul and win the throne, you are gravely mistaken," Orcus said, drawing his black sword again. "And I'm not the only one."

As if on cue, more bounty hunters stepped out from the darkened woods around them, and before long, they were surrounded by replicas of Killian. Except, instead of blue, they all had eyes as black as night.

Ella had never seen Killian shrink back before, but at the sight of the group of bounty hunters closing in, he lowered his sword.

"Killian?" Ella's voice shook when she realized they were trapped. And when Killian didn't respond, it confirmed her fear.

"Take me," Killian finally said, turning to Orcus. "If you take my soul instead of hers, all of the souls I've claimed will be transferred to you, and the throne will be yours."

Orcus' thick brows pinched together. "Do you peg me for a fool? You well know that our soul cannot be claimed unless we voluntarily give it away."

Without another word, the flame of Killian's sword extinguished, and he threw it to the ground. "I volunteer."

Orcus staggered back as if Killian's words had crashed onto him. "Have you gone mad?"

"So, what will it be, boys?" Killian asked, scanning the clearing for all the other hunters. "Who wants the throne?"

"That will be me." One of the bounty hunters stepped forward with a wicked grin. But before he reached Killian, a flaming sword pierced his back. His breath hitched in his throat, and he fell to the ground, revealing another hunter who had stabbed him from behind.

"Not so fast," that hunter said with a hiss like that of a rattlesnake. "The throne is mine."

"No, it's mine!" Yet another hunter said, jumping in front of Killian. But instead of turning toward Killian, he turned toward the rest of the hunters and braced himself for a fight.

Suddenly, countless swords set ablaze with flames burning red, but instead of aiming toward Killian, they aimed them at one another. "The last one standing takes Killian's soul," one of the hunters challenged.

"You bunch of imbeciles," Orcus barked from across the field. "Can't you see that is what he wants?"

The men considered Orcus' words for a moment, but then faced one another and braced themselves. "May the best man win!"

A war cry erupted in the clearing, and flames shot from every side. Killian grabbed Ella and jumped onto Azul, urging him to gallop faster than he'd ever done. The abrupt movement threw Ella back, and she pressed herself onto Killian's chest.

"Hold on!" Killian yelled, urging Azul to go even faster. His hooves left the ground as he began to fly, and Killian held Ella securely in front of him. But then Orcus' horse rammed into them, throwing them off

Azul and onto the ground. Ella scraped her knees against a tree root and grimaced in pain.

Before Killian could hurry to her side, Orcus jumped from his horse and grabbed Ella from behind. His glass blade was at her neck, forcing Killian to a halt.

"You hurt her, and I swear—"

"Are you sure you want to threaten me right now?" Orcus dug his blade into her neck, and she winced.

Killian balled his fists but held his ground.

Orcus smirked. "Didn't think so. Now, quit wasting my time and put these on."

Orcus threw a chain made of dark glass at Killian's feet. Orcus' glass was different from Killian's. Perhaps their glass was unique to each of them, which meant that Killian would most likely not be able to break free from those bonds.

"Killian, don't do it," Ella begged, even though the sharpness of the blade was almost breaking her skin. "Please. Don't."

Killian picked up the bonds and shackled his wrists as well as his ankles. Then looked up at Orcus with an unafraid expression. "There. My soul is yours. Let her go."

As Orcus' hand dropped, so did his mouth. "My, oh my." He walked toward Killian, then stole one last glance over his shoulder at Ella. "You're in love with her."

Their eyes locked for the span of a heartbeat, then Killian fell to his knees as his shackles flashed red. It was as though that glass was sapping his strength. His shoulders sagged and his head hung low.

"Killian!" Ella screamed, falling to her knees in front of him. She lifted his sweaty face and waited for him to open his gorgeous blue eyes again. He did, but he was so weak. "Killian, what did you do?"

Despite the exhaustion, he flashed her a crooked smile. "I would die a thousand deaths for you, my love."

Then his smile faded and his eyes rolled back, and his strong body fell to the ground with a loud thud.

Ella gasped in horror, but before she could reach for him again, Orcus picked Killian off the ground and threw him over his shoulder. "You, my lady, have done the impossible." He bowed his head, and Ella could sense a deep respect and admiration from the simple act. "You have brought down Killian, the son of Hades. Who was once a flaming god, is now nothing but a cinder. And it is all thanks to you. For that reason, I will make your name known in the Underworld." Orcus thought about it for a moment, then a smirk grew across his face. "You will be known as Cinder… Ella."

And without another word, he mounted his horse and flew toward the heavens, taking Killian with him.

Ella wiped the tears from her eyes, then growled a resounding, "No!" No more sacrifices for her sake. No more letting the people she loved die.

Ella picked up Killian's sword from the ground and gripped its hilt firmly.

She could not allow yet another person she loved to give their life in exchange for hers. She had allowed it too many times before, but no more. This time, she was determined to fight back, and rid her soul of all guilt once and for all.

19

KILLIAN

Dark swirling mist covered the rocky floor of Killian's cell, the air heavy and moist. The humidity was so high it drowned out any lingering scent of Ella on his clothes. Killian rubbed the back of his neck with a heavy sigh.

He was back.

In the short time he had been away, he had already forgotten how quiet the Underworld was compared to Earth. No rusting leaves. Or steady heartbeats. Not even the humming of a bumblebee.

Only stillness. If he really focused, he could just about hear the mist roaming the ground like a dragon's breath.

But his heart was not heavy because of his surroundings. He did not care about being imprisoned, waiting to see Hades and meet his fate. He had no regrets.

His heart throbbed because he would never see Ella again. Or have a life on Earth with the woman he loved. For so long, his one directive was to claim enough guilty souls for Hades in exchange for his mother's freedom. So, not only had he failed Ella, but he also failed his mother.

The only two women in his life he had ever truly loved.

But at least Ella was safe. That thought alone brought him peace.

He wondered how long it would take for her to forget about him and move on. Would she marry a prince? A huntsman? He hoped that she would not go back to working as a maid. She was far too resourceful for such a small role.

He tried to picture her happy. Living on a small farm, rearing animals and sewing clothes for her eight children. All of them would have her golden curls. And everyone would come to her for glamourous gowns.

Even as he tried to picture the happy scene, Killian's mouth could not even twitch upward because he wasn't part of that life. No matter how much he wanted to, he wouldn't be part of her future.

Perhaps it was a kindness that his life was ending.

He couldn't even imagine the agony it would've been to live an eternity missing her.

Even if Hades decided to pardon him and offer a reward for his many centuries of loyalty, his heart would throb and ache for as long as he existed. And nothing could beat the anguish of being ripped away from Ella.

"No one is allowed in here," one of the guards said in a deep voice.

Killian looked up at a cloaked figure standing down the dark hall. The figure threw their hood back, revealing a slender woman's face bathed in soft blue light. The guards drew back aghast.

"Queen Persephone, my apologies." He bowed nervously. "I did not recognize you."

The woman's expression remained impassive. "I am here to speak with my son. You will stand outside and ensure no one interrupts us," she said, her voice thunderous with authority. Her dark eyes flashed blue, and the guard stepped back again. "Yes, of course. Your Highness."

He scrambled out of the iron door, and it squealed shut behind him.

Killian rose to his feet and leaned against the glass bars of his cell as his mother approached. When she reached him, she slid her hands between the bars and clutched his arms. Her eyes softened, as did the tone of her voice. "Killian, what have you done?"

"Do not concern yourself with me," he replied, dipping his head and resting it on two bars. The glass was cool against his hot skin.

"I am your mother," Persephone said. "I shall always have concern for my son, and it will do you well to…"

Killian looked up. "I failed you, Mother."

Persephone ended her lecture with a look of surprise. "How so?"

Killian sighed. "I wanted to become Ruler of the Underworld so I could set you free. All these centuries of claiming souls… I did it all for your freedom, Mother. But I failed you, and for that, I will be eternally sorry."

Persephone rested her hand on Killian's cheek and gave him a warm, motherly smile. "My sweet, Killian. Even if you had set me free, I wouldn't have left."

Killian gave her a puzzled look. "How could you say that? He captured you and forced you to marry him against your will."

Persephone's lips curved. "He captured me, yes. But he never forced me to marry him. I made that choice on my own."

"Why would you…?"

Her eyes softened. "I fell in love with him."

Killian stared at her, baffled. He was expecting her to say many things, but that was not one of them.

Persephone sucked in a breath as she seemed to read his face. "Love is not black and white, Killian. It has layers upon layers of complexity. You, better than anyone, should know that." She motioned toward the bars. "If love were simple, you wouldn't be in this cell. You wouldn't have willingly offered up your soul to Hades."

Killian averted his eyes from his mother's discerning stare. "I couldn't let them take her. She's too…"

"I never thought I would see the day my brave Killian fell in love," Persephone said, caressing his face. "For that reason, I rejoice."

Killian sighed and shut his eyes. His mother was the queen of looking on the bright side of situations. A talent no doubt needed in order to survive an eternal marriage to Hades.

Persephone touched his cheek again. "Allow me to talk to your father. He will summon you shortly, but I'm certain we can come to some sort of agreement."

Killian lifted his head and swallowed against the painful lump in his throat. "You offer false hope, Mother. Ella is free to live out her life in peace. That is all I want."

Persephone tilted her head. "Is it?"

Of course, it wasn't. He wanted to be free to live out his days on Earth and be with Ella. Even if only for one human lifetime. But the lump in his throat forbade him to utter a single syllable.

Persephone seemed to read his thoughts, though. "I came here to tell you to keep your spirits up, my son. There is still hope."

Then without another word, Persephone lifted the hood of her cloak and left Killian alone with his thoughts once more.

"Well, that was touching," a woman's voice echoed inside Killian's cell, and he swung around.

His illusion of Ella was leaning against the far wall with a mocking expression. Killian groaned in frustration. "Not you again."

"Pleasure seeing you too," she replied with a snarky tone. "Too bad this might be the last time."

"Well, if dying will finally help me to get rid of you, at least that's one thing in the 'pro' column," Killian said, falling back on the small bed in the corner and closing his eyes.

"Don't be a jerk. I didn't come here to fight with you," she snapped.

"Then why did you come?" he asked, not bothering to open his eyes. He figured if he managed to fall asleep, maybe she would disappear into oblivion.

Besides, he didn't like that she looked like Ella. He

was going to die soon, and he didn't want the last face he saw to be of an illusion. He wanted to take his last breath thinking of the real Ella. Of her floral scent and the taste of her lips…

"I came to thank you," the woman said, interrupting his thoughts.

He groaned with irritation, but perhaps if he played along, she would take pity on his sentenced soul and leave of her own accord. "Thank me for what?" he muttered.

"For saving my sister's life."

Killian's eyes shot open, and he lifted his head to look at her. "What did you say?"

The woman rolled her eyes with a heavy sigh. "All right, I lied. I'm not a figment of your imagination, Killian."

He sat up, hanging on her every word.

"My name is Rapunzel, and Ella is my twin sister," she said. "So, thank you for sacrificing your life for her. And I admit it, I was wrong about you."

Killian blinked several times, wondering if Hades had already begun playing games with his mind. But for Hades to even be able to do that, Ella's sister would have to be…

Killian's eyes shot up toward her again. "Are you here? In the Underworld?"

"Oh, no." Rapunzel scrunched up her nose as she

ran a finger over the bars, then inspected it. "I wouldn't be caught dead in this place."

The irony of her words was not lost on Killian, but he really needed her to stop being cryptic. "We went to the Tower of Gold. You weren't there."

"Oh, I haven't been there in a very long time," she said, walking about in the cell, her hourglass figure moving with grace.

"Then where are you?" he asked.

She flashed him a smile. "Right now, I'm inside your head."

Killian narrowed his eyes and crossed his arms. "If you're not a figment of my imagination, how are you inside my head?"

She let out her own frustrated grunt. "So many questions. You really have been spending a lot of time with my sister."

"If you're alive, why haven't you returned home?" Killian pressed. "Or at least reached out to your sister so she knows you're alive."

"And have her come and get me?" Rapunzel scoffed. "Yeah, because that worked out so well last time."

Killian knew she was referring to the time Ella got caught in Midas' field and was sent to the gallows. He wondered if she blamed Ella for the death of their father. "She was trying to save you."

"There is no saving me," she said, the edge in her voice gone. "So, it's better if my sister thinks I'm dead."

"You can't possibly think she'll be better off—"

"My sister is only safe because I'm not part of her life," Rapunzel said, the edge back in her voice. "If I were to return home, she would be killed for simply looking like me. Trust me, it's safer for her if I keep my distance."

"Then why appear to me?" Killian asked.

"You…" Rapunzel flashed him a devilish smile. "Ever since I learned you were after my sister, I had been trying to get into your head. But you were like a locked fort. Until, of course, you went into the dream world and left your mind wide open."

"And trying to seduce me was part of… what plan exactly?"

She shrugged. "That was me trying to keep your paws off my sister. You men from the Underworld are despicable, to say the least."

Killian couldn't argue with her on that. "I don't blame you for wanting me out of your sister's life," he said. "But my love for her is true."

For once, she offered him a genuine smile. "I know. I can see that now. And for what is worth, I think you both would've been very happy together if things were different."

Killian lowered his eyes to the floor, the reminder

of his fate suddenly weighing heavily on his shoulders. "Your sister is going to need you," he said. "When I'm gone, she will be consumed by sadness, and she will need someone to be there for her. To get through the pain."

Rapunzel seemed to consider his words with a nod. "My sister will survive. She always does."

If nothing else, at least they did agree on that.

"Well, I think you should listen to your mother." Rapunzel gave him a lopsided grin. "If she says there's still hope, hold on to that. She seems like a smart woman. Meanwhile, I wish you the best on your trial of sorts."

The corner of Killian's lips lifted. "Thank you."

Rapunzel flashed him one last smile. "Goodbye, Killian."

20

ELLA

Ella caressed Azul's mane as he flew over the kingdom. The red light of the blood moon bathed the Kingdom of the Shores in a crimson glow. It was eerie, but it reflected her feelings perfectly. Her heart bled at the thought that her sister might be dead. And that Killian's soul would perish if she didn't get to him in time.

She had lost many people through the years, but the thought of losing Killian just about destroyed her. She simply could not bear it.

She pushed Azul to fly faster until Shores Beach finally came into view. "All right, Azul," she said, caressing his mane. "Show me the entrance to the Underworld."

Azul glided down toward a cavern surrounded by water, then soared through a dark tunnel until they came out in a large pool of water with a mystical glow. Azul landed on a small patch of sand, and Ella dismounted, finding her footing on some rocks.

"Can you take me down there?" she asked, turning to Azul.

He neighed, then shook his head. Ella frowned as she turned her attention to the pool. The water glistened with a blue glow, and she could see the pool was bottomless. Without being able to breathe underwater, she would most likely drown.

But still, she had to try. She had to fight for him. Even if she died, at least she would die trying.

Ella wasted no time stripping off any unnecessary clothing, then dove into the water. It was warm, unlike the ocean, and she wondered if it had anything to do with the flames of the Underworld burning underneath.

She sucked in a breath and dove under water. As she swam deeper, the cavern began to darken, so Ella touched the rocky walls and followed it down, as far as she could go. But her ears began to pop and her lungs deflate. She had heard stories about a riptide that led through the entrance of the Underworld, if she could only find the current. But as she held out her hands, she felt nothing other than still water.

When her lungs ached to the point she couldn't

take it anymore, she swam back to the surface. As she crawled out of the water, Azul came to meet her.

"The portal is too deep," she said, out of breath. Azul nudged her with his nose, and Ella wasn't sure if he was encouraging or comforting her. Regardless, giving up was not an option.

She rose to her feet, and when her knees wobbled, she grabbed onto Azul. He lowered himself to support her.

Ella bit against a scream of frustration as her mind worked overtime to come up with a new idea. But as she looked around the vast waters, all hope was lost. Her heart flooded with despair. Without the ability to breathe underwater, there was no way to access the Underworld alive.

She looked down, pinching her brows as a terrible thought sprang to mind. But before she could scramble the thought into a sentence, a voice startled her.

"Ella."

Lexa bobbed in the water, and her silver tail glowed, lighting the surrounding waters in an unearthly glow.

"Lexa, what are you doing here?" Ella said through a breath. She rushed to the water's edge and sank to her knees. Her heart lifted a little. It had been so long since she saw a friendly face. She looked at Lexa's tail again. "I thought your father gave you legs?"

Lexa's serious expression broke for a moment and she smiled. "I can transition freely now. But I am not here to talk about that. I've been looking for you."

Ella's heart squeezed and her eyes widened. "Me? Why?"

"I'm so sorry, Ella. I am responsible for what's been happening to you," Lexa confessed, tears welling in her eyes. "I sang the forbidden song. I'm the reason the Underworld wants your soul."

Ella swallowed hard, surprised by Lexa's emotion. "You couldn't have known my heart was racked with guilt."

Lexa swam closer and reached out to hold Ella's hands. "I thought I was offering my own soul… I'd never… If only I could make it up to you…" She looked away, unable to finish her thought.

Ella's chest throbbed at the sight of Lexa's distress, but her mind cast back to Killian. There was no time to talk while he was in the Underworld. If she didn't get there soon, who knew what would happen to him.

Ella squeezed Lexa's hands. "Maybe there is something you can do."

Lexa's face brightened. "Anything. You name it."

Ella looked Lexa hard in the eyes. "Your father, King Poseidon. He's Hades' brother, correct?"

Lexa's eyes squinted as she studied Ella's face.

"Yes..." she said slowly. "But he can't save you. Trust me. I've asked."

Ella withdrew her hands and stood up, nervous energy soaring through her body and willing her to start pacing. "I don't need him to save me. I simply need him to get me to the Underworld."

Lexa was quiet, but only for a moment. "It's no use," she said. "He refuses to leave Atlantis, and you can't breathe underwater. There's no way."

"Can't you summon him to meet me?" Ella asked, giving Lexa a pleading look.

Lexa bit her lip. "He won't come. The last time he left Atlantis..." She broke off and dragged a hand over her face. But then her head snapped up and she locked eyes with Ella. "There might be a way."

Ella sank to her knees, her heart racing. "Tell me."

Lexa sucked in a deep breath and turned to point at the mouth of the cavern. "Poseidon is not just a king. He has made a solemn vow to be guardian of the sea."

Ella squinted into the horizon, wondering where Lexa was going with this.

Lexa's voice turned mystical. "It is his responsibility to ensure balance and harmony. If the elements were to be disrupted, he would come."

Ella cocked her head to the side and squinted at Lexa. "You make it sound like that's simple. But I'm just a human with no powers. How do I disrupt the elements?"

Lexa stared at Ella. "You may be a mere human with no powers, but he..." She nodded to Azul. "...is not a mere horse."

Tingles rushed down Ella's arms as she caught onto Lexa's thought. But before Ella could thank her, Lexa had already disappeared into the depths of the water. Her silver glow faded, leaving Ella alone with Azul once more.

When their eyes met, she gave his shoulder a soft pat. "Let's hope this works."

AFTER GUIDING AZUL OUTSIDE OF THE CAVERN, HE hovered over the ocean. Ella leaned forward and whispered into his ear. "All right, Azul. We'll need to gallop on the water. Can you do that?"

Azul's hooves brightened with a blue glow, lighting up the water beneath them. Ella charged toward the surface, and everywhere his hooves touched, the water shone like a nebula. She galloped in a loop, creating a large, bright ring on the surface of the water.

Lightning cracked the sky above, and Ella pushed Azul to run faster. She needed to disturb the natural elements as much as possible.

When thunder followed, Ella smirked. It was working. "Faster, Azul. Faster!"

The sky roared again, sending vibrations into the ocean. Ella then pulled out Killian's sword from Azul's sheath and held it up. When yet another lightning strike lit up the dark clouds above her, she threw Killian's sword toward the center of the ring. An electric blue string struck the sword, setting it ablaze. The whirlwind inside the ring caught fire and the blue flames from the sword grew upward like an awakened monster, coating a slow-forming cyclone.

Ella was so focused on her speed that she didn't notice the towering wave that formed in the distance. It crashed over her, throwing her into the water. By the time she broke through the surface again, the wave had also extinguished the fire cyclone.

She looked around, wondering if it had worked. Then she spotted a shadowed figure bobbing on the water a few feet away. Azul hurried to her side, and she clung to him.

A golden crown rested above the shadowed figure's head, and a trident was in his hand. "King Poseidon!" Ella shrieked. It worked. She couldn't believe it had worked. "I'm sorry for disturbing the natural elements in your realm, my lord. I couldn't think of any other way to summon you. And I'm in desperate need of your help."

"Who are you?" Poseidon asked, his thunderous voice sending vibrations into the water.

Ella pulled herself up onto Azul so she could have a better view of Poseidon. "My name is Ella," she said, respectfully bowing her head. "I need your help to enter the Underworld. I have heard that only gods can move through realms unharmed. Perhaps there's a way you could send me there?"

"Ella…" He cocked his head as if her name sounded familiar. "My daughter has spoken to me about you. About your soul."

"My soul has been spared."

Poseidon gave her a puzzled look. "Then what is your business in the Underworld?"

"Someone I love took my place, but I cannot allow him to give up his soul for mine," Ella said. "I need to save him."

"My brother will never allow it," Poseidon said. "He may love his games, but he will not break his rules."

"I do not wish to break his rules," Ella explained. "But surely, there must be something I can do to save the man I love."

Poseidon considered her words for a moment. Perhaps he was familiar with the power of love. "I do not have the answer you are looking for."

"But you do have the means to make it happen." She knew.

"I may be able to get you in, but I have no authority to get you out," he explained. "If you don't find your own way out, you both will be trapped down there for eternity."

Ella shuddered, but then shook off the fear. "I understand the risks. I still need to try."

Poseidon nodded. "As you wish." He then raised his trident and began to swirl in the air. The winds picked up around them until another cyclone formed a few feet away. The swirling winds drilled into the water, creating a gaping hole in the ocean.

"What is happening?" she asked.

"It's an air tunnel," Poseidon explained. "Jump inside and allow the current to take you to the bottom. It should take you to the Underworld without you having to breathe underwater."

Ella sucked in a nervous breath, then guided Azul to get closer. Once she was on top of the dark abyss, she braced herself. That was it. Her last resort. Closing her eyes, she leaped into the hole and screamed all the way down.

Ella opened her eyes to find herself lying on a rocky ground by a lake, inside what looked like a cavern. The lake glowed a bright shade of blue with a heavy fog hovering above the surface.

Ella pushed herself to sit up, her drenched clothes sticking to her body. Then a scraping sound of glass came from her right, and she turned toward the sound. Killian's sword dragged against the rocky floor. She picked it up and it tugged in her hand. She rose to her feet and held up the sword in front of her.

"Take me to Killian," she whispered. Of course, she knew the inanimate object couldn't hear her, but perhaps it could sense the urging in her soul. Her desperate need to find Killian, to see him again, even if only one last time.

The sword tugged a little harder, and Ella followed the pull like a compass. After several turns, and hiding from every sound, she descended some narrow stone steps that led to a dark tunnel. The reflection of the torches burning on the walls bathed the tunnel in a blue glow.

On arriving at what looked like a dungeon, Ella looked into the glass cells. Men and women with gray, chalky skin stared back at her. They probably knew she couldn't do anything for them because no one bothered asking her for help. They didn't even move from where they sat. They simply watched her walk past them in silence, and the thought that they were all in line to lose their soul made her shudder in fear.

"Ella?" Killian's voice was unmistakable, and she turned toward the sound. His face was pressed to the glass bars of his cell, and Ella hurried to embrace him through them. "What are you doing here?" he asked.

She grabbed his face and kissed him in response. He claimed her mouth with such intensity, it took her breath away.

"You shouldn't have come. How foolish of you." His words came harsh and rebuking, but his kisses were nothing but hungry. Desperate. Thankful.

"I couldn't let you die for me," she said against his mouth. "I brought you your sword so you can break yourself out of here."

He rested his forehead with hers, then shook his head. "My sword won't break me out of here," he said. "These bars are made of the same material."

"Then how will we—"

"Where did you come from?" A hand grabbed Ella and yanked her away from Killian. She tried grabbing onto him, but her wet hands slipped from his arms. "You're not supposed to be here," a guard hissed, shoving her away from Killian's cell. Then his eyes fell to the sword in her hand. "Hand over your weapon."

Ella gripped the sword with renewed strength, but then caught Killian's face over the guard's shoulder. He gave her a single nod, and she lifted the sword at an angle as though she was about to run the blade through him.

The guard threw his head back and laughed. "It will take a lot more than your strength to pierce me with a sword."

"You're right," Ella said. "That's why it won't be my strength." When she pulled her hands back, the sword floated in midair. The guard's eyes widened in horror, but before he could move a muscle, Killian stretched out his hand, summoning his sword to come to him.

The sword swished through the air and pierced the guard in his chest, throwing him back. He fell to the floor with a thud, and Ella hurried to grab the keys from his belt.

After setting Killian free, Ella ran into his arms, and he tightened his embrace around her. "Come on. Let's get you out of here," Killian said, yanking his sword from the guard's chest as he walked past. "Before Hades finds you."

21

KILLIAN

Killian's chest swelled every time he glimpsed at Ella. Her damp curls lay flattened over her shoulders, and he wondered what it took for her to make it to the Underworld. Her expression was so intense as they raced through the tunnels, it filled him with adrenaline.

Seeing Ella again gave him renewed strength. He slashed his sword at any guards that crossed their path. He would burn the whole place to the ground if it got Ella to safety. She was all that mattered.

They urged forward, and the rocky floor climbed into a steep incline. But the guards kept coming and they were growing in number.

Killian fought tirelessly, sinking his blade into flesh after flesh, slicing limbs and kicking so hard that bones were snapping. The air flooded with shouts and howls, but all of it was drowned out by Ella's delicious scent.

Her aura was blood red, and she had an entirely new smell. It burned his nose but in the most delightful way, like warm spice. It filled him with strength. Like a fireball, it encircled his body, raging faster and allowing him to clear their path faster than ever.

But as they reached the mouth of the cavern, they were entirely surrounded by multitudes of Underworld guards. They swarmed them, and as Killian spun around, looking at them all, he knew that an escape was not possible. Even if they did make it out, Killian knew that Hades would send his army for him.

A new idea struck him like a bolt of lightning, as though Zeus was somehow nearby, channeling him with hope. He cut a path through the guards behind them and the two of them ran at full pelt. The tunnels echoed with hyena-like laughs and thunderous booming sounds of boots smacking the ground in a march.

"There are too many of them," Ella said through ragged breaths. "How will we ever escape?"

"We don't need to escape them," Killian said in a hushed voice as he shouldered a door and it burst open. A soft blue glow flooded his vision. He held up a hand to shield his eyes and urged Ella forward.

The small circular room had nothing but a metal stand. Atop sat a simple helmet.

To any ordinary person, it could have been mistaken for an old battle helmet. But Killian knew better. He lifted it from the stand and handed it to Ella. "Put it on."

Ella's brows lifted as she inspected it. "I hate to dash your hopes, but this won't do much against an army of the Underworld."

Killian nodded. "Put it on," he repeated.

Ella did as she was told, and as he expected, she disappeared from his view.

Before Killian could say anything, the room flooded with guards, their glass swords glowing red and aimed at him. Killian raised his palms. "All right. I give up."

The guards halted in their tracks, their beady eyes boring into his soul.

Killian kept his breathing slow and resisted the urge to look around for a glimpse of Ella. He could still sense her presence. Her sweet scent encircled his body. He knew she was close.

He blinked slowly and kept his voice steady so as to not show any sign of weakness. "Take me to Hades."

The guards sneered at him, and whispers flooded the space. Then they marched forward and took Killian's arms. "It will be my pleasure," one of the guards said with a slight chuckle. "He's ordered for your imminent execution, and we're all going to be there to watch."

Hades sat on his throne, with his right hand resting on his knee as Killian entered the great hall of the Underworld. The ground was made of glass created a millennia ago. Killian could see the white wisps swimming through the endless waters below.

He caught a glimpse of his mother standing far off in the shadows. Her eyes glowed like two moons as he met her gaze.

"Well, well, well..." Hades said, rising to his feet. His long royal blue robes flowed like water over his body as he walked. "Killian, you have always done things your own way. But I never pegged you to be a martyr."

The guards by Killian's sides shoved him to the ground, and Killian sank to his knees. Hades walked up to him and rested a bony finger under his chin, lifting his head to look him in the eye.

Hades' eyes glowed a deep blue, like a blazing fire. His body radiated fury even though his voice remained impassive and calm.

"After all these years..." he said, lowering his face

to whisper in Killian's ear. "You had one soul left to attain… and all this would have been yours."

Killian didn't bother responding.

Hades leaned back to give Killian a disappointed look. "You know I am rather fond of you. But it appears that my fondness has grown a blind spot. I never saw this coming."

He started to walk away and flicked his hand. The guards tightened their grip on Killian, and a masked executioner marched forward.

Persephone ran out from the shadows and threw herself in the way. "Hades. You will kill your own flesh and blood?"

Hades turned and his eyes flashed upon the sight of Persephone knelt with her face mere inches from the executioner's ax. He glared at the executioner. "Stand back from your queen, you fool!"

Then he turned to Persephone. "My dear, you know that there are eternal laws of which I am bound. The boy murdered scores of his brothers. He has broken sacred vows. My hands are tied."

Persephone began to sob. "I cannot stand by and watch you kill my son. *Our* son."

Hades flicked his hand again. "I do not expect you to, my eternal love."

Two guards moved forward and grasped her up by

her arms. Persephone protested with loud screeches, but Killian shushed her.

"It's all right. I accept the consequences of my actions," he said. "Go. You do not need to witness this."

Persephone's teary eyes locked with Killian for a moment before the guards carried her out of the hall, her soft cries still ringing in Killian's ears.

He clenched his fists and braced for impact as the executioner raised his ax. He closed his eyes and thoughts of Ella suddenly flooded his mind. As did her scent. Like sweet spices filling his entire being.

"Wait!" Hades shouted, and Killian shot his eyes open.

The executioner looked at Hades, with the ax hovering high above his head. Hades hummed, thin-lipped, and his face paled. "It appears as though I have changed my mind." He looked at Killian pointedly. "Or rather, someone has changed it for me."

Killian noticed a cut on Hades' neck and crimson blood seeping from it.

Killian held his breath. *Ella, what are you doing?*

He tuned into the sound of her sharp breaths and caught her whisper to Hades. "Let him go."

Killian's heart began to race while Hades hummed again. "Tempting proposition. But first, take off my helm and show yourself to me."

Ella appeared into view, throwing the helmet on the floor with a clang. The guards staggered back with a gasp. Swords rose in the air and they began to march forward, but Hades raised a hand.

"Leave us and get back to work," Hades demanded. "There will be no execution today."

Several guards murmured to each other as they filed out of the hall, but the executioner took his time with a long, disappointed grunt. Finally, he trudged away, leaving the three of them alone.

Hades sighed. "I can see why you're attracted to her, my son." He eyed Ella through a reflection of the glass with a look of amusement, but she scowled back.

"Well, do we have a deal?" she asked, her eyes flashing at him.

Killian shook his head and rose to his feet. He hadn't heard her deal, but his gut already knew that she had offered her soul in exchange for his. "Ella, no. I'm not letting you do this."

Ella frowned more deeply, keeping the blade pressed to Hades' neck.

"Father," Killian said, softening his voice. "I'll make you a new deal."

Hades blinked slowly, seeing that Ella still had him pinned to her with the blade at his throat. "I'm listening intently."

Killian squared his shoulders. "There's no place for

me here, not after my failure to deliver you one last soul," he said, looking down. Though he would have done it all again for Ella.

"You're right, I cannot allow you to dwell here anymore," Hades said. "Your soul count has been reverted to zero, and I no longer recognize you as my family."

Killian would have been more emotional if he'd had a relationship with Hades. But the truth was, the man was cold and distant ever since he was a child.

"You may pity me for the way things have turned out," Killian added, "but the truth is, I have no regrets." He stood taller to look at Hades eye to eye. "It is you that I pity, Father. You're a prisoner here. Forced to guard the Underworld. The only reason I am here is because you enslaved my mother."

"She loves me," Hades said acidly.

"She shouldn't," Killian replied with a scowl. "You're a soulless monster incapable of love."

For the first time, Killian sensed hurt in Hades' eyes. "Is this your deal? I stand here and listen to your tirade of abuse?"

"No," Killian said, shaking his head. "I want to live on Earth."

Hades snorted. "And you expect me to allow you to walk away with her?"

Ella remained poised, her hand steady on the handle of the blade.

"I offer up my immortality," Killian said. "I choose one life. A mortal life. With Ella."

Hades' nostrils flared, and he looked at Killian as if he had said a foul word. But Killian was not done. He stared at Hades deeply. "And when I die, my soul will come here and belong to you."

"You will have us both," Ella added.

Killian nodded. "Just allow us free passage away from this place. One mortal life. It'll be over in an instant for you. And we'll be yours for eternity."

Hades hummed in thought. "Two souls."

Killian knew he couldn't deny it was a good deal. The Underworld would see it as the ultimate punishment. Being forced to live a life as a mere mortal, only to end up in the endless waters as a wisp in the Underworld. To any immortal, it was a fate worse than death.

But to Killian, he would rather live a limited number of years with his love than an eternity alone.

"Deal," Hades said finally.

Killian's heart leaped, but Ella hesitated to release the knife until Killian nodded to her.

Her face broke into a weepy smile, and she ran to him. But just as she was about to throw herself into his arms, she lurched to a halt with a high-pitched gasp.

Killian blinked rapidly as he looked down at a glass blade poking out from her chest.

"On second thought," Hades said, ripping the blade from her body. "I'll take one soul now… and have yours later."

With a devilish wink, he put the helm on his head and disappeared.

Killian caught Ella as she crumpled in his arms. "No. No. No. Ella!" He cradled her as he lowered her limp body to the ground.

Ella gasped like a fish out of water. "Killian…" she said weakly, tears rolling down the side of her eyes. "Killian…"

"Ella, stay with me. Stay with me!" Killian closed his eyes and pressed his hand over her chest. He could hear the throb of her heartbeat. The dripping blood flooding her chest cavity. She was bleeding out before his eyes, and he had never felt more hopeless in all of his existence.

Blood spewed from her mouth, and she choked.

"Stay with me, Ella!" He laid her flat on the ground, then placed two hands over her chest. His hands began to glow a bright blue. "Fight, Ella. Fight!"

He closed his eyes and tuned into her heart. The beat had already grown weak. But he pushed aside any doubts and fears. Instead, he allowed the vibrations of his hands to move outward. He pictured swirls of blue mist enveloping Ella's hemorrhaging heart. Then he sensed the mist turning to glass, just as he had done countless times, making glass blades.

This time, though, he crafted the glass into a case around Ella's heart. The bleeding slowed, and Killian closed the opening with a thin, flexible band of glass.

A faint beat vibrated against his hand, and he shot his eyes open. His love was soaked in crimson blood, and her face was whiter than snow, but at least her heart was still beating.

He scooped her up in his arms. "Hold on, my love. Hold on," he whispered in her ear. "Don't give up. Please, stay with me. Fight to live. For me. Live… for me."

22

ELLA

When Ella opened her eyes, it took longer than usual for her vision to clear. But when it did, she thought for certain that she was dreaming, because how else would she have been back in her childhood home?

The walls were still the same soft yellow as she remembered, and the white furniture hadn't changed. Even the white treasure chest in the corner where she used to store her dolls looked exactly the same.

As she sat up and caught her reflection in a mirror across the room, she saw that she wasn't a child. She was an adult, and her curls were as golden as they had ever been. But when had she changed into a long, silk garment?

Her brain shifted in her skull, and she grabbed onto the bed for balance. Something wasn't right, but her memory of the events that led her there was hazy. And her breathing was heavier. There was a tightness in her chest unlike anything she'd ever experienced.

That was when a flash of memory struck her brain —Hades' blade piercing through her chest.

Ella gasped, then hurried to the mirror and began to remove the silk robe until her chest was exposed. Her skin just below her collarbone was smooth, without any trace of a blade ever having sliced through her.

But she was absolutely positive that it happened. So, either she died and woke up in some sort of after-life, or she'd been healed.

"Neither," a woman's voice came from behind her. Ella swung around to find a familiar face staring back at her.

"Aurora?" Ella blinked several times to make sure her eyes weren't playing tricks on her. "Is this…?"

"The dream world, yes," Aurora said, leaning against the open window. "Seems like you've once again fallen into a deep sleep. What happened?"

"Hades…" Ella's memory was so clear, she found herself brushing the tip of her finger over the spot where Hades' blade should've scarred her. "I'm fairly certain he killed me."

"You're not dead. This realm is only for those who find themselves stuck on the stage just before death,"

Aurora said, looking out the window. "Which means you might be in a coma."

Ella's mouth dropped open. "A coma? Does that mean I'm stuck here?"

"Not yet. But if you don't wake up soon, you will."

"How do I wake up?" Ella asked, trying to remember what Ensley had said about the dream world. "I need a jolt. Something strong enough to pull me back into consciousness. Wait, I need to fall!"

Ella hurried toward the window, but as she peeked outside, her heart sank at the realization that she was on the ground floor. And her childhood home didn't have but one story.

In the distance, just at the foot of the hill, Ella could see Belle's burned cottage. It was also one story.

"There are higher buildings in the next town over," Aurora said. "But I doubt you'll have time to travel."

Ella shook her head, panic rising within her. "Then what can I do?"

"Perhaps there is something we can try, but first…" Aurora pulled out of her sheath a small, rolled-up parchment paper and handed it to Ella. "Will you keep this for me?"

"Sure." Ella took it. "What is it?"

Aurora shrugged. "Something I'll only need if I ever make it out of here."

Ella nodded, then shoved the paper into the pocket of her silk robe. "I hope you do one day."

"Thank you." Aurora smiled as she approached, then placed a hand on Ella's shoulder. "You're a good person, Ella. I hope we stop meeting like this."

Ella chuckled, but before she could respond, Aurora pulled out a knife and pierced it into Ella's chest. Ella gasped in horror.

Then in the blink of an eye, she was lying on a different bed, in a different room, and she shot upward, adrenaline coursing through her body as she struggled to breathe.

"Ella!" Killian's voice entered her mind, then he came into view. "Ella, darling." He hurried to her side and cupped her face. "Breathe."

"Killian..." She clawed at his arms as if she was drowning. "I can't..."

"Breathe, Ella." He took in a deep breath in front of her, urging her to do the same, then slowly exhaled. "Follow my breathing."

She did as she was told, then finally air found her lungs again.

"There you go." He smiled, brushing his thumbs over her cheeks. "You're all right."

As relief washed over her, and she could finally breathe again, she focused on Killian's face. He had deep, dark circles under his eyes, and it made her wonder how long it had been since he last slept.

"Killian…" She reached up to touch his face. His cheeks were wet, and that was when she noticed there were tears. "Are you crying?"

He rested his forehead on hers and pressed his eyes shut. "I thought I had lost you," he whispered, his voice trembling. "But you came back to me." He opened his eyes and held her gaze. "And… your soul is clear as day."

Ella pulled back, her eyes widening in surprise. "It is?"

Killian nodded. "Yes, my love. We are free."

"We?" she echoed.

"Yes. You are free from your guilt, and I am free from Hades." He smiled, brushing a thumb over her bottom lip. "We are free to live the rest of our mortal lives together."

"Oh, Killian!" She threw her arms around his neck and pressed her lips to his. But as her heart raced, a tightness pressed inside her chest.

She pulled back with a wince, and Killian held her arms to steady her.

"What's wrong?" he asked, watching her closely.

"I'm not sure," she said, rubbing her chest as if the movement could somehow relieve the pressure. "Something's wrong with my heart." She looked up to meet Killian's eyes. "What did Hades do to me?"

Killian frowned. "He pierced your heart with a sword. But I was able to stop the bleeding."

Ella cocked her head. "How?"

Killian brushed one of her curls behind her ear. "I patched the wound with glass, then encased an even thicker layer around your heart just to be sure."

Ella stared at him with eyes unblinking. "My heart is inside a layer of glass?"

Killian nodded, and she placed a hand over her chest.

"Does it still beat?" she asked.

"Yes," he said, resting a hand over hers. "It still beats. And it's stronger than ever."

"Will it go away once my heart heals?" she asked.

Killian shook his head. "I can't manipulate the Underworld elements as I used to. I'm not immortal anymore."

"So, I will have a heart of glass for the rest of my life?"

"My love, even if I could remove it, I wouldn't."

"Why not?"

He cupped her face and peered into her soft eyes. "Do you have any idea how many souls I've taken from this world? How many enemies I've made? If they ever find out that you are the most precious thing to me, they just might come for you. And that heart of glass will give you a measure of protection that I will no longer be able to provide. And if anything ever happens to you…"

In seeing his distress, Ella grabbed his face and pressed her lips to his. "Nothing is going to happen. And thank you for saving my life."

He took her hand in his, then pressed it to his chest. His heartbeat was strong against her palm. "Feel that? That was you saving mine. I'm alive because of you."

Moved by his words, she pulled him down onto the bed with her and deepened the kiss. His tongue found hers as he lay above her.

Laughter came from outside, and Ella placed a reluctant hand on his chest. "Where are we?" she asked.

Killian lay next to her on the bed and propped his head up with his hand. "The Elven Island," he said with a shrug. "In all the centuries I've been alive, they have always had the best healers. And I wasn't going to take any chances with your life."

"And they offered to help?" Ella asked, unable to mask her skepticism. "Do they know who we are? What we've done?"

Usually, elves kept to themselves and out of any drama. They were peaceful people. Which was why Ella was surprised they agreed to help, considering the ordeal she had gone through. She couldn't imagine they hadn't heard of the King's death and the bounty on her head by the Prince himself. Even though her alleged crime was absolved, drama was drama. And Killian, having been from the Underworld, certainly, enemies would come looking to avenge their loved ones' souls.

"As soon as I told them what I had done to your heart, they were too fascinated to turn us away," Killian said. "They couldn't get this room ready fast enough."

That explained it.

Elves were curious creatures. Always looking to expand their knowledge of the Earth's properties, or in this case, the Underworld's. Knowledge was elven currency after all.

"We'll be safe here, for now," Killian assured her, then pressed his forehead to hers. "In the meantime, I have made arrangements to buy your father's property back."

Ella's eyes widened. "The one up the hill from Belle's cottage?"

Killian pinched her chin. "Yes, my love. I will buy that back for you. However long it takes to pay it off."

"Oh, Killian…" Ella's heart soared. "I love you so much."

Killian watched her for several heartbeats, then tugged on the drawstrings of her cotton dress, letting it open up to reveal the long scar running between her breasts. "I love you more than you could ever imagine," he said, pulling the material away from one of her shoulders and kissing her skin.

The heat of his mouth sent tingles all over her body, and her eyes fluttered closed. "What if they hear us?"

Killian leaned in and nibbled on her earlobe. "I guess we'll find out."

Ella shuddered under his touch, allowing him to trail kisses up her neck. She sighed as his calloused fingers grazed her bare stomach.

"Oh, my Ella," his whisper was hot in her ear. "You are absolutely perfect."

That was when she realized the tip of his finger was tracing her scar. His touch heated her skin, sending goosebumps all over her body. Even on the verge of death, she had never felt so alive.

"Killian…" Her breathy voice oozed with need. "Are you sure we're alone?"

Killian pulled back to give her a dark smile. "Do you want me to stop?" he asked, dropping his eyes to her bare body as she lay before him. She gripped the back of his neck, and pulled him close, then kissed his mouth with a sigh.

"I don't want you to ever stop," she whispered, edging closer to him. Killian removed his shirt and allowed her bare skin to press against his chest, making everything zing.

A rush of emotions flooded her as his hands lifted her thighs. She wrapped her legs around his waist and reveled in the feel of him fitting so naturally between her. His strength, his need, his desire, so evident in his touch. For a moment, they stopped kissing and peered into each other's eyes. He wrapped his arms around her body and buried his face in her neck, inhaling her scent with appreciation. With her guilt and despair gone, Ella imagined that her scent must've been like breathing fresh air.

"I cannot sense you anymore," Killian said, his mouth against her neck. "So I'm going to need you to tell me what you're feeling."

Ella savored the heat of his tongue against her collarbone and tangled her hands in his hair. "I feel like…" Her voice was breathy. "My heart is going to explode."

Killian smiled against her skin. "Good thing I encased it in an unbreakable glass, then."

"Killian, please…" She arched her back, pressing her body even tighter against his. "I need you."

When she opened her eyes, she caught him watching her amusingly.

She scowled. "If you love me as you say, why are you torturing me?"

"Because…" He brushed a soft curl from her face. "I want to savor every moment with you. I want to memorize every inch of your body. And that, darling, takes time."

His words fueled her with an insatiable need for him, and a rush of passion rose within her, setting her body ablaze. She grabbed fistfuls of his hair and pulled him into her. "I cannot take this any longer."

Killian's eyes darkened in such a delicious way, a burst of pleasure exploded within her at the mere anticipation of being claimed by that beast of a man.

"Answer one question for me, and I will spend the rest of my life claiming you," he said, watching her with hungry eyes.

Ella bit her bottom lip as her breathing quickened. "Out with it."

Killian flashed her a devilish smile. "Will you spend the rest of your days by my side… as my wife?"

A gasp hitched in Ella's throat. And for a moment, she was speechless. "I don't…" she breathed. "I wouldn't…"

A confused crease formed between Killian's brows. "You wouldn't… marry me?"

"No. I mean…" She sucked in a deep breath. His question had taken her breath away. "I wouldn't be able to live a single day without you."

"So, then, your answer is…"

"Yes!" She beamed. "My answer is yes! A million times yes—"

He caught her words with his mouth and kissed her hard. She parted her lips, inviting him deeper, and he obliged effortlessly. The taste of his tongue was invigorating, and it filled her with an urgent need that vibrated in her core.

"I will love you forever, Ella," he growled against her mouth.

She reached up to rest a hand on his cheek, then she uttered the words that were finally his undoing.

"I am yours. Forever."

EPILOGUE

TRISTAN

In the cool spring morning, birdsong flooded the skies, and golden beams of sunlight poured in through the evergreen trees of the Chanted Forest.

As the old carriage rocked back and forth over the uneven terrain, Prince Tristan gazed out the window at the thick overgrowth, teaming with wildlife. A squirrel scurried up the trunk of an oak tree, passing a woodpecker too busy hammering for bugs to notice he was not alone.

Tristan had heard about the Queen of the Chanted Forest. Her name was Snow White, and for such a new queen, her reputation was impressively marvelous. Rumors had it that she was so attuned to wildlife, they were drawn to her like a magnet. Some said she even possessed the ability to understand them.

Looking around the lush green foliage and all

manner of creatures roaming in and out of view, Tristan supposed that some of it had to be true. The forest was thriving and it was a far cry from the days of her predecessors.

Unlike the Evil Queen, Snow White was known to be kind and generous and adored by her people. Tristan wondered if marrying a huntsman had anything to do with how much the people accepted and respected her.

His father would've been proud of her ability to win the hearts of the people. After all, that was the reason he had wanted Tristan to marry Lexa. Tristan understood the advantages their unity would've had for both of their kingdoms, and even though she was indeed a beautiful woman, her eyes didn't sparkle for him. There was no zing between them when they danced, and that was enough for him to know that she wasn't the one.

He wished his father understood. Perhaps if he had respected Tristan's decision to let Lexa go, he wouldn't have gone after her at Neverland. He wouldn't have gotten entangled in Neri's lies. He would've still been alive. But the man had the prize in his sights and nothing and no one could change his mind.

His father's stubbornness was what cost him his life. Or at least that was what Tristan kept repeating in his mind over and over again, for months, so that he didn't become consumed with guilt.

His jaw tightened as another memory flashed in his mind's eye. The devastation of the bitter truth hitting him in the chest. He killed his own father.

Granted, his mind was controlled by someone else because of pixie dust, but still, it was his own hands that murdered his father.

Tristan looked down at his open palms. No matter how often he'd scrubbed them, they still felt dirty. And when he held his father's crown for the first time, the golden metal instantly became stained with blood. Tristan knew it was all in his mind because none of his father's advisers could see it, but that was enough for him to have it put away. He hadn't been able to touch it ever since.

That was months ago.

That was one of the reasons he hadn't yet arranged for his coronation. Although becoming King was inevitable, he couldn't fathom the thought of seeing his father's blood sliding down his crown and onto his royal garment in front of all his subjects, even if it was only inside his own mind.

But he also couldn't prolong the coronation any longer. King Midas from the Golden Kingdom to the north had taken advantage of the Kingdom of the Shores' vulnerability and declared war. Midas wasted no time moving his troops into the Shores' territory, and the people were already losing their crops as well as their homes. Families had been divided, and lives had been lost. Tristan couldn't stand to watch his kingdom suffer any longer. But also couldn't rise to power with a haunted mind.

The only way he could become the King his people needed him to be, was to cleanse his haunted mind once and for all. But for that to happen, he needed to find the memory of that night. The night his father died.

Between the time his father threw the pixie dust at him on the lower deck of the ship, to when he found his father's bleeding body on the upper deck, there was nothing but a stolen void inside Tristan's mind.

Ella had mentioned something about having found her own memory of that night. Perhaps, she could elaborate on how she went about retrieving it because that was what he needed as well.

When the carriage rocked violently again, Tristan cringed in frustration. But not at the old carriage he'd paid for at the marina. Or at the driver. No, his anger rose because had he taken a royal carriage, his identity as a prince would be revealed. And ever since his deal with Rumpelstiltskin, going outside of the palace walls had become too dangerous.

The deal made with Rumple was a document

which stated that in the event that Tristan died without an offspring, Rumple was to inherit the throne.

But it was a trick.

Rumple had manipulated matters so that Tristan would be put to death that same night.

What Rumple didn't account for, however, was for Ella to have been merciful toward Tristan. Despite everything he'd put her through, she pleaded for his life and kept Killian from piercing his sword through Tristan's heart. He owed her his life.

But that didn't mean Rumple gave up on his plan.

Even though the document stipulated that Rumple himself could not kill Tristan, it didn't say Rumple couldn't hire low-life men to do his dirty work. And Tristan had experienced many *random* attacks in the past few months which left him no doubt that Rumple was more eager than ever to do away with him.

So, not only did Tristan have to find a way to get his memory of the night his father died, but he also needed to find a wife, sooner rather than later, and produce an offspring to negate Rumple's contract.

Tristan rubbed his throbbing temples for the rest of the way until the carriage finally came to a stop. The driver's voice came from outside. "We have arrived, sir."

Tristan looked out the window to find a home at the top of a hill. A large green field stretched within a wooden fence. Horses and cows grazed the pasture inside it.

Throwing a hood over his head, Tristan stepped out of the carriage. He sucked in a nervous breath because the people he came to see were no doubt going to be surprised at his visit. And at their last encounter, he had almost died.

A woman with long golden curls stepped outside, holding a basket of clothes. She began hanging them on a string tied between two trees. But it wasn't until Tristan approached that he noticed her bulged belly.

"Ella?" Tristan called out, his voice careful not to startle her.

She swung around with a smile, clutching her bump, ready to greet the visitor, but at locking eyes with him, her smile fell from her face.

Tristan immediately lifted his hands. "I come in peace," he said, keeping his voice soft and unthreatening. He even offered a friendly smile for good measure. "I just want to talk."

She must've sensed his honesty because her features relaxed and her eyes softened at him. "You have questions about your lost memory," she said. It was more of a statement than a question.

Tristan nodded with a frown. "I wasn't sure who else to seek."

"That's all right. Come on in," she said, motioning

toward the door, leaving her clothes basket on the grass outside.

Tristan entered the home, then waited for Ella to guide him as to where to sit.

"Would you like some tea?" she asked, motioning to the sofa.

"I do not wish to bother you," Tristan said, pulling the hood from his head as he took a seat. "I also do not wish to take much of your time. I simply come seeking answers about that night."

Ella reached for a kettle that seemed to already have been boiled and grabbed it by the handle. "I believe I already told you everything I know," she said, pouring the fervent liquid into a ceramic mug. "I don't think I left anything out."

"Maybe." Tristan nodded. "But the night you told me everything, I had been drinking. I only remember flashes of information, but not the details."

After sprinkling some mint leaves into the mug, she handed him the drink.

He took it appreciatively. "Thank you." Then his eyes roamed around the place once more. "Where's Killian?"

"Out, hunting," Ella said with a pleasant smile. And for a moment, Tristan wondered if she'd meant to paint an image of her assassin husband with a hunting knife.

Tristan swallowed dry at the thought that Killian could walk in at any moment and use that same knife on Tristan.

"So, you want details," Ella said as she took a seat on a rocking chair across from him. When her eyes settled on him, she sighed. "Are you sure about that?"

Tristan nodded as he blew into his cup. "Yes. I need every detail you can remember. No matter how dark. Don't sugarcoat it on my account," he said. "I believe it's the only way I will find closure and be able to move on."

Ella considered it for a moment, resting a soft hand on her belly as she began rocking back and forth on the chair. "The tricky thing about memories is that we all have our own. It's about perspective," she explained, looking down as though remembering words spoken by someone else entirely. "When I retrieved my memory, I could only see what my own brain registered from that night. Even though I saw what you—Neri—did, I do not possess the reasons behind it."

Tristan sighed and placed his drink on the coffee table between them, watching as the steam danced above it. "There must be something I can do," he pressed.

"There is," Ella said, piquing Tristan's interest, and he lifted his eyes to her again. "The fairies told us about the sundrop flower. They prepared it under the moonlight, and when we drank it, we were sent to a dream world where all of our memories reside. As well as our deepest fears."

Tristan watched her, enthralled. "What was it like?" he asked.

"For me…" Ella let out a humorless chuckle. "It was a nightmare involving a Golden Tower, my dead parents, and me barely getting out. If Killian hadn't come for me, I would've gotten stuck in there like Aurora—"

"You wouldn't happen to know where I could find one of these sundrop flowers, would you?" Tristan asked.

"Give me one good reason we should help you?" a thunderous voice came from the door, making Tristan jump to his feet.

"Killian." Ella said her husband's name as though trying to keep a lion at bay. "We've been through this."

Tristan lifted his hands. "I truly am sorry about what I put Ella through. I would never have done it had I known the truth. If there's anything at all that I can offer as compensation…."

Ella smiled kindly. "There's nothing—"

"There is one thing," Killian cut in, pulling out his hunting knife. Tristan stepped back, causing an amused grin to spread across Killian's face. "Relax. I wouldn't kill you in front of my wife."

The menacing look in his eyes gave Tristan the impression that he would not even hesitate to cut his throat had Ella not been there.

"Have a seat," Killian said with an authoritative tone as he motioned to stand next to Ella's rocking chair.

Tristan took a seat, hesitantly.

"I have made many enemies through the years because of my line of work," Killian said. "In the event that those enemies come for me, or my family, I would like them to have a secure place where they could flee."

He placed a large hand over his wife's baby bump, and she rested hers over his. And suddenly, Tristan understood. They were just two parents trying to protect their unborn child.

"Of course." Tristan nodded. "My palace will always be open for your family. For you too, Killian." Tristan thought to add, considering Killian had asked for a safe place for his wife and child, but not himself. "If you agree to leave the past in the past, I will do the same." Tristan stepped forward and offered his hand to Killian. "From this moment on, your family will not only have protection within my palace walls, but you may choose any property in my kingdom and it will be given to you. In the event that you need to leave this one behind."

Killian looked down at Tristan's hand for a long time, then took it in a firm handshake. "Thank you."

Relief washed over Tristan. For a moment, he thought Killian might have been contemplating breaking every bone in Tristan's hand. "Well, I better be on my way," Tristan said, pulling back and securing his cloak. "Thank you for letting me know about the sundrop flower."

As Tristan turned to leave, Killian raised a hand. "Wait," he said. "I might have something you can take with you."

Killian walked over to a cabinet in the kitchen and pulled out a jar with a silver liquid inside.

When he returned to her side, Ella's eyes widened. "When did you—?"

"I took it from the fairies before we left," Killian said, handing it to Tristan. "In case we needed it again. I didn't want to have to go back there."

Tristan took the jar and examined a silver flower floating on the surface of the water inside. "I've never seen a silver flower before," he said.

"The flower is normally yellow," Killian said. "But after they boiled it under the moonlight, it turned silver. That's how you know the water is ready to drink."

"Fascinating," Tristan muttered. Then lifted his eyes back to Killian and Ella. "Thank you so much for this."

"Be careful in there," Ella said with a frown. "The dream world… is a very dark place."

Killian took her hand, and Tristan wondered what had happened to them there.

"I will," Tristan said, shoving the jar inside his bag. "Thank you."

He threw the hood of his cloak over his head and walked out the door. The sun had already begun its descent, but they just needed to make it to the marina. Once back on his boat, he would be among his trusted crew and no longer in danger.

As he approached the carriage, the driver was sitting in the exact spot he had been when Tristan left.

"To the marina," Tristan said, then climbed into the carriage. He leaned back on the hard seat and closed his tired eyes as he waited for the carriage to move.

But it never did.

Tristan opened his eyes, the eerie silence prickling his skin as he leaned forward. "To the marina," he ordered the driver once more, but the carriage still didn't move.

Tristan peeked out the window to catch the driver finally moving. Except he *wasn't* moving. He was falling.

His limp body collapsed to the ground with a thud, and Tristan jolted back into the carriage. A loud bang came from the roof as though heavy boots landed on it.

Then more footsteps followed, surrounding the carriage.

Tristan reached for his sword, but it was stuck. The space was too tight.

Then the door flew open, revealing a bearded man with jet-black hair. He flashed a wicked grin at the sight of Tristan. "I've been waiting for you," he said with a growl as he stepped forward.

A wave of painful grunts came from all around the carriage, and the man's grin fell from his face. Then a guttural sound ripped from his throat as his breathing stopped. He fell into the carriage, face down, and Killian came into view, standing at the door with the man's blood dripping from his hunting knife.

"Let me guess," Killian said.

But he didn't have to finish. Tristan nodded. "Rumpelstiltskin."

— Keep reading Tristan and Aurora's story in Upon a Dream, book seven in the Fairy Tales Reimagined series!

If you enjoyed this book, please consider leaving a review! Reviews help us find new readers.

Made in the USA
Las Vegas, NV
21 August 2024